299 Days: The Change of Seasons

by

Glen Tate

Book Seven in the ten book 299 Days series.

Dystopian Fiction & Survival Nonfiction

www.PrepperPress.com

299 Days: The Change of Seasons

ISBN 978-0615934785

Printed in the United States of America.

Prepper Press Trade Paperback Edition: December 2013

Prepper Press is a division of Kennebec Publishing, LLC

- To the real "Amber Taurus," the den mother of the Washington State liberty movement.

This ten-book series follows Grant Matson and others as they navigate through a partial collapse of society. Set in Washington State, this series depicts the conflicting worlds of preppers, those who don't understand them, and those who fear and resent them.

The Change of Seasons is the seventh book in the *299 Days* series, where summer has ended and reality has set in at Pierce Point. For many people, this means scrambling to survive the long winter with even less food. Some were smart enough to spend the summer preparing for the changing season and the expanding effects of the Collapse; others were not so smart, and their desperation and fear grows stronger by the day. Grant Matson reflects with pride on how he has provided for his family while guiding Pierce Point into a community that functions well on its own. Celebrating this accomplishment, Grant and others join to offer the community a Thanksgiving dinner, which is met with gratitude and exhilaration. This mood is short-lived, however, as circumstance quickly begin to unravel, beginning with the disappearance of a beloved community member, followed shortly by a self-defensive killing by another.

The situation is just as bleak, or worse, in other parts of Washington State and the country, as innocent people are imprisoned and murdered, women and children become commodities, and what is left of the government looks even less like the once-beloved United States of America.

As the threat of a civil war becomes imminent, Grant, the Team, and the 17th Irregulars at Marion Farm bond over their duty to protect the country and are soon a fully-formed combat-ready unity, excited to go into combat but uncertain of what will happen to them. Grant dreads what he knows is coming, but he understands that he has been called to sacrifice - potentially his life and probably his marriage - to stop the Loyalists from hurting more people.

Books from the 299 Days series published to date:

Book One – *299 Days: The Preparation*

Book Two – *299 Days: The Collapse*

Book Three – *299 Days: The Community*

Book Four – *299 Days: The Stronghold*

Book Five – *299 Days: The Visitors*

Book Six – *299 Days: The 17th Irregulars*

Book Seven – *299 Days: The Change of Seasons*

Book Eight – *299 Days: The War*

For more about this series, free chapters, and to be notified about future releases, please visit **www.299days.com**.

About the Author:

Glen Tate has a front row seat to the corruption in government and writes the *299 Days* series from his first-hand observations of why a collapse is coming and predictions on how it will unfold. Much like the main character in the series, Grant Matson, the author grew up in a rural and remote part of Washington State. He is now a forty-something resident of Olympia, Washington, and is a very active prepper. "Glen" keeps his real identity a secret so he won't lose his job because, in his line of work, being a prepper and questioning the motives of the government is not appreciated.

Chapter 216

"Call in the 'Hit'"

(August 2)

After they lifted off, Nedderman used the helicopter's intercom radio to ask Mendez where they were going. "I'll punch them in," Mendez said, referring to the coordinates. They had left so hastily that they didn't have time to do the normal pre-flight procedure of going over the plan. They had to hit the target fast because word could get out that it was coming. Nothing stayed a secret very long at Joint Base Lewis McChord, or "JBLM" as everyone called it. The teabaggers always seemed to know what the still-loyal American forces were doing.

Chatting on the radio was frowned upon, but Nedderman couldn't resist. "I'm looking forward to this," he said to Mendez. Nedderman loved killing teabagger insurrectionists.

"Me too," said Mendez. "Me too," he repeated.

"Olympia airport?" Nedderman asked, referring to where the military units operated from.

"Nope," Mendez said. "We need to boogie before the mission is compromised, so we're meeting the contractors at a landing zone outside of Olympia."

"Okay," Nedderman said. The trip from Camp Murray, which was within the JBLM complex, to Olympia only took a few minutes. They flew in silence, each man running through his mental checklist of what would happen if he died in the next few minutes. They'd been through it a million times, but each time they thought about dying, it was like the first time they'd ever pondered the concept.

"There they are," Mendez said, after spotting some men at a landing zone in a clearing near the water. Right where they were supposed to be. That wasn't always how things worked.

Yellow smoke, from a smoke grenade, appeared down by where the contractors were.

"That's the sign," Mendez said with a smile. Everything was going according to plan. What a relief.

Nedderman took great care while he was touching down. He had to avoid power lines, trees, and, because helicopters were most vulnerable during takeoffs and landings, he had to be on the lookout for enemy fire. The teabaggers were everywhere.

The contractors were in the tree line surrounding the landing zone, staring at the approaching helicopter. The yellow smoke swirled around from the rotor blades. Nedderman skillfully set the helicopter down and looked over at Mendez with a smile for a job well done. Mendez didn't smile back.

Instead, he swiftly took out his pistol and shot Nedderman, who looked at Mendez in horror. Mendez shot him several more times, holstered his M9 pistol calmly, and looked around.

Almost instantly, two of the contractors came up and tried to pull Nedderman out of the cockpit.

Mendez signaled for them to leave Nedderman strapped to the cockpit; he was dead and couldn't do any damage. Then Mendez signaled for them to get in, which they did. After the contractors' team leader counted and ensured that all of his men were in the helicopter, he signaled to lift off. He put on the headset so he could talk to Mendez on the helicopter's intercom system.

"All in," the team leader said. "Call in the 'hit.'"

Mendez switched from the intercom and radioed back to base and screamed, "We're hit, we're hit. Ambush! Ambush!" He switched back to the intercom and asked the team leader, "Where we going?"

"To see the Attorney General," the team leader said with a huge smile.

Chapter 217

Meatball Sub

(August 2)

"The Governor thanks you for your service," Sean Patterson, the Governor's Legislative Director, said sarcastically right before he smirked to mock and humiliate the teabagger asshole standing in front of him. "We have a new, and," Sean paused and then said, even more sarcastically, "exciting... assignment for you." Sean barked like a dog and said, "You get to guard the Governor's dog!"

Captain Brad Finehoff had been expecting this. Up until a few minutes ago, when he was rudely summoned into Sean Patterson's office at Camp Murray where all the state officials had fled to, Brad had been the chief of the Washington State Patrol's very elite EPU, the Executive Protection Unit, which was the state-level equivalent of the Secret Service that protected state officials. He had worked incredibly hard for the past twenty-three years and now was being treated like a child by an evil and thoroughly corrupt little politician who took great delight in tearing other people down. Especially strong men; the very slight and frail Sean Patterson seemed to have a chip on his shoulder about those types.

"Woof! Woof!" Sean kept saying, acting like a spoiled little child. "Won't it be fun taking care of Rover?"

The Governor's dog was actually named "Rover." That was because, after hours of political strategizing, her aides decided to come up with the blandest name possible so as not to offend anyone. The name of the "First Dog," as Rover was called in the EPU, had become a symbol of how dysfunctional Washington State government had become before the Collapse. The First Dog was kept in the old Governor's Mansion in Olympia, which had been evacuated of all essential personnel. Now it was just a symbolic building, but was still guarded by a massive force because it was a juicy target for the Patriots, or rebels, or whatever they were. It looked like the mansion in Olympia would be his new duty station. He wondered if he really had to take care of Rover.

"I will gladly serve in any capacity I can," Brad said in shock. "But ..."

"Yes?" Sean said. "But, what?"

"Why, sir?" Brad pleaded, as he noticed his lip was quivering. "Why am I being re-assigned?" He was fighting back the tears. He hadn't cried in decades.

Sean looked out the window at the barbed wire and machine gun nests surrounding Camp Murray. "Well, Trooper," Sean said, knowing that Brad was not an entry-level Trooper, but instead a Captain, "it seems that your son is still missing." Brad's twenty-five year old son, Russ, had been missing since May Day.

"Have you heard something? A clue?" Brad asked with great enthusiasm. "Is he okay?"

"No, we don't know anything," Sean said with a roll of his eyes, which was an incredibly cruel thing to do to a parent with a lost child. "Maybe you know where he is."

Brad looked dumbfounded. "If I knew where he was, he wouldn't be missing, sir," Brad said. Sean's behavior was confusing him.

"Okay," Sean said, disengaging from the argument, "I guess you don't know where he is."

"How does my son's disappearance have anything to do with me being reassigned to Olympia?" Brad asked.

"I dunno," Sean said, sarcastically again. "Why do you think?"

"I'm sorry, sir," Brad said, "I honestly don't know." Brad had no idea why this little snot of a man was being so cruel.

Sean stared at him. "Your son is hiding out at some insurrectionist camp, isn't he?"

"I have no idea," Brad said. "If I knew where he was, I'd go get him. If he's being held hostage by terrorists, then I'd be the first through the door with the entry team. I mean, that's my son they're holding."

"Keep up the game, Trooper," Sean said, once again refusing to acknowledge that Brad was a Captain.

"Game, sir?" Brad asked.

"Dismissed," Sean said with a wave of his hand.

That was it. Twenty-three years of sacrificing to protect state officials and now he was apparently being demoted to guarding a dog named Rover. Brad left the room.

As he gathered his belongings from his quarters at Camp Murray, Brad thought about all that had happened. His son, Russ, was an aide to the conservative state Senator John Trappford. Brad figured that it was only a matter of time before his son's very unpopular political position made it impossible for him to remain on the Governor's protective detail. There had been whisperings before the Collapse about Brad being a "known conservative," though Brad had been never political. He found most politicians to be quite unpleasant.

His fellow EPU agents openly wondered how Brad could remain the Governor's bodyguard when he was a "known conservative." Desperation was the answer. The State Patrol, as big as it was, didn't have much bench strength when it came to the protective details. Before the Collapse, the EPU was tiny because there weren't too many threats against the Governor, just a few crazies. Now there were lots of threats, as evidenced by the fact that the Governor was hiding out in a fortified military base.

The tiny EPU grew enormously when the Collapse hit. The State Patrol hastily trained up a new, and mammoth, EPU when the riots started. Brad knew his days were numbered in the EPU when they didn't even ask him to train the new kids. And they were kids, all in their twenties. They didn't remotely have the experience it took to be an effective member of a protective detail. They were young ladder-climbers who wanted to make a name for themselves on an elite assignment they were not qualified for. Brad shrugged as he took his last load of items out to his unmarked police cruiser. The lack of experience on the protective details wasn't his problem now.

Brad forgot to get the fan he loaned a co-worker so he went back to the entry gate. He got out his swipe card to get through the first layer of gates. It wasn't working. He tried it again. It still didn't work. Of course not. He was no longer welcome near the Governor. He sighed and drove off to Olympia, to start Rover Duty.

After the shock of being fired so rudely had subsided, and he drove farther away from Camp Murray, Brad became more and more relieved. He couldn't stand being around those people anymore. For the first fifteen years or so, things were fine. The various governors and their families were genuinely nice people. Their staffs were polite and hardworking. Many of them seemed like the kind of people who were working in government to solve problems and help people. But, as the years went on and state government grew and grew, it seemed like the people running it got more arrogant. They had egos and threw temper tantrums.

The worst part for Brad was watching the corruption grow. It started with little things, like people getting their friends out of tickets and an occasional DUI. Then Brad started to notice that gifts were rolling in from lobbyists. And the trips! All the trips the politicians went on, paid for by the lobbyists and unions and God only knows who else.

Brad accompanied the Governor and other officials on all of the trips. These excursions were where the corruption started to turn really ugly. Everyone had girlfriends or boyfriends, and they partied hard. At first, they kept the drugs away from Brad and the EPU agents, who, after all, were law enforcement officers. Then, slowly, they stopped hiding their activity.

Eventually, the wild parties, along with the drugs and prostitutes of every kind, started popping up at the Governor's mansion. Brad couldn't believe what he was seeing. He started to feel abnormal because he wasn't doing cocaine, ecstasy, and oxycodone with transvestites like everyone around him. Even some of his EPU agents were getting high on the job. It wasn't the honorable service for honorable people he remembered from when he started in the unit.

Brad wasn't alone. As the Collapse approached, he found a small group of his EPU agents who were as disgusted with everything as he was. They became a tight group. However, after the Collapse, Brad went up to Camp Murray, but the others remained in Olympia, so he lost touch with them.

As he approached the outer ring of the defenses around the Governor's mansion, he saw two men, and one woman, in suits with their backs turned. When he was closer, they turned around and Brad immediately recognized them: Jerry, Mike, and Chrissy; his EPU friends who were disgusted with everything like he was.

Brad rolled down the window and said to them, "Looks like it's reunion time." They didn't smile. They looked nervous. They got in Brad's car.

"How you guys doin'?" He asked. They were silent. Finally, Mike said, "Let's go to Mecconi's," which was a nearby sandwich shop.

"Okay," Brad said. "Is everything alright?" He was the guy who just got demoted, yet he felt like the happiest one in the car compared to his three somber passengers.

Jerry, Mike, and Chrissy were still silent until Jerry said, "Parking at Mecconi's is so much better now that no one can get near the capitol campus." The other two nodded solemnly.

"Hey," Brad said as he pulled into the Mecconi's parking lot, "what's going on?"

"Meatball sub?" Chrissy asked. "You still like the meatball sub, Brad?" She remembered Brad's favorite sandwich from the hundreds of times they'd eaten there.

The three unbuckled their seatbelts and started to get out. It was like they were robots or something weird. Very weird.

Brad stayed in the car. After a few seconds, they noticed that he was still in the car and turned around and returned to him. Brad rolled his window down.

"What the hell is up?" he asked them.

"Come in for a meatball sub, Brad," Jerry said and tugged at his left ear with his left hand. That was the signal they used back when they worked together. It meant, "Just roll with this. Trust me."

Brad knew instantly that whatever was going on was planned and was going to be okay. He got out of the car and started to walk toward the others.

Mike made the hand symbol of someone talking on a cell phone and then motioned to keep the phone in the car. Brad nodded, took his cell phone out of his pocket, and threw it in the car. The Bluetooth in the phone could only record conversation from about ten yards, so leaving it in the car would mean their conversation couldn't be heard by whoever might be listening. Lately it had been common for the authorities to record, and sometimes listen to, the conversations of sensitive personnel. The authorities were paranoid about Patriot spies and thought everyone, even trusted people like EPU agents, could be one.

Brad was trying to catch up to the other three, but stopped suddenly. They were getting into another car, Chrissy's personal car, instead of going into Mecconi's. Mike motioned for Brad to join them, so he did.

When Brad got in the front seat of Chrissy's car, they let out a cheer and started high-fiving him.

"Welcome back, brother," Jerry said. "We missed you."

"What the hell is going on?" Brad asked.

"Something better than a meatball sub," Chrissy said as she drove. Mike and Jerry smiled and nodded.

"And that would be...?" Brad asked, starting to feel a little annoyed by this charade. He had just been demoted in a career-ending humiliation and now his friends were acting all mysterious and weird. Chrissy drove a few blocks to the industrial area of town, known affectionately as "Bum Town," and parked in front of the Union Gospel Mission. It was teeming with homeless men. She didn't seem the slightest bit afraid.

The homeless men saw the government-looking occupants of the car and started to run, likely because they were used to not being treated well by government agents.

The three got out of the car. Brad stayed in the front seat. He refused to go in because he had no idea what was going on and no one would tell him, which was unlike the EPU unit. They always communicated about everything – who was going where, who was taking lead, taking the rear, who would wait in the car – because they had to move and operate that way. It made the silent treatment he was receiving extremely odd and very unsettling.

Finally, Mike noticed Brad was still in the car and turned around. He yelled at Brad, "You coming, or what?"

Brad lost his temper. He rolled down the window and yelled, "What the hell is happening, here?" He paused for their reaction; they just smiled. "I'm not going anywhere until I know what's going on," he said. They smiled even more.

Jerry rolled his eyes and gave Brad the ear-tug signal again. Then Jerry signaled for Brad to hurry up and get into the mission. Once again, Brad unquestionably reacted to the ear-tug and went into the mission.

It smelled horrible inside. Brad had been in the beautiful and meticulously maintained Camp Murray for several months. He hadn't been around people who hadn't showered for weeks.

Jerry, Mike, and Chrissy looked so out of place in their suits in this sea of derelicts and dirty street people, yet they seemed completely at ease.

Brad was thoroughly confused at this point. He looked at Mike. "What am I doing here?"

"Going into the kitchen," Mike said. He tugged on his left ear.

Chrissy and Jerry went into the kitchen first, as if they were checking the room for a threat. They didn't draw their weapons, but they moved like they were securing the room. Mike got behind Brad to cover any threats from the rear. Brad felt like he was under strict protection and his team was securing the kitchen for him. Brad started to wonder if he really should go into the kitchen, but then remembered the multiple ear-tugs. He pushed the swinging kitchen door and strode in, confident that his team was taking care of him, just like they always had.

To his surprise, there was a homeless man standing there with a Mecconi's bag.

The homeless man, who had a long beard, a hat, and sunglasses smiled.

"You want a meatball sub?" he asked. Then he pulled off his

fake beard.

"Russ!" Brad screamed as he ran over to hug his son. He hugged him so tight he thought he would snap him in half.

After he caught his breath and came back to his senses from the shock of seeing his missing son, Brad asked, "What are you doing here?"

"Asking you to work for the Patriots, Dad."

Chapter 218

Render Unto Caesar

(August 2)

They were still absent. Another Sunday had come and gone and the Matsons were absent from Olympia Christian Church. Rev. Martin Tibbs was looking out into the growing number of empty chairs as the Collapse wore on, but he understood. Despite the sharp increase in people attending church immediately after the Collapse, people were starting to run out of fuel to get to church and it was dangerous to walk there, even in Olympia where there were more police than elsewhere.

The Matsons, though, were a different case. They were absent not because of scarce fuel, but because, rumor had it, they were wanted by the government. Martin was afraid for them. He always liked them. He remembered helping them through the difficult time when they learned their son, Cole, had autism.

Martin also fondly remembered baptizing Grant a few years ago. There weren't too many men in their mid-thirties getting baptized. He liked Grant's recent-convert enthusiasm for the Gospel, even if he did swear a lot.

Martin remembered being fascinated with Grant's political views. He never cared too much about secular politics; humans were sinners, so politicians would fight for money and power. Nothing new there; that's what flawed human beings do. No use getting caught up in the details of which politicians were doing which bad things. None of that earthly stuff ultimately mattered.

Martin just accepted the government as a part of life. In his Olympia congregation, most parishioners were either government employees or contractors. They didn't dislike government; they were part of it. But Grant was different. He seemed to have example after example and persuasive argument after persuasive argument, why government had become too big. Giant government crowded out the church's ability to help people, Grant would always say. Martin was starting to see things Grant's way.

At seminary, Martin was repeatedly taught that Christians must "render unto Caesar." That meant, he was told, that Christians must be obedient to the earthly governments that ruled over them, which were the Romans in Jesus' time. Besides, earthly government was just temporary, to be replaced for eternity with a supremely just and merciful ruler. Life on earth was full of injustices that Christians must suffer through, so putting up with corrupt, and sometimes evil, government was just what Christians needed to do.

Grant's examples and arguments got Martin thinking. A few months before the Collapse, Martin read the "render unto Caesar" passage with a fresh perspective. There were actually two parts to that passage, not just the single "render unto Caesar" part. The full passage said, "Render unto Caesar the things that are Caesar's, and unto God the things that are God's."

What are God's things? Martin asked himself. Everything. If God has everything, how could earthly government crowd out God and take over? Wasn't God still in charge of everything? Of course. So, Martin concluded, Christians should generally honor government, except when government starting being unjust and corrupt and doing things God wouldn't want. God would not want people to submit to injustice and corruption.

This was a watershed thought for Martin. He started to see all the horrible things that government was doing. Killing innocent people, allowing (and, in some cases, committing) rape, and working with gangs to steal. God would never want that.

In the days after the Collapse, Martin started to pray about what he could do. He asked God how he could preach the sermons he felt were necessary; sermons that would get him in trouble with the government. He was willing to sacrifice his liberty or even life, but he wanted to do something effective, not just be a martyr without accomplishing anything. He needed to figure out a way to have a free pass to preach what needed to be said without getting in trouble.

Then one day, he heard a knock on his office door. He had the strangest feeling that the answer to his prayers had arrived. He opened it and a well-dressed man extended his hand.

"Hi," the man said, "I'm Logan Henson with FEMA's Clergy Response Teams. Do you have a moment?"

Martin had heard of the Clergy Response Teams. They were an official department of FEMA that worked with clergy of all denominations to get information out to people through the churches. Martin had assumed that meant getting out information about how to prepare for a tornado or things like that, but he quickly learned that the Clergy Response Teams were asking clergy to tell their congregations about how people of faith need to follow instructions from their government. The message was that the government is a large and very effective charitable organization that helps people, just like Jesus did. Martin was uneasy about churches, especially his, being used to get the government's message out.

"We're here to help," Logan said.

In an instant, Martin knew exactly what he would do. He would lie to this man, and God would forgive him. He would lie a lot and it would be okay. He hated lying and hadn't done it since childhood, but he knew he needed to do it now. He was amazed at how easy it was to put on his "game face" and start lying to this man.

"Great," Martin said to Logan. "How can I help you help my congregation?"

That's what Logan wanted to hear. He loved it when a clergy member played ball. This was his last church to visit today and then he was done. This one would be easy and he'd be home early this afternoon.

Logan explained, to a very attentive Martin, how the Clergy Response Team could help. They would provide a weekly update for Martin to hand out each Sunday. The handout would describe all the things the federal and state authorities were doing to help people and how the "terrorists" were trying to thwart all this good work.

"Sounds great," Martin said. "I'd be happy to."

Logan explained the other programs that FEMA offered to churches, including grants and loans, in some cases. Martin listened carefully and showed great enthusiasm.

"Lastly," Logan said, as he closed Martin's office door and lowered his voice, "There is a program we have that you might be interested in."

"What's that?" Martin asked.

"Do you have any parishioners who might be hoarding food or doing things that are not best for the whole community?" Logan asked. "Maybe parishioners who have expressed anti-government sentiments."

Martin laughed. "Oh, not in my congregation," he said, instantly thinking of Matt Collins, a friend of Ron Spencer's and a suspected Patriot. "This is Olympia, after all," Martin said. "Most of my people are state employees. We all fully support the Recovery."

"Every single parishioner?" Logan asked.

"Absolutely," Martin said and, extremely uncharacteristically, slapped Logan on the back like a used car dealer.

"Good," Logan said and clapped his hands. "I could tell this was a good church."

Martin gave him a thumbs-up, yet another uncharacteristic gesture from the normally scholarly reverend.

"Do you have any questions?" Logan asked.

Martin thought for a moment. "Just one," he answered. "How can I get more involved in the Clergy Response Teams?"

Logan clapped his hands again and explained to Martin how to participate in FEMA's Clergy Council, which was an advisory board for the area Clergy Response Teams.

"I'm so glad you came by," Martin said at the end of their conversation. "I look forward to working with you. You know, 'render unto Caesar.'"

Logan smiled. He loved hearing that.

In the next few weeks, Martin networked all he could with the Clergy Council. Most in his congregation fully supported his efforts; a few were leery of the church being so involved with a government agency. Martin winked at them and assured them that it was for a good cause.

Only two months after he met Logan and started helping FEMA, Martin had a list of all the Olympia-area clergy working for the agency. He knew all the FEMA liaison staff like Logan. He asked them to sign the church's guestbook with their home addresses, "for when the mail is working again, after the Recovery, so we can have you over for a potluck." The FEMA liaisons gladly gave Martin their home addresses.

Today was a warm and beautiful August day. Martin got in his little car and, with gasoline provided by FEMA for his services, he drove to a bar in a bad part of town. Martin hadn't been to a bar in several years, so he wasn't sure how to dress or act. His denomination let him drink, but he didn't go to bars. He found the bar and went inside, feeling strange.

Martin saw the man he was supposed to meet. "Hey," he said, and almost spilled the beans by saying the name of who he was meeting, "How are you?"

Matt Collins started walking toward him.

When he got close, Matt said, "Thanks for not yelling out my name." He laughed, knowing that Martin was a rookie at all this cloak and dagger stuff.

They got a little table in the corner where no one could really see them. The music was so loud no one could hear them, either.

"So," Martin said right off the bat because he was nervous and wanted to get out of the bar as soon as he could, "Can you get some information to the yellow team," a phrase that meant the Patriots due to the yellow "Don't Tread on Me" flag they used.

"Maybe," Matt said. He didn't know his pastor very well. He knew that Martin was working for FEMA. But Martin had pulled him aside two Sundays ago and, in the privacy of his office, swore on a Bible that he wanted to make contact with the Patriots and was not trying to get anyone in trouble. Matt could tell that Martin was no polished spy and judged that he was sincere.

"I have one condition," Martin said as he started to pull a piece of paper out of the envelope he had been carrying. "It's important."

"What is it?" Matt asked.

"You don't kill anyone," Martin said. "No killing."

"Okay," Matt said, having no idea if that request could be honored. But he really wanted that list of FEMA liaison home addresses.

"What will you do to them?" Martin asked. "Maybe scare them?"

He tried not to laugh out loud at Martin's naivety. "Scare them?" Matt said without laughing. "Yeah, we'll – well, maybe someone – will let them know that they shouldn't be doing this." Matt realized that Martin was being a thoroughly decent man about this, and was risking his life to get the information to him. Matt owed it to Martin to do all he could to honor Martin's very reasonable request. "You have my word, Reverend, that no one will get killed."

Martin sighed with relief. He had been praying about this for days. He could justify the lying to the FEMA people and his fellow Clergy Council members, but killing was not allowed. He couldn't be part of that.

"What will you do with the addresses?" Martin asked.

"We're putting together a list of bad people," Matt said. "This information will be added to that list."

"Yes, but what will you do with the list?" Martin asked. He feared the answer. Matt was silent.

"For most of the list, the ones already on the list, I can't guarantee bad things won't happen to them," Matt said. "But, for you, Reverend, I will make sure no one on your list gets hurt." He was serious. The Patriots he worked with weren't blood-thirsty monsters. They would understand; and they clearly appreciated getting the information, even if it came with strings attached. Humane and decent strings, actually.

"Okay," Martin said as he handed Matt the piece of paper with the addresses. After a few words of thanks and pleasantries, Martin left the bar.

A scheduled Clergy Council meeting the following morning was cancelled because, that night, most of the FEMA liaison staff on Martin's list had "FEMA Lima" spray painted on the front door of their houses. They were terrified and many were talking about moving to Seattle where it was safer. Others said if the capitol city of Olympia wasn't safe, then nowhere was. This led some to start thinking that the Legitimate Authorities couldn't keep them safe, which led them to rethink their allegiances.

Word of the spray painting and the new security concerns spread quickly through Olympia, including Martin's congregation. He gave a rousing sermon that Sunday entitled, "Render unto Caesar: the Second Half." It talked about how the second half of the passage was that God was in charge of everything. Normally, that message would have raised eyebrows and put Martin under suspicion, but, just as Martin had realized after praying, he had a "free pass" to preach almost anything he wanted because he was a trusted member of the Clergy Council.

"Problem solved," Martin whispered up to the sky.

Chapter 219

Car Wash Josh

(August 3)

"AAG 3009," nineteen year-old Josh Kohlman quickly wrote in his little notebook. He wrote down the time and date, too. He also wrote "every Wed. - lunch." And then the big prize: "gold triangle." He was thrilled to write that down. This would be valuable, he thought. Very valuable.

Josh closed up his notebook, put it back in the little Ziploc bag he kept it in, and stuffed it in the cargo pocket of his shorts. He worked at the carwash and was standing in the one place that the surveillance cameras didn't cover. The Ziploc bag kept the notebook dry when all the mist and water was swirling around.

Now came the hardest part: doing his crappy carwash job for a few more hours until he could get all this valuable information to where it needed to go. Time inched along until, finally, the end of the day came and he was off.

Josh worked at the Olympia Eco-Wash, the only remaining carwash in town. The other ones had gone out of business, but the Eco-Wash was owned by a connected person who just happened to get all the permits necessary to operate. His competitors didn't.

Because the Eco-Wash was the only remaining carwash in Olympia, many of the VIPs went there to get their new, shiny government cars washed. Of course, the very highest-ranking VIPs had security details wash their cars, but many of the second-tier VIPs had to wash their own cars, so they routinely came to the Eco-Wash.

That's where Josh came in. He was a Patriot. He had his future stolen like everyone else in his generation. He grew up in the 2000s, when everything seemed fine. The economy was booming and his family and friends always had plenty, but when Josh was in high school, everything started to fall apart. His mom lost her job at the Washington Association of Business, which was where he had met all kinds of interesting people and learned about the Patriots.

Josh wasn't bitter; he was determined. He didn't whine about his future being stolen and didn't want to "get even" with the people who did it. Instead, he wanted to end what was going on. He didn't care how it ended, he was just determined to end it – even if that meant he had to work hard and risk his safety in the process.

Josh thought long and hard about what he should do to end what was going on. He was a peaceful young man and didn't want to hurt anyone, but the more he thought about it, the more he realized that he couldn't do anything purely peaceful. He couldn't just vote for someone to change things. People voting for "free" stuff was what caused the mess. He couldn't print up pamphlets because no one in Olympia seemed interested. He wasn't prepared to join a guerilla unit because, well, he just wasn't. He had the weird feeling he was placed in his present situation for a reason. But what good was a young carwash attendant to the Patriots?

Then it hit him. One day, he realized how many fancy government cars came to his carwash. He couldn't believe how exposed they were: their license plates just sitting there, along with the dates and times they came. All Josh needed was information on the license plates to know who the drivers were. That information was a closely held secret, so once again he assumed he was useless at his stupid carwash job.

Then one day, he was talking to Eric Benson, who used to work at WAB with Josh's mom. Eric was like an older brother to Josh.

"I have all this great license plate info," Josh said, "But I can't do anything with it."

"I can," Eric said with a smile. He knew someone in the Department of Licensing who was working for the Patriots. Eric didn't tell Josh that; no need to provide information that could be tortured out of him.

"Dude," Eric said, "you get me the license plates and the times they are usually at the carwash and I'll take it from there."

There it was, Josh thought. His role. The way he could help end this.

Josh started off slow at first. He had to figure out how to take down the license plates and times people came without getting caught. After a while, he noticed the one place the video cameras didn't cover. Then he discovered something big.

The government people had parking passes for various parking lots. Most parking lots were for the rank-and-file drones, but some parking lots meant the driver had an important job. A gold triangle, for example, meant the driver got to park at the Legislature. The driver was either one of the remaining legislators (the handful of Patriot legislators had resigned after the Collapse and formed a government in exile) or a key staffer in the House or Senate.

Josh, who was a very smart kid, learned the parking pass codes from talking with people. He found out where they worked and then put the parking pass symbols together with their jobs. The Patriots had people working at the capitol who confirmed the parking pass codes.

Josh eventually got his hands dirty with some direct action. He worked with Eric to identify a state bureaucrat, Bart Sellerman, and Eric shot him in the carwash. The police, what was left of them, came out to the carwash two days later and took some pictures. Sellerman wasn't important enough in the state hierarchy for anyone to think it was a political assassination. It was just another random killing, like the few others that took place on any given day. So taking pictures two days later was the entire investigation; that was it. Josh had been nervous that a killing at the carwash would bring attention to him, but it didn't. This emboldened him.

After a while, Josh's license plates, trip information, and especially parking pass codes, were having a huge impact. For reasons no one in the government could understand, VIPs were getting ambushed while they were driving around. The Patriots were smart enough not to hit the VIPs only while they were driving to and from the carwash. The Patriots had surveillance teams who, knowing the car and license plate, could shadow a car for a few days and learn the driver's routine for the week. Then, a Patriot ambush team would hit the car on a weekend at the grocery store, or other seemingly random location.

The Limas assumed that someone close to the targeted VIP was working for the Patriots. This threw off the scent and caused the Limas to waste scarce investigative resources trying to figure out which person close to the VIP had compromised them. This, in turn, caused the Limas even more problems because innocent people connected to the VIPs were being thrown in jail, creating morale problems for the government. The Patriots even got some recruits from the innocent people thrown in jail under these wild goose chases.

It only took a couple of these ambushes for the mid-level VIPs to become terrified – and demand that they, too, get security details. The government couldn't possibly extend security protection to more people. So many of the VIPs lost their vigor for working for the government. They started to question whether the government could protect them, which led them to question working for the government even more.

Many VIPs switched to private cars, although quite a few had been driving government-issued cars for so long they no longer had their private cars. But Josh could help with this, too. He was a friendly and chatty guy; he got to know his customers, so he knew when a person who worked for the Department of Emergency Management was now driving a different car. He took down the new license plate and got it to Eric. Now VIPs in private cars were being hit. This caused even more terror. Pretty soon, VIPs were resigning from their government jobs. This was the best outcome: the government was weakened and no one got hurt.

Josh became so valuable that the Patriots devoted scarce in-city armed teams to protect him. He didn't even know he was under protective surveillance. He never noticed the "homeless" men in the parking lot of the adjacent vacant building near the carwash. Then again, homeless camps were everywhere, so Josh wouldn't have noticed.

The Patriots even recruited a beautiful young lady to be Josh's girlfriend. She drove up to the Eco-Wash in a hard top Jeep, telephone numbers were exchanged, and they ended up moving in together. Now the Patriots had a close eye on Josh for several hours a day. Josh quickly figured out what was going on, both with the homeless protectors across the street and the pretty Jeep girl, but didn't have any complaints. He was being protected, had a gorgeous girlfriend, and even got to drive her Jeep on the weekends. Not bad for a guy with a stupid car wash job.

Chapter 220

"Sorry. Nice E."

(August 3)

Damn, I love my job, Eric Benson thought to himself as he was taking off her clothes. Then he caught himself enjoying it. A normal man might consider ditching the job at hand and just revel in what was about to happen, but I'm not normal, he thought. He was singularly focused on his job. He was fueled by hate, not pleasure.

Eric had always been different than others; a lot different. He had an overriding personality trait that might seem like a good thing at first, but it wasn't. Eric could not stand people being treated unfairly. If he could control himself and just stick up for the little guy, he would have been an admirable person. But he couldn't control it. The instant he saw an injustice, he would go from a nice, normal person to a raging avenger. The even scarier part was that he really loved the feeling of beating on a bad person. The feeling was intoxicating when he was hurting someone who was hurting an innocent person.

When he was a kid growing up in Chicago, he would always get in fights with bullies who were tormenting kids. This was an admirable quality. But there was a second, less admirable side to him: He would fight with teachers and other authority figures over minor inequities. If a teacher, perhaps innocently, handed out a punishment to a child Eric thought was innocent, he would jump up out of his seat and scream at the teacher. Then, when he was punished, he would argue loudly, and sometimes physically, that he was the good person here and the teacher was the bad one. Then he would get in more trouble. And the cycle would continue.

It got so bad that once, in middle school, he hit a teacher. This landed him in juvenile detention, which was the absolute worst place he could end up. Injustice and unfair treatment was a daily occurrence there. He punched counselors and a guard and got even more time piled onto his sentence. He spent most of eighth grade in "juvie" as they called it. Finally, he realized that if he didn't control himself, he'd be in jail forever and would be miserable for his whole life even though he didn't do anything wrong. Ironically, that wouldn't be fair, he realized. He chuckled in his juvie cell when he realized this. That chuckle saved his life.

From that chuckle onward, he worked very hard to control his anger. At first, he failed more than he succeeded. Then, he started to learn how to talk himself into not getting angry. He would tell himself, "Don't let them win." He wasn't controlling his anger to be a good person; he was doing it to be effective. "I can't fight bullies if I'm in jail," he would tell himself. He would talk to himself when he was getting angry, and usually talk himself down. It took practice, but he was getting the hang of it.

Eric quickly realized that once he got the anger under control, he would be unstoppable. He could right all the wrongs he wanted if he could get into a successful position in life. The more power he had, the more good he could do.

Eric thought about how he could do that. He was extremely intelligent, hardworking, good looking, athletic, and charming (when he wasn't mad). Those were the qualities he needed to be successful, then powerful, then a righter of wrongs. That was his plan.

After that horrible year in the eighth grade, he transferred to another school and got a fresh start. He started excelling at everything. He went from failing grades to straight As, got on sports teams, and even became popular. His parents were amazed and relieved.

Eric kept working and working at being successful. He would have conversations with "Angry Eric," as he called the dark side of his personality. He would tell Angry Eric to keep a lid on it just a little while longer until "Nice Eric" could get them into a position of power where Angry Eric could be unleashed to right wrongs.

High school was a great time for Eric. He was valedictorian, homecoming king, and a varsity football and basketball player. He got into a great college and was at the top of his class.

As college life came to an end, he had to decide what he wanted to do for a living. That is, how he could become powerful and then right wrongs. At first, he thought about going into business and getting rich. Then he'd be powerful. But just making money didn't appeal to him.

True warriors want to be in battle. They want to be where the action is. Eric looked around American society trying to find where the injustice was. It was with the legal system, of course, which was a big pile of steaming and squirming injustice. It was a target-rich environment.

And, as corrupt as the legal system was, Eric realized that he could actually do some good things for people. In fact, the more corrupt the system was, the more he could help people who were getting screwed.

He got into law school very easily. There were plenty of opportunities to work on "justice projects," but they were all for left-wing causes. Eric, who grew up in Chicago, always saw big government mistreating people. He also saw how the elites, who were often white, used minorities and the poor to keep their hold on power.

He looked at the liberal law students touting leftist causes and quickly realized they were junior examples of the elites who ran things. The rich and privileged kids just wanted to become the next generation of the rich and privileged. He wanted to be successful so he could help people, not turn into one of the elitists. He knew Angry Eric would explode and get out of control if Nice Eric tried to do that, so he took a different track than virtually any of his fellow law students. He started volunteering to help the small businesses that were being attacked by the government. He fought for a tow truck company owner who had the audacity to actually put in a winning bid for some city work – work that was supposed to go to a favored company. He usually lost these cases because the judges were corrupt as hell. But Angry Eric was being calmed by working on them.

Then something amazing happened. Eric actually won a case. Government had become so used to winning that they were getting sloppy. In one case, on behalf of a black beauty shop owner being harassed by state regulators at the behest of competitors, the state regulators actually spelled out what they were doing in an email. Then they turned it over in pre-trial discovery because they assumed they'd still win. However, the judge, who was black and whose mother had been screwed just like the business owner in Eric's case, actually ruled for Eric's client. Eric won. He beat the bad people. He had helped the little person.

The feeling was intoxicating. He felt years of pent-up Angry Eric finally breaking loose. He wanted to punish the regulators. He wanted to get them fired and seize their house to pay the judgment. He wanted to hurt them. Not physically. Well, yes, physically, Angry Eric admitted to Nice Eric.

He didn't hurt anyone, but he realized that actually winning these battles was what he wanted to do. He loved it. He wanted more of it.

He heard about some business association in Washington State that fought these kinds of battles and actually won on occasion. He got on a plane and nailed the interview. It wasn't long before he was a hard-charging attorney for the Washington Association of Business.

Washington State was another target-rich environment for fighting injustice. It was like Chicago, except the naive people of Washington State didn't think their government was anything like "corrupt" Chicago. Washington State government might have been more subtle and less severe, but Eric could see that it was the same thing, just a different degree.

Eric had a few really good years at WAB. He teamed up with Grant Matson to win some cases and help people.

But something frustrated Eric: WAB, as aggressive as it was, wasn't aggressive enough. More and more, Angry Eric was telling Nice Eric to take these fights from the courtroom to the streets. To start bustin' some skulls. Go after union thugs, bureaucrats, and government lawyers. Nice Eric always persuaded Angry Eric that the time wasn't right.

But it was getting closer to being the right time. Eric watched as all the pieces were falling into place as the Collapse approached. He watched as government got bigger and bigger. It clamped down on civil liberties more and more. He could see that government would be out of money soon. Very soon.

That's when Angry Eric started to win some of the arguments with Nice Eric. "This will be our time!" Angry Eric would tell Nice Eric. "When there are no cops around, we can punch some fuckers in the mouth! They deserve it. They've hurt people." Angry Eric would wait for Nice Eric to have a response; Nice Eric was having a harder and harder time doing so. Nice Eric was starting to agree with Angry Eric. As conditions in the days leading up to the Collapse worsened, Nice Eric increasingly lost the arguments.

The days surrounding the Collapse were the last straw for Eric. He couldn't believe that, with all the leftists out rioting and trying to destroy the WAB building, the rest of the WAB guys would just sit there. Were they out to fight for the little guy, or just watch their beautiful office building burn to the ground by the very people out hurting people? Was all their political and legal bluster just bullshit? Or were they going to fight against the bullies?

Nice Eric finally lost it when he left the WAB offices on his last day. He pleaded with the WAB guys to go fight, but they wouldn't. Eric stormed out of the office and finally let Angry Eric take over. He put his key in the car and said out loud, "OK, you win." Angry Eric didn't gloat. He just said, "We've got this. Let's go." Eric promptly went out and killed a state bureaucrat, Bart Sellerman, who had bullied one of Eric's clients. It felt amazing. Angry Eric was delighting in it.

"We need more of that," Angry Eric said to Nice Eric after watching Sellerman's head explode in the car wash.

"Yes," Nice Eric said. He was fully on board with the new post-Collapse plan for righting wrongs. It was about killing people. And loving it.

The carwash hit was a one-time thing. Sellarman just showed up at the carwash right when Josh predicted he would; it was too easy. Too convenient. That probably wouldn't happen again. Eric needed to think about how to do more. He came up with a plan.

He knew who he needed to meet, but he didn't know how to get access to that person, so he worked hard on getting to know someone who knew the ultimate person he was interested in. The person who knew the ultimate person was a beautiful young woman named Michele, who after weeks of observation and planning, Eric "accidently" bumped into at a college coffee bar. A week later, they were dating. Exactly according to the plan.

"You gonna turn me on?" Michele softly asked Eric as he was undressing her.

"Oh, you bet," Eric said and he proceeded to do so. Very well.

Eric allowed himself to enjoy the amazing sex they had, but he was determined to stay focused on the job at hand. After they were done, Michele asked him, "So, you wanna maybe move in with me?"

"Thought you'd never ask," Eric said with a smile. And then they went at it again. Even Angry Eric had to admit this was pretty awesome.

"What will your roommate think?" Eric asked Michele after round two. "You know, about another person living here?"

Michele's roommate was Maddy Popovich. Maddy and Michele were students at Olympia's extremely left-wing Evergreen State University. Maddy was the leader of Students for Democratic Action (SDA), a radical communist group. SDA had ties to the Red Brigade, the left-wing terrorist group.

Maddy was a very effective leader on campus and managed to rile up over 2,000 students who served as foot soldiers in the Left's army of thug enforcers in Olympia. They were the very people who burned down the WAB building back in May. They were the very people whose mouths Angry Eric wanted to smash.

"Maddy'll be fine with it," Michele said, having no idea how Maddy would react, but wanting Eric to live with her. Maddy was rarely in their tiny apartment, anyway. She was always at some rally or meeting. Maddy probably wouldn't even notice Eric was there.

"Well, okay, then," Eric said as he kissed Michele. She tapped him on the shoulder. "Twice is enough for me, baby," Eric said. Michele understood.

As Michele drifted off to sleep, Angry Eric was energized and telling Nice Eric what needed to happen.

Two weeks later, Angry Eric's plan happened. Maddy was found dead in her apartment after being murdered in a violent and horrific way. Michele was found there, too, but had died in a painless way.

She had, "Sorry. Nice E," written on her forehead.

Chapter 221

Angie

(August 4)

"I don't know what she sees in him," Granny whispered to Molly Prosser one day out at the Prosser Farm. "I mean, I'm happy for him, but what's the attraction here?"

Granny felt terrible for saying that about Dennis, who was a really nice man. But Dennis' new girlfriend, Angie, was … well, out of his league. Dennis was a good man, but not a looker. Angie, on the other hand, was stunning. What could she possibly see in him?

"Stop being a gossip," Molly whispered back. "You sound like some small town old lady. Just be happy for him."

"I am, I am," Granny said. "I just wonder, that's all."

By this time, Angie and Dennis came up to Granny and Molly's picnic table. They were having a Sunday picnic like they had been doing that summer. The weather was beautiful and the food was superb – well, superb for a post-Collapse picnic. About a dozen families nearby came over. The kids played, the dogs ran, and the grownups got to talk and relax. It was magnificent.

"Granny," Dennis said, proud as can be with his chest puffed out a little, "have you met my girlfriend, Angie?"

"Pleased to meet you," Angie said, sweetly. She seemed very nice, but Granny couldn't help noting, Angie seemed a little out of place. It wasn't just that she was so beautiful, but she just looked … out of place.

"Angie, would you care for a glass of iced tea?" Dennis asked politely.

"Sure, honey," she said to him. He swelled with pride when he heard that. He, Dennis, had a pretty and nice girlfriend. He was a still a bachelor in his mid-thirties. He had started to wonder if he'd ever meet someone nice. And now he had. He was on top of the world.

Now that Angie was alone with Granny and Molly, Granny decided to do some digging on this girl.

"So, Angie, tell us a little about yourself," Granny said and then smiled.

"Oh, I'm pretty typical," Angie replied. "I was an art student at

Evergreen," which meant the liberal college in Olympia, "and now, with all that's going on, I'm not a student there anymore." She shrugged. There wasn't much more to say.

"Are you from here?" Granny asked.

"No…" Angie was searching for the best name to call Granny. "Do you go by 'Granny' or something else?" she asked.

"Oh, 'Granny,' is what I go by," she said. Angie had manners, Granny realized. That was a scarce commodity among today's young people.

"I'm from Southern Oregon," Angie said. "Ashland. You know, where the Shakespeare festival is every year."

Neither Granny nor Molly had ever heard of that.

"Oh, of course," Granny said, pretending to be cultured. "The Shakespeare festival."

"So what brought you out here?" Molly asked, "To the farms?"

Angie squirmed a little. She did not feel comfortable answering that question. "Well, I needed a job," she said. "You know, with the college closed down and all." She shrugged.

"What brought an art student out to a farm?" Granny asked, a little too bluntly, and she felt sorry for that.

Angie expected that question and had rehearsed an answer. "You know," she said cocking her head to one side, "I didn't know. I just knew I needed a job." She shrugged again.

Granny wasn't feeling like her questions were being answered. It wasn't that Angie seemed evasive, it just seemed like there was no answer to the questions.

"Have you found a job out here?" Molly asked, trying to be a little nicer than the slightly too blunt Granny.

"Oh, yes," Angie said as her eyes lit up. "I'm helping Dennis at his place."

"Doing what?" Granny asked. Again, a little too bluntly.

"You know," Angie said, "stuff." She started to shrug again, but stopped mid-shrug. She didn't feel comfortable shrugging anymore.

"Household chores," Molly said, trying to rescue the conversation. "That kind of thing?"

"Yes, yes," Angie replied, relieved that Molly was helping her along in this uncomfortable conversation with Granny.

"Oh," Granny said with a smile, "I understand. That's great." The ice had been broken. Granny just seemed awkward, not mean.

By this time, Dennis was back with two Mason jars of iced tea.

"Here you are, honey," Dennis said. He had never called a woman "honey" before and was very thankful he finally could. He was so happy his hands started to shake a little, causing him to spill a few drops of iced tea.

"Oops, silly," Angie warmly said to him and grabbed a rag and wiped up the few drops of iced tea. "There, honey," she said with a smile. Dennis smiled back at her. He couldn't stop smiling.

This was shocking to Granny and Molly, who had known Dennis his whole life. He had never had a girlfriend and now was swapping "honeys" with a beautiful woman. It was so out of character.

"So how long have you two been dating?" Granny asked them.

They looked at each other to see which one would answer. "Go ahead, dear," Angie said, "Tell her the story."

"Well," Dennis said as he slightly puffed out his chest again in pride, "I was on guard duty a couple of weeks ago at the Delphi guard station." He looked at Angie as if to ask if she wanted to tell the next part.

She accepted the invitation. "I was walking down Highway 101 looking for a job or whatever," she said, lowering her eyes a little. Granny noticed this, and it confirmed what Granny was thinking.

"I was walking during the day because it's much safer than at night," Angie continued. "You know how bad things are in Olympia, especially at the college."

Granny and Molly had heard stories of the students being basically abandoned out there. No food trucks were coming in, so the students were getting in their cars, if they had any gas, and trying to drive back home. Most didn't get very far. Quite a few just started walking toward town. They would camp out in large groups. It was summer so they just needed a blanket to put on the ground.

"What did you do during the time until you came to Delphi?" Molly asked.

"Well," Angie said, "like a lot of the students, we camped in various places for a few weeks."

"It got old fast," Dennis interjected. "Angie didn't have anywhere   to   shower."

"Yep," she said. "It got old. Then I found a job in town."

"What kind of job?" Granny asked. She was getting more and more comfortable being direct like that. She needed to find out about Angie. For Dennis's sake.

Angie looked down and then looked up and said, "I, um, worked for a guy in town. I did, you know, general things for him." Granny and Molly nodded. They were starting to figure things out.

"What kind of work?" Granny asked.

"I went out shopping for him," she said. "The lines are so long for everything. I'd wait an hour to get him gas, and then another hour for groceries. That kind of thing."

"How old was he?" Granny asked, closing in on the kill.

Angie was getting uncomfortable. She looked down and then up at the sky, as if she were thinking.

"Well," she answered, "let's see. I think he said he was forty or something."

"Why couldn't he get his own groceries and gas?" Granny asked. Her tone was polite, but she was determined to get some answers.

"He had a big job," she said. She paused and nodded.

"Doing what?" Granny asked with a smile.

"He was some guy for the state," Angie said. She knew Granny would ask her for more detail, so she started to think what he did for a living. She kept looking up at the sky. She seemed to remember the answer and said, "Some highway planner guy or something."

"Oh," Molly said, hoping to soften the line of questioning, "so he had a lot on his FCard, probably."

"Sure did," Angie said, once again glad Molly was rescuing her from Granny's direct questions.

"That must have been a good thing to have," Granny said, steering the conversation back in the direction she wanted.

"Yeah," Angie said, once again looking down, "I guess."

Dennis was oblivious to all of this. All he knew is that he had a pretty girlfriend. He was finally in love. Finally. He wanted to marry Angie.

"So how long did you stay with him?" Granny asked.

"How long did the job last?" Angie shot back, too smart to fall for the trap Granny was setting. Angie did not like this Granny lady's questions. She understood Granny's need to find out about Dennis's new girlfriend, she just wished she had better answers to the questions.

"Yes, dear," Granny said. "Of course. How long did the job last?" Granny was playing along. She wasn't going to cause a scene or make Angie mad, which would be bad for Dennis. She wanted Dennis to be happy.

Angie looked up at the sky again, as if she were counting.

"Let's see. Early June to not that long ago. So that's, like five weeks."

"Why did the job end?" Granny asked. Another fair and logical question, even if Angie didn't want to answer it.

Angie decided to tell the truth. She was an honest person and didn't want to lie. "His wife came back," she said. Granny and Molly were silent. Dennis was oblivious.

"His wife came back?" Granny repeated.

"Yeah," Dennis said, "so he didn't need Angie's help anymore. His wife could do stuff." By "stuff," Dennis meant waiting in lines; Granny and Molly suspected "stuff" meant something else.

Angie nodded. She was relieved that was now out in the open.

"Oh," Granny said, still trying not to cause a scene. "So then you moved on and came out here?"

"Yep," Angie said. "I started walking down Highway 101, thinking that people in the country were better off than in the city. You know, more food and everything." She pointed around her at all the gardens and cows.

"Well," Granny said with a reassuring smile, "You came to the right place. We have plenty of food." She wanted to soften things and be nice to Angie. She didn't dislike the girl; she just wanted to know what Dennis was getting himself into.

Someone yelled, "Who wants pie?" and Angie, sensing her chance to break free from this uncomfortable conversation, jumped up and said, "We do!" She turned to Dennis and said, "I'll go get us some, honey."

"Sounds great, honey," he said. He loved to hear that word. Over and over again.

Dennis looked around and saw Angie was several yards away going to get the pie. "So?" He quietly asked Granny and Molly, "What do you think?" He was beaming.

"She's lovely, Dennis," Granny said. "A sweet, sweet girl. She's perfect for you. We're so happy." Molly nodded.

Dennis clapped his hands and yelled, "Wahoo!" Getting the approval of Granny and Molly for Angie was the second happiest day of his life; the happiest day being when he met her at the gate.

"Some people want to talk to us," Angie yelled from the pie table as she motioned for Dennis to join her. He got up and said, "Gotta go." He trotted over to be with this magnificent girlfriend.

When Dennis was far enough away, Granny asked Molly, "Are you thinking what I'm thinking?"

Molly nodded slowly.

Chapter 222

The Think Farm

(August 4)

"Of course!" Brad Finehoff shouted to his son, Russ, who was disguised as a homeless man at the Union Gospel Mission. "I've been waiting for this opportunity." Jerry, Mike, and Chrissy clapped. They were gambling that Brad would accept Russ's offer; if he didn't, they would be exposing themselves as Patriots. But, like with the tugs of the left ear, they knew each other well.

Brad paused and, after realizing that his missing son was now alive and well, asked Russ, "Oh, and where the hell have you been for the past ninety-four days?"

Russ started to answer and Mike put his finger up to his lips, signaling Russ to be quiet. Brad saw this and nodded.

"Now isn't a real good time to talk, Dad," Russ said. "I mean, I'm in Olympia and I'm not exactly super welcome here."

"Got it," Brad said. He looked at Jerry, Mike, and Chrissy, put two fingers up in the air and pointed toward the door, which was the signal to get their protected guest out of the room. As they'd done a thousand times together, the closest one to the door, Mike, went out with Chrissy behind him and Jerry maneuvered around to take up the rear behind Brad and Russ.

They quickly and discreetly exited the mission. Most of the homeless men got out of their way and put their hands up as they passed. They didn't want any trouble with these people, who were obviously with the government.

By the time Jerry was at Chrissy's car, she had already started it and Russ was getting in. Brad was heading toward Chrissy's car when Jerry said, "My rig" and pointed toward his truck, which Brad recognized. It had been pre-staged at the mission because they knew they'd run out of room for all five of them in Chrissy's car. Besides, they wanted to split up the cargo, with Russ in one vehicle and Brad in another in case something happened to one vehicle. A final, and very important, reason for two vehicles was to check for a vehicle following them. The vehicle in the rear would drop back a few vehicles behind the lead vehicle and keep track of the vehicles around it. Then the rear vehicle would move up to the lead and the vehicle formerly in the lead would drop to the rear. This way they could tell if one of the vehicles they were keeping track of was speeding up to follow the rear vehicle that was now up in the lead. The EPU unit did this so often that they didn't even notice they were doing; it was how they rolled.

Brad grabbed the little radio under the passenger seat of Jerry's truck, where it always was. It wasn't the government-issued ones they usually used, but the controls worked the same as the ones he was familiar with. Jerry concentrated on driving while Brad worked the radio, which was used to keep in contact with Chrissy's car. They only talked on the vehicle-to-vehicle radios if they needed to. Chatting was looked down upon.

Brad was finally able to take in all that had happened that day. His career ended, his friends joined the Patriots, his missing son was found, and now Brad was joining the Patriots, which, of course, was a death sentence if he got caught.

At least he was with his son and his team. The only thing that would have been better would be being with his wife, Kathy, but she had left him a decade ago, when Russ was in high school. She couldn't handle having a husband who was never around. Her leaving had made Brad even more devoted to his EPU team: if it had cost him his marriage, he might as well enjoy all the time he could with the people who had stuck with him all these years.

Russ was included in that category. When Kathy left, Brad and Russ were on their own. They took care of each other and became even closer, which was why it was so hard when Russ turned up missing right after the May Day riots.

Brad was trying to stay silent so Jerry could concentrate on driving, but he couldn't contain himself. He settled for merely saying, "I bet there's a hell of a story waiting for me about how that homeless dude with the sandwich ended up in that kitchen." Jerry looked over at him and smiled.

They quickly arrived at a nearby welding shop. They drove up, and Mike said, "Albatross pepper," from Chrissy's car on the vehicle-to-vehicle radio. Right on cue, the large garage door of the shop opened and both vehicles drove in. The garage door closed right behind Jerry's truck.

Brad instinctively took off his seat belt and was looking around for what to do next. Normally he knew every detail of what to do next – where to go when he got out of the vehicle, who was in the lead, who was in the rear, and where they were going next. It was very unusual and unsettling for him to not know these details. But, he would just roll with it, knowing that his team was taking care of everything.

As Brad was exiting the passenger side of Jerry's truck, he saw two men in work overalls signaling for him to follow them. Mike turned around and put his hand behind his head, which was the signal to follow the other's lead. Brad did so.

Russ and Brad met up with the two men and headed through a door into the office of the welding shop. Brad still had no idea what was going on. Brad, who was always armed with at least his service weapon, a Smith and Wesson M&P .40, felt comfortable having these strangers take him and his son somewhere. But, still wanting to know what the plan was, he turned back to get an indicator from his team. Mike pointed toward Brad and Russ, and then at the two men, and said, "You're going with them. You'll know they're on the right team if they know what you were having for lunch." Brad nodded and, along with Russ, who looked so strange dressed up as a bum, walked out of the office into a welding shop van waiting on the street outside. One of the men opened the panel door and Brad and Russ got in the rear seat. There was a new man in coveralls driving, in addition to the first two who had guided them into the van.

Brad felt perfectly comfortable when his team was around, but now they weren't. He immediately swung into "possible threat" mode and felt for his pistol, which was right where it was supposed to be.

"What'd I want for lunch?" Brad said to the driver.

"Meatball sub, sir," one of the two men in coveralls said.

That reminded him about his lunch that he never got to eat. "Where is it?" he asked Russ.

"Where's what?" Russ asked.

"My lunch," Brad said.

Russ smiled, which looked so strange in that fake beard, and said, "I kinda ate it." Things were just like normal, Brad thought. His always-hungry son ate his lunch.

Brad was starting to relax – to the extent he ever relaxed when he was on a protective detail. Then it hit him: he was on a protective detail, not protecting the Governor or some other state official, but his son. And he was working for the Patriots. Doing what, he wasn't sure. But he knew it would be worthwhile.

Brad wanted to ask Russ everything about what he had been doing while he was missing, where they were going to, and what lay ahead, but he knew that conversation would come later, when they were in a secure place. It was excruciating to sit silently and not talk to his son. Russ had been instructed in advance to just remain quiet during the ride.

"What's our cover story?" Brad asked the men in coveralls. They had to have an explanation for why men in a welding van had an EPU agent and bum.

"Stranded motorists," the first man in coveralls said.

"Pretty crappy cover story," Brad said. "Where's my car, what kind of car is it, why don't I have the keys on me, and why would a bum either be riding with me or have a second vehicle?"

"We're winging some of the details," the second man in coveralls said. "This isn't like the old days when we had tons of resources." He sounded like he had been an agent of some kind before the Collapse.

Brad was silent. It was true that no one had the resources to plan out things like they used to, when they had plenty of money, personnel, and no threats against the people they protected. Then again, the government didn't have the resources, either. The government was winging it, too.

"If we're stopped," the driver said after a few moments, "We shoot our way out of it."

"Roger that," Brad said. That was a plan. Of sorts.

They drove in the van for about half an hour, which took them out into the countryside. They slowly pulled up to a long driveway that served several homes judging by all the mailboxes at the junction between the driveway and the road. They were in a heavily forested area and the houses were spread out so each home was hidden.

A few yards from the beginning of the driveway was a broken down car in the way. The first man in coveralls got on the radio and said, "Gazelle pasta."

"Space command," was the reply on the radio. A teenage boy appeared out of nowhere and started the ignition in the car and moved it so the van could come down the driveway. As they were passing by, Brad noticed about twenty heavily camouflaged and extremely well-armed soldiers. They weren't duck hunters; they had current-issue military fatigues and radios. A few had camouflage paint on their faces and looked like the special operations guys Brad's EPU unit sometimes trained with. These men were pros.

They passed several houses that looked like typical country homes in the area. They were nice but not ostentatious. They were typical houses from the building boom in the mid-2000s when nice homes were built on wooded five-acre parcels all around Olympia. The houses were not noteworthy; they blended in perfectly.

About two hundred yards down the driveway, there was a second checkpoint. It was in front of a belt-fed machine gun under the canopy of a big evergreen tree so it couldn't be seen from the air. Three soldiers were manning it with anti-armor rocket launchers. The driver exchanged code words with the men at the second checkpoint and they kept driving slowly down the driveway.

They pulled off the main driveway onto a smaller one and toward a nice house tucked away in the woods. As they pulled up, Brad immediately noticed only one vehicle parked in front of it. That made sense, he thought, because drones or satellites would notice a throng of vehicles in front of a house. Brad realized that even though his former employer, the Legitimate Authorities, had limited drone and satellite capabilities with all the personnel shortages, they still had some. And if they were looking for some extremely high-value targets, or HVTs, they could use these whiz-bang toys to find people – but only a handful of people, out of the tens of millions who no longer were loyal citizens of the United States.

"We're home," Russ said as the van stopped at the house.

The men in coveralls got a cowboy hat out from a bag and handed it to Brad. "Just in case a drone has been tracking the van and wants to see who our passenger is," the driver said. "Super unlikely, but it's an easy precaution to take." Brad put on the hat. He felt weird wearing a cowboy hat in a suit and getting out of a van with his son dressed as a homeless man, but he also felt reassured that his hosts were professionals who were taking good care of them.

An attractive woman in her early forties came out the front door of the house in shorts and a t-shirt with a diet Coke in her hand. She looked like a soccer mom getting ready to take the kids to a day at the beach. She was quite a contrast to the camouflage-faced soldiers hiding in the woods a few hundred yards away.

"Welcome, guys!" she said. "Nice to see you. A cowboy and a bum; what is it? Halloween?" she said with a laugh.

"Trick or treat," Russ said, getting out of the van. He pointed to Brad and said, "Amber Taurus, please meet my dad, Brad Finehoff."

Brad walked up to her and shook her hand. He wondered if they were at the right house. Surely, a super-secret den of HVTs wasn't hosted by a soccer mom with a diet Coke in her hand.

"Welcome to the Think Farm," Amber said. "We call it the Think Farm because it's a public policy think tank but we're hiding out here on the little farms we have." Amber had been a liberty activist before the Collapse and galvanized her like-minded neighbors to let her have some "guests" out.

"We're glad to have you, Brad," Amber said. "I've heard a lot about you."

"Glad to be here," Brad said, suddenly wondering what exactly he would be doing out here.

"Come on in," Amber said. "I've got sandwiches for you if you're hungry."

"Great," Brad said. "Some homeless guy ate my meatball sub."

Amber looked puzzled.

"It's a long story," Russ said.

"Well, come on in," Amber said as she motioned for Brad and Russ to enter her home.

When they entered, several people in the house came to greet them. They were college-looking kids and it looked like Amber was their den mother.

Brad recognized a few of the kids as friends of Russ from when he worked on the staff of the Republican caucus in the Legislature. One was Carly, the former intern at the Washington Association of Business. Brad said hi to her. He realized he had a cowboy hat on and a suit. No one thought it looked odd; they knew that new visitors wore cowboy hats in case any drones were hovering above the Think Farm.

"What's it like back in Olympia?" one of the kids asked. Russ gave a good report, giving them his observations about little things with political significance like the graffiti and the increasing garbage on the streets. "More burned out cars," he added. He went on to describe the alertness of the guards. A pretty good Intel report, Brad thought. He was proud.

After the kids discussed the conditions in Olympia, Amber said, "Brad, we need to get you to your quarters and to our afternoon meeting."

Brad nodded. "Go ahead, Dad," Russ said. "I'll catch up with you at dinner." Brad said his goodbyes and walked out the front door with Amber.

The van was still there. "They'll take you to where you'll be staying," Amber said. "It's two houses down the road." She looked back at her house and said, "Don't worry. You'll be staying with grown-ups." Brad laughed.

The van took him two houses down the road. He came to a house very similar to Amber's. He got out, wearing his cowboy hat again, and met a man who introduced himself as Jason. Brad recognized him from many legislative receptions the Governor attended when he was on her EPU detail.

"Welcome to the capitol of New Washington," Jason said. "Here are two other former members of the House, Matt and Dave." Jason also introduced Brad to a former judge, a few former county commissioners, and some former staffers for various elected officials.

"We're all 'formers,'" Jason said. "As in former office holders because, in our case," he said, motioning to himself, Matt, and Dave, "the House voted a few days after May Day to eject me from my seat and appoint one of their own people." He rolled his eyes.

Brad took off the cowboy hat. It seemed too ridiculous to be wearing it inside. "So, what do you guys do out here?"

"We are figuring out how to rebuild after we win," Dave said. "Rebuilding politically. We spend hours talking about the new constitution we'll enact, elections, the size of the new government, and how we'll reconcile with the Limas who want to live in our territory." It sounded strange for him to say "our" territory.

"What territory we want is a big topic," Matt said. "Do we want to try to govern the whole state, or leave Seattle to rot?"

Brad listened as they discussed the pros and cons of trying to take and govern Seattle. It was fascinating. They all seemed convinced the Patriots would win. They were already working on the details of governing, getting private industry to rebuild infrastructure, starting a court system, a new police force, and even relations with other states and nearby Canada.

"So, what will I be doing out here?" Brad asked them after a while.

Their answer stunned him.

Chapter 223

End of Summer

(September - October)

As autumn settled in, a new normal developed at Pierce Point. All the things that became earth-shatteringly different when the Collapse hit were now nearly commonplace. The daily 9 to 5 existence disappeared, and was replaced by gardening, bartering, and learning how to survive without Starbucks. Office jobs quickly seemed like a thing of the past. This had an enormous impact on everyone's lives. There were no more alarm clocks, no more commutes, no more lunch hours, and no more quitting times. No more hard structure to the day. It was like being on vacation — sort of.

Despite this change in pace, the Collapse was no vacation, as in carefree fun and games. The lack of structured work days came with a price: there was now a lot more work that people had to do themselves. People were much busier, but it was a good kind of busy. They started walking everywhere instead of driving. They had to spend time finding food and cooking it because there were no more restaurants. They canned, dried, smoked, and froze food.

Gathering firewood became a constant chore because the pre-Collapse ways of heating a home could no longer be counted on. Those relying on heating oil were out of luck; petroleum was now being used exclusively for gasoline and diesel. Natural gas was still flowing most of the time because it was one of the utilities protected under the Utility Treaty. The problem with that was that a natural gas furnace relied on electricity to power the fan.

The electricity stayed on most of the time throughout the summer, but it was inconsistent. The hackers continued attacking the grid periodically. The bigger disruption to the electrical system was that the government couldn't get replacement parts out to the electrical companies.

Woodstoves and fireplaces started becoming very popular. Quite a few people started little businesses supplying firewood. Luckily, there were lots of woodstoves and plenty of firewood in Pierce Point.

Repairing things, like the chainsaws that were now necessary to provide firewood, was another thing that was done during the hours that people used to check email at their work desks. There were no more repair people to come out to a person's house and fix something like a broken door. People had to fix things themselves or find people nearby who could. Since almost no one knew how to do things like that, even out at rugged and relatively self-reliant Pierce Point, it often required relying on people who knew how to fix things, which could take a few days, or longer.

In Pierce Point, finding these people was often done by walking or riding a bike to the Grange and writing a help wanted note on the bulletin board. Then, if the phones were down, like they often were, walking or riding a bike to the Grange the next day to see if someone had responded. And then maybe another walk or bike ride somewhere to contact the fix-it person. People with fix-it skills were in very high demand and were starting to make a nice living.

Even harder than finding a person who knew how to fix things was finding the replacement parts. Before the Collapse, getting a new door just meant a quick trip to a home improvement super store. Now it might take a few days. It might mean visiting neighbors and asking if they knew of a door not being used at an abandoned house, what its measurements were, and then removing it. All this had to happen before a person could even attempt to use the door. It might take a few weeks to replace the door.

In addition to simple tasks taking days or weeks, people's new jobs for the community, like guard duty or kitchen duty at the Grange, took much of their time. Most people were working a lot more even though they were technically unemployed.

Due to the generally slower pace, the lack of a daily grind, and the unpredictable nature of how long various tasks would take, punctuality was soon thrown out the window.

All of this walking and biking, and the more vigorous lifestyle in general, meant that people were in the best shape of their lives. Despite the stress that people were under, they were generally sleeping much better, because they were so exhausted at the end of the day.

The exercise wasn't the only reason people were in much better shape. They weren't eating crap all the time. Instead of drive-thru value meals, people were relying a lot more on vegetables from gardens, lean deer or elk meat and fish. They drank water instead of sugared soda.

Aside from the health benefits, the widespread weight loss and nicely tanned skin from the summer sun had other benefits, too. Men and women who used to be uninterested in each other were suddenly rediscovering each other. Before the Collapse, slender and tan was sexy, but rare. Now many more people were in that category and they were getting noticed by the opposite sex.

Sex came roaring back. Immediately following the shock and stress that occurred after the May Day collapse, sex had been the last thing on most people's minds. But, as things started stabilizing in Pierce Point around mid-summer, people rediscovered it, especially since there wasn't much else to do without TV worth watching, movies, restaurants, or anything else that involved driving places. People went back to doing what they did before all of those distractions.

The new way of life was somewhat freeing to some women, too: most quit wearing makeup. There were no more semi-trucks of makeup restocking the shelves, so people had to make do with what they had on hand when the Collapse started.

At first it was hard for some women to go without makeup, but they slowly got used to it. The men also got used to seeing women without blush and mascara, although they never cared nearly as much about women wearing makeup as the women did. Besides, the general trend of slender and tan more than made up for the lack of makeup in most men's eyes.

The notable exception to the lack of makeup was the women on TV. They still had painted faces. They started looking stranger to all the people who didn't have any makeup around. Women with makeup on TV were just another indicator that the government running the TV networks was out of touch with real people.

Another social phenomenon from the Collapse was that most men started growing beards. They didn't have the time or shaving supplies to shave every day. One exception was that Loyalist men were often clean shaven. Loyalists had the shaving supplies because they were first in line to get things. Shaving became a status symbol to Loyalists, as it showed they had the power to get the necessary supplies. Loyalists thought the bearded men were barbarian teabaggers. The men on government TV were clean shaven, except the villains, who all had beards. The clean shaven men on television made it even more artificial for people out in rural areas where most men were bearded. The division in the country between the ruling class and the ruled class popped up in the most unlikely places: facial hair and makeup.

Another unforeseen outcome was that being fat became a

positive status symbol, at least among Loyalists. Before the Collapse, most Americans were fat. The question was whether they were very fat or just fat. During the Collapse, when most people lost weight, some Loyalists still had access to all the food they wanted and they still had people to do all their physical work for them. Well-connected Loyalists could get gas so they could drive instead of walk, like everyone else had to. So some Loyalists who had the luxury of being fat showed it off as a status symbol.

Weekends were no longer what they used to be. Before the Collapse, people went to work during the week and tried to avoid their offices on the weekends. After the Collapse, weekdays and weekends started blurring together. People did what they needed to do — get food, repair things, do guard duty — when it needed to be done, which was seven days a week. No one could take off Saturday and Sunday and leave the gate unguarded. People had a much more relaxed pace during each day, but they had that relaxed pace seven days a week. About the only thing that happened on the weekends that set those days apart was that some went to church and funeral services on Sundays.

And Sunday dinners. A strong tradition one hundred years ago, the Sunday dinner was back. After the Collapse, most people would have a big meal Sunday afternoon with their family and friends. It was a mini-Thanksgiving, but with whatever food they had, instead of turkey and stuffing. People brought different foods and shared them. The Grange often held a big Sunday potluck for the people who didn't have families. The guards also had a version of Sunday dinner. Guards who didn't have family and weren't working on Sunday would come down to the fire station on Sunday afternoon.

It was odd. So many traditional American things returned during the Collapse. Sunday dinners, church attendance, beards, healthier people, less reliance on technology, and lots of good old fashioned American self-reliance.

At the same time old traditions resurfaced, other traditional American things faded away. No one cared if people were married or not. Non-official "war marriages" as they were called and shacking up started becoming more acceptable.

There was no detectable racism at Pierce Point. That had faded over the decades. Now most communities, including Pierce Point, had people of many races in them. In Pierce Point there were several Mexican families who had been there for decades. Most people didn't know a white-only world. People — at least out in Pierce Point — were smart enough to know that good people and bad people come in all colors.

The one role race was supposed to play never materialized. The government tried to use race to mobilize Loyalists by warning that teabagger Patriots were evil racists out to hang blacks and Hispanics. That message worked in Loyalist-held cities, but not out in the rural areas, like Pierce Point. To most people out there, it seemed absurd to think that Patriots were Klansmen. Rural people saw with their own eyes how ridiculous that was.

One thing that people firmly agreed on was the fact that winter was coming. The mornings were now crisp and the days were cooler. It got dark earlier. Leaves were starting to fall, along with the rain. In Western Washington, it would be cloudy and rain on and off from October until mid-spring.

People knew things would be tougher in the winter. The gardens would stop producing their bounty. In addition, hunting and fishing were already yielding less food because everyone spent the summer hunting and fishing.

Getting food during the winter was a big concern, but the government said everything would be fine. Most people in the nation knew the government had just barely held things together during the summer. If struggling during the summer had been the best the government could do, then the winter would be a disaster. There was no way the government could get food out by truck when the snow and ice hit in the Midwest where most of the government food came from. With no heating oil and only spotty natural gas, people in the Northeast and Midwest would literally freeze to death. Winter colds and flu viruses would be able to kill people who lacked medicine. People were stressed and undernourished, and without medicines. These things were becoming a big deal; a deadly big deal.

People in Pierce Point were working overtime to get enough food put up for the winter. There was increasing chatter about when to open up Gideon's semi-truck of food. Residents who had not been volunteering at the Grange, and therefore didn't have a meal card, were now very interested in volunteering.

For the first time, it looked like the Grange might not have enough food for all the people eating there with meal cards. There wouldn't be mass starvation, but things would get sparse. Tensions would rise. This would lead to arguing; possibly violence. Maybe Pierce Point was like the Loyalist government in one way: things were relatively easy during the summer, but the winter would be different.

On top of all this, there was going to be a war.

Chapter 224

Kit Kat

(Late October)

Grant was trying his hardest to attend to his Pierce Point duties, though he was distracted by the activities at Marion Farm. He had to force himself to focus on Pierce Point. After all, Pierce Point was a civil affairs success story and he had to make sure it was still working as the great example of what could be done when people didn't rely on the government. More importantly, he had to make sure his family was fed and defended. He found those things to be amazing motivators.

As part of his day job at the Grange, Grant trained with the Team whenever he could. He even went out on a couple of calls with them (all of which turned out to be false alarms). Grant talked regularly with Rich, Dan, and the Chief to make sure the guards, beach patrol, and Team had everything they needed to do their jobs. He made sure the communications system between the security forces was working. He had never truly realized how important good communications were until now.

He also presided over three or four trials a week; a few criminal trials, mostly for smaller things, no murders or rapes. Hanging people early on swiftly created a law-and-order atmosphere, which was good.

Brittany and Ronnie from the meth house were released from jail early for good behavior. They had a hard time in jail because they were cut off from their various drugs and the withdrawal was horrible. Brittany came out of it better because she wasn't as addicted as Ronnie. She even started having Pastor Pete come by and became a very active church member after she was released. The church gave Brittany a place to live and they fed her. They gave her a job as the "administrative assistant," but she didn't have much to do. It was just a nice way to give her charity, but she took the job seriously and worked diligently at it.

After his release, Ronnie was depressed and was basically waiting around to die. He did odd jobs at the Grange and went to be by himself in an abandoned mobile home he had refurbished. No one heard from him for long periods of time, which was how he liked it.

Most of the trials were mental health commitments and a few

terminations of parental rights. After an initial spike in mental health commitments resulting from the lack of medications, the number of commitments went down. The commitments never completely diminished because there were still plenty of people who were mildly mentally ill who were finally breaking down. Also, some people who were not mentally ill were cracking under the pressure of life after the Collapse. The mental ward was starting to fill up.

There were only a few terminations of parental rights. Most of them were kids being taken out of the homes of people being committed to the mental ward.

Grant was proud of the parental termination system they had developed. It took a lot of credible evidence for a jury to take kids from their parents because parents are supposed to raise kids, not the government. Removing them from their families was only to be done out of absolute necessity. Pierce Point's system was so much better than the old government one, which seemed to let kids get abused for years before intervening, or, on the flipside, to overreact and take kids on a whim. The old system was all about jobs for social workers, not safety for kids. Pierce Point had stripped down the bureaucracy and ensured no one had a profit motive in the child protection system. Taking away the profit motive seemed to eliminate the problem, as did keeping things small, like a tight-knit community that actually knew the kids and parents and truly cared about them. That was undoubtedly better than a giant countywide or statewide system of anonymous faces. And a profit motive.

The main thing Grant worked on was political unity. Without unity, there would be fighting and that would be the end of Pierce Point. Unity was essential.

And by "unity," Grant meant "people who think like I do." Was that "bossy" or "close minded"? He didn't care.

Long ago, Grant had gotten over any guilt about insisting that Pierce Point operate on a Patriot set of principles. This wasn't some debating club with the luxury of asking everyone to share their feelings and gently consider opposing viewpoints. This was survival. Taking too long to decide life-and-death matters, or having constant debates that divided everyone, would get people killed. Pierce Point needed leadership, not a moderator of philosophical discussion.

Grant wasn't a dictator, though. This was especially true since there were other leaders in the community, like Rich and Dan. There was no way for one person to emerge as a dictator. That was by design; checks and balances.

While he wasn't a dictator, Grant was very firm in how he approached his leadership role. His view was that if Pierce Point wanted to succeed, they needed to do it the Patriot way using the smallest government possible, self-reliance, liberty, law and order, a strong defense, and charity. People at Pierce Point didn't need to be total Patriots and believe exactly what Grant did. No, they just needed to do things the Patriot way. Because it worked. Period. The Loyalist way … well, that's how things got screwed up.

If someone wanted big government, dependence on others, and oppression, then they could move to Frederickson, or Olympia, or Seattle. Leave. Good riddance.

Besides, Grant had a very personal stake in the Patriots prevailing at Pierce Point. He was a wanted man. The Loyalists would haul him off to jail or maybe shoot him on the spot if they captured him. Snelling had been going down the path of turning Grant in to the authorities before Wes … announced "Lima down."

That was how Grant chose to characterize to himself what happened to Snelling: Lima down. It sounded so bland and businesslike. "Killing people who disagree with you" didn't have as nice a ring to it. And Grant was concerned about the war turning into a political bloodbath of petty vendettas. Even when the person involved, Snelling in this case, was actually trying to get Grant killed. He still hated to see this political killing, but he was ready to do it and knew he'd be doing more of it in the future.

Therefore, given how crucial political unity was, Grant spent lots of his day-job time on politics. There were no more open Loyalists at Pierce Point. If they existed (and they surely did) they were keeping quiet. Some rumors went around about Snelling's disappearance and how the Team may have killed him. That seemed to silence the Loyalists. Good. Grant hadn't wanted to kill Snelling, but now that he was dead, at least there was some good coming from it.

Grant constantly tried to figure out who the Patriots were and, more importantly, the ULPs, which stood for "Undecided/Leaning Patriot." ULPs were the people Grant concentrated his efforts on. For every open Patriot, there were probably ten ULPs. They were the key to political unity at Pierce Point. And political unity was the key to survival.

There were also the "U"s: Undecideds. These were the truly undecided people who didn't care about politics, which was the majority of people at Pierce Point. They just wanted to make it through the Collapse and hopefully have a better life when it was all over.

Grant remembered how the majority of the population back in the Revolutionary War was also undecided. They waited to see who was winning and then started coming out in support of the soon-to-be winner. There was no use getting mad at the "U"s for being spineless. People just needed to accept that this was how most human beings act in such situations.

At Pierce Point, the "U"s would look at the growing number of ULPs turning into open Patriots. The "U"s were the big prize and the ULPs were the key to winning over the "U"s.

Grant would find out what ULPs needed and try to make sure they got it. A ULP needs some canning jars? Grant would try to make sure they got some. Upon delivery, he would say something not very subtle like, "The government couldn't get this for you." He would stop and take plenty of time to talk to ULPs and let them know all about the good things: the guards, the food, and the social events.

Everyone knew Grant was a Patriot and was trying to persuade them, though he wasn't doing it in an obnoxious car-salesman way, or in an intellectual and theoretical "Thomas Jefferson once said…" way. Instead, Grant would try to persuade people in a "here's what's working" way, with plenty of "remember what didn't work" sprinkled in.

His practical approach to persuasion was working. People saw results. The government had absolutely no credibility at this point, so just about any alternative to it would be persuasive. People in Pierce Point, who could still intermittently use the internet and phones, knew from the outside world that they had it very good out there. Instead of cowering in their homes hiding from gangs and waiting for the next shipment of food to try to buy with their FCards, people in Pierce Point were getting by. School—at least a part-time, volunteer one—had started in September. Some of the families out there thought that the structure of school and resemblance of normalcy would be helpful for the kids.

When Halloween rolled around, it was obvious how well Pierce Point was doing. When he started prepping a few years earlier, Grant began taking all the extra Halloween candy they had—and there were way too many bags of it—and vacuum sealed it. He had told Lisa that he was taking it to the homeless shelter, but he had actually sealed it and put it out at the cabin. He just knew that something as simple as Halloween candy would have a big impact during a disaster. It would be a luxury, even.

Sure enough. When the post-Collapse Halloween arrived,

Grant had several hundred miniature candy bars and other goodies. Other families had a little Halloween candy and chipped in, too. When they pooled their candy, there was enough for all the kids at Pierce Point to have a couple of pieces.

They had a big Halloween party at the Grange, which was nicely decorated, and everyone came in costume. And they didn't arrive in the fancy pre-Collapse, store-bought, costumes. They came in real ones that people actually took the time to make. Lisa had mouse ears that Eileen made her and Grant was a farmer with a John Deere hat and overalls. Manda came as a princess and Cole was a pirate.

Grant took great joy in handing out the candy at the Grange Halloween party. The kids hadn't had much, if any, candy in months. After going so long without sugar, the candy tasted overly sweet. Grant allowed himself one Kit Kat. It tasted sweeter than anything he'd ever eaten. Just seeing that red wrapper and snapping apart the sticks of the Kit Kat took him back to days past when things were normal. Back when he just went to the store and got himself a Kit Kat whenever he wanted one.

Dozens of parents profusely thanked Grant and the others who donated the candy. "This feels like a 'normal' Halloween," a single mom told Grant. "That means everything. The kids need to have 'normal' things," she said. Soon after, Grant noticed she had switched from ULP to Patriot on Drew's list. The government couldn't get her kids Halloween candy, but the Patriots could.

Grant would gleefully tell Ted the details of how well Pierce Point was functioning, which Ted reported to Boston Harbor. He wanted HQ to know that Grant was handling the civil affairs job at Pierce Point extremely well. Ted also wanted HQ to know that this area was hospitable to even more troops. He wanted to get the biggest and best equipped unit possible. Not for his ego, but to have a better chance of winning the fight that was coming.

Things on the home front were going well for Grant. He and Lisa were getting along magnificently. She had almost fully adjusted to her new life and living conditions. She had realized a long time ago that she was lucky to have a man like Grant who had made all the preparations he did. She wouldn't tell Grant that, though; it might go to his head.

The one thing that still stood between Grant and Lisa was his continual lying. He wasn't telling her what he was doing at Marion Farm. While the guilt ate him up at first, he was slowly adjusting to lying to her as the months went on. He had to. He'd been through that in his head a million times.

Manda and Cole were doing very well. Manda and Jordan were full-on boyfriend and girlfriend. She was still doing a fabulous job of taking care of all the kids. Jordan was doing an excellent job as a gate guard. Cole was continuing to improve every day with his talking. He was a very happy kid and was taking care of the younger kids, too. It was heartwarming.

Drew and Eileen were fully at home upstairs in the cabin. They loved having the grandkids around and they had made many friends out at Pierce Point.

Grant, Lisa, and Drew had meal cards at the Grange. (Actually, they didn't physically have cards; everyone just knew they could eat there.) That meant Eileen, Manda, and Cole were on their own for food. Mary Anne brought over produce from her garden and other people's, and Eileen got food from people for helping them with canning and drying. Lisa got quite a bit of food in barter for her medical services. The food coming from others accounted for about half of their food.

The other half of the food for Eileen, Manda, and Cole was the stored food in the shed. Thank God, Grant thought, that they didn't have to rely exclusively on the stored food because it was running out.

They had about half of it left, but Grant's quick calculations were that it wouldn't last through the whole winter; maybe just about through the winter, but not until spring. Grant searched for solutions.

Drew still had some cash, although almost no one was taking it. Grant had some guns and ammo he wasn't using (the butter knife guns). They hadn't been using FCards because, up until this point, they hadn't needed to. Maybe between the cash, guns, and starting to use FCards, they could stretch their stored food to spring. Maybe. Probably. Hopefully.

Chapter 225

"I Brought Friends"

(Late October)

Guard duty at the Delphi Road exit was becoming more interesting. Outsiders were increasingly coming down Highway 101 and trying to find food and security in the country. There were not waves of human refugees or anything like that. It started out as just a few people coming up to the gate each week, then increased to a few each day, followed by a dozen or so each day. Despite this increase, the vast majority of people in the Olympia area were still staying in their homes and getting their FCard food.

The guards could usually turn back people from the gate simply by telling them to move on. A few times, they had to show force by chambering a round from a shotgun, which was a universally understood sound. One guard would keep his shotgun unchambered so he could rack it when necessary to persuade people.

One time, however, this did not work. A group of five rowdy, and probably high, young men and two women arrived at the gate right after dark in a van. They taunted the guards. One of the rowdy men pulled out a pistol and started running toward the guards. They cut him to pieces. It was loud and violent. He was hit so many times it was impossible to identify him when they were done. His friends ran back to their van and sped off.

Most of the guards who fired the deadly shots hated doing it, though a couple of them really enjoyed it. It was understandable why the guards, who were normal people during peacetime, had turned into people who enjoyed shooting bad guys. The guards spent the day thinking about all the dirt bags out there who were trying to steal their stuff and hurt their families. They wanted to take out the "zombies," which was what they had started calling the people coming up to the gate.

The guards who enjoyed shooting the man were rotated off the front line. The leaders of the Delphi Road guards didn't need people starting a firefight just because they enjoyed killing people.

The other guards, the ones who reluctantly killed the "zombie," were not exactly pacifists. They realized that it had to be done. There was no way they were going to let just anyone come into their relatively safe and well-fed community.

The night after the shooting, Brian Jenkins, one of the WAB POIs hiding out at Prosser Farm, was waking up in the dark RV he was sleeping in with some other guards. It was the last day of his week-long guard stint. He had been sleeping when the shooting happened. He was glad he didn't have to kill anyone.

In a few hours, Brian could go back home to the Prosser Farm and be with his family. He was surprised by how quickly the farm felt like home to him. The former lobbyist got his boots on and grabbed his rifle.

Suddenly, the alert went off. People were scrambling around and yelling. Someone was at the gate. "Vehicle! Vehicle!" Brian instantly wondered whether this was the van coming back to avenge the death of their friend.

He flew out of the RV and took up his position. He fell down because he was trying to run in the dark. He was lucky he didn't hurt himself. The stinging on the palm of his left hand where he hit the ground added to the adrenaline of the situation. He was worried he wouldn't be able to hold up his rifle and do what might be necessary.

Brian had never killed anyone. Every time the alert went off, he wondered if that would be the day he would have to kill someone … or be killed himself. It was an unusual thought for a former white-collar guy like him.

Everyone scrambled to their positions. Brian could see some headlights flashing on and off until they went off completely and just the yellow running lights were on. The vehicle was idling. Brian wondered if the vehicle was getting ready to ram the gate.

There was a silent standoff for about a minute; a very long minute. The guards stood there and watched the vehicle idling with its running lights on and then the bushes started rustling. They all knew who it was.

Some of the pickets—the forward sentries who were hidden in front of the gate—came back. "It's a van," they said.

The guard commander, Ned Ford, yelled to the guards, "The van ain't even trying to sneak up on us. Could be a diversion." Ned had been an infantryman in Vietnam and had vivid memories of ambushes and tricks that got people killed. He was determined that nothing like that would happen here on Delphi Road.

The headlights flashed again and the passenger door opened. It was drizzling and dark so it was hard to see anything. A person with his hands up was walking very slowly toward the gate.

They shined their big light on the van and saw the outline of the person. The bright light not only allowed them to see but, as an added bonus, blinded the driver so he couldn't ram the gate.

The person got closer. About twenty yards from the gate, the person yelled. It was a woman, not a man as they originally thought in the dark. "It's Carly. I'm here for Ben."

Ned had been expecting this. A young woman named Carly had come to the gate back in the summer and Ben, one of the guys staying at the Prosser Farm, said to let her in if she came back. It was important. That's all he would say.

Ned had a hunch that Ben was a wanted Patriot and that his covert visitors were doing something important. Ned would do anything he could to help the Patriots, after what had happened to his daughter.

"Proceed," Ned yelled. "But the van stays put."

Carly nodded. She motioned to the driver to stay parked and kept walking slowly with her hands up. Way up. She was nervous.

Brian came up to Ned. After Carly first arrived, Ben told Brian, Tom, and Jeff about why she came. Ben and Laura had decided that he would go with Carly to a new hideout where he could be the interim governor when the time was right. The plan was that the WAB guy who was on guard duty during any given week would greet Carly and then go get Ben. It was Brian who was on duty this week. Ben was packed up and ready to go on a moment's notice.

"I got this," Brian said and Ned nodded. Brian surprised himself with how calm and confident he was.

"Carly, it's Brian," he said. Carly nodded and kept walking slowly with her hands up. It was hard for her to see with the light shining almost directly in her face.

She got about five yards from the gate. Brian slung his rifle, a 30-30, and walked up to her.

There was enough light to see her. She had lost weight and looked fantastic. Brian was so glad to see one of his favorite WAB staffers safe and sound.

"Welcome, Carly!" He said as he hugged her. Brian had honestly expected all the other WAB people who didn't make it out to the Prosser Farm to be dead or in jail by now. Seeing her was a sign of hope that they might get through this.

"Awesome to see you, Brian," Carly replied. She was very excited, but still very nervous about all of the guns pointed at her.

Brian motioned for the light to be turned away from them. Carly got her composure and said, "Let's go off where we can talk privately." When they were far enough away from the other guards, she looked like she was going to ask someone to marry her.

"So?" she said with great anticipation.

"So?" Brian asked. "What?"

"Ben," she said. "Is he going to do the new job?"

"Oh, yeah," Brian said. "He's in."

Carly jumped up and down. She was part political genius, part guerrilla fighter, and part excited twenty year-old girl.

"Awesome!" she finally said after she stopped jumping up and down. She suddenly got very serious.

"Okay," she said. "Here's the plan." She pulled Brian closer and whispered. "The original plan was to take Ben and his family to a safe place with all of us. But," Carly looked ashamed of herself, "I kinda told a few people at the Think Farm where you guys were. I'm so sorry!"

Brian felt his face get hot. Right after they came out to the Prosser Farm in May, Brian was terrified of the authorities finding them. Now, almost six months later, he realized that the Loyalists didn't have the resources to hunt them down. Besides, he trusted Carly, and he trusted John Trappford's organization, which was now being called the "Think Farm." Her admission didn't make him as mad as he thought it would.

"That's okay," Brian said. He would rather she hadn't told anyone, but Carly probably had a good reason for doing so. Let's hope so, he thought.

"I told them," Carly said, "because the Think Farm might not be as safe as your place. We have a couple dozen people there and we have some concerns that the Limas know we're there."

"Limas?" Brian asked. Was she talking about beans?

"Loyalists," she said. "Or 'Legitimates' or whatever they call themselves. You know, the phonetic alphabet? L is Lima. The Ls? You know. 'Lima' a military term for the Loyalists."

Brian and the rest of the WAB people had been largely cut off from the outside world. They didn't know updated things, like the term "Lima."

"So ..." Carly paused, "I told them about your setup at the Prosser Farm. I described it and the guards here. They agreed that Ben and his family would be safer at the Prosser Farm than moving them to our place, which might be compromised. And, you know, not putting all the eggs in one basket. We want to spread out our people."

That made sense to Brian. He had to trust Carly. Besides, he had thought numerous times, the odds were that they'd get caught at some point. He was ready to die if he had to. He wasn't ready for his family to die, but he had resigned himself to the fact that he probably would.

Carly pointed to the van. "I brought friends." She smiled, but it was a nervous smile, like she was hoping for Brian's approval.

Now Brian was getting nervous. Carly had told people where they were hiding and now "brought friends"?

"Carly," Brian started. He was going to say "I don't think this is a good idea," but she cut him off.

"They're former EPU," Carly said.

"They're all former EPU, I should say," she continued. "They left the State Patrol when things got too corrupt for them."

Brian still wasn't convinced this was a good idea. He started to say so, but Carly cut him off again.

"They're led by Russ's dad!" she gushed. She paused for his reaction and then jumped up and down.

"Russ Finehoff?" Brian asked. Russ was a good guy and a fellow conservative or libertarian, or whatever the hell the Patriots were. Brian recalled that Russ's dad was in the State Patrol and was in the EPU. Russ would always tell stories from what his dad saw. Stories about rampant corruption, including extravagant and disgusting parties with drugs, prostitutes, and anything else the partygoers wanted. Well, Brian had to admit, maybe Russ's dad was OK.

"Who else is in the van?" Brian asked.

"Former EPU troopers handpicked by Russ's dad," Carly said with excitement. She was very proud of how they had put together this plan. It had taken weeks of preparation.

"Who are they?" Brian asked.

"Well, there's Jerry Schafer, Mike Turner, and Christina Espinoza," Carly said. "And Russ's dad, Brad. All solid. All Patriots. All experienced EPU. They want to guard the new Governor — Ben!" Carly started to jump up and down again.

Seeing Carly jump up and down, Brian wondered whether she and her slightly immature enthusiasm was being used by the Loyalists to find the WAB families and kill them. This would be the way to do it. Have a team of assassins drive right to the Prosser Farm in a van.

Brian realized he couldn't make this decision—which could get them all killed—on behalf of the WAB families. This decision affected all the families, so he needed to consult with them.

"I'm sure they're fine, Carly," Brian said, which wasn't how he really felt. "But I need to talk to Ben." He almost said Tom, too, but he didn't want to let on that Tom was at the farm in case Carly was being used by the Loyalists. "And," Brian continued, "We need to decide if we want to let several well-armed strangers, who happen to be former high-ranking government employees, come to our hide out."

When Brian put it that way, Carly realized that it was kind of unrealistic to think Brian would just welcome the van load of agents to drive right up to where his family was hiding out.

"Okay," she said, feeling deflated. This great plan they worked up might be failing. She wanted Ben to be the governor. She wanted to be out at the Prosser Farm with all her WAB friends. She wanted to be in on the history they would be making out there. For the next hundred years, school kids would learn about the first governor of Free Washington hiding out on a farm with a small group of brave advisors and guards. Carly would be part of that story. She would be part of history.

"I'll go back and talk to Ben and the others," Brian said. "You guys need to hang tight for a while; an hour or two."

Carly nodded. She was devastated. This plan wasn't working.

"If this plan makes sense for our families, we'll do it, okay?" Brian said to Carly. He didn't want her to be so sad, but he didn't want his family to get slaughtered, either.

"I'll go back to the van," Carly said, hanging her head low.

Brian nodded. He motioned for her to come back to the area where the rest of the guards were.

"Hey, Ned, our guest here is going back to the van and they're going to hang out for a while. I need a ride back home to talk to some people."

Ned nodded and arranged for a little car that didn't use much gas to take Brian back to the Prosser Farm. When Brian arrived, everyone was asleep. He nonchalantly got Ben, Tom, and Jeff into a room and told them about Carly and her "friends."

"It's risky," Jeff said. His family would also be killed if the EPU agents happened to be assassins, so he had a big stake in this decision. Not to mention, he'd have to feed and house the agents.

"But, so is hiding out here," Jeff admitted. "I mean, we're about ten miles from Olympia. We're not bulletproof out here. We could probably use the expertise of the agents in defending this place." Jeff was also thinking that if the Patriots—assuming the van load of people were Patriots—thought this was important enough to send the van then it must be important. Jeff wanted to help the cause.

"I dunno," Tom said. He wasn't a very trusting type. He saw all the risks. He had always thought that Carly was a little immature, despite being a great intern. He could easily see her being tricked by the Loyalists. "I'd rather not have anyone out here."

"But they already know where we are," Brian said. "Carly told them. Probably not our exact location, but this van drove up to the Delphi Road exit. They could easily find out that a former WAB staffer owns a farm out here. They can get us any time they want." Plus, Brian didn't say, the Loyalists probably had a few operational drones with missiles. They still had a few operational helicopters, too, so the Loyalists didn't even need to drive up to the gate to attack the Prosser Farm.

The realization that the Loyalists could attack them any time they wanted was sobering, especially to Tom who thought they might be more anonymous out there than they really were. "If the people in the van are trying to kill us, they'll have a tracking device on them. So even if we killed them at the gate," Brian said, not believing that he had just said that, "they'll easily send a bigger team to come and get us." The room was silent. They couldn't believe they were actually having this conversation.

"Then again," Brian said, "I find it hard to believe that with all the shit the Loyalists in our state have to deal with now, like feeding a couple million people who are about to revolt, they'd take the time to recruit Carly, set up an elaborate ruse using Russ Finehoff's dad, and then send four agents on a mission to kill a bunch of women and children."

Brian wanted to say, "C'mon, guys. Let's not flatter ourselves. We're just some trade association staffers who the politicians don't like." But he didn't. Because he knew they were more than that. Rebel Radio, now being distributed by copied CDs, was fueling the resistance. They knew that from all the graffiti Dennis reported seeing when he went into town.

It was silent for a while as the men thought over this very important decision. Ben left the room and came back with Laura. He told her what was going on. They had already talked and jointly decided that Ben would agree to be the interim governor.

"I need to quit just thinking about myself and my family," Ben said. He looked right at Laura and said, "Sorry, hon, but it's true."

She nodded. She knew he was right.

"It's bigger than just us now," Ben said. "It's a real chance to fix this state. To stop all of this." Ben looked very serious and then said to Laura, "Hon, we've been looking for a sign that we're supposed to do something."

Laura nodded in agreement.

"Do you think this is the sign?" Ben asked, already knowing the answer. She nodded again.

"We're in," Ben said as he looked up toward Tom, Brian, and Jeff. "Life is full of risks right now," he said. "But the one risk I'm not willing to take is sitting around and missing out on putting this state back together. And, for some weird reason, that means me being the interim governor. Let's do it."

Tom nodded slowly. And reluctantly.

Jeff simply said, "Yep."

Brian gave a thumbs up. He wanted to talk to his wife about this, but realized that domestic tranquility could not have a veto over an important security decision like this. He'd just have to deal with the domestic consequences, if any.

"I'll be back," Brian said, doing his best attempt at an Arnold Schwarzenegger impression from Terminator. He was trying to relieve the serious mood. It didn't work. As Brian left, everyone was quiet, like they were waiting to see if they would die in the next hour or two. It was a fair question.

Brian got in the car and his driver took him back to the gate.

"What's going on?" the driver asked Brian as they pulled away from the Prosser Farm.

"Nothing," Brian said. "Nothing." They were silent the rest of the drive to the gate.

Brian got out at the gate and told Ned that the van could come in.

Ned was surprised. He had assumed the van was there to pick up someone, not come into the farm.

"Are you sure?" Ned asked. "There's no taking this decision back."

"We're sure," Brian said. "Let them in."

Ned thought about it for a moment. A van load of some people who were new to the area. "I'd like to meet the occupants. I need to know who is out here," Ned said.

That seemed reasonable. "But you're the only one who can see them," Brian said, anticipating that the agents didn't want everyone out there to see them. For all the agents knew, there were Loyalist spies at the gate.

"Sure," Ned said. Brian's reluctance to let anyone else see the occupants of the van confirmed what Ned was thinking. These were Patriots of some kind. Probably more high-level Patriots needing a place to hide, Ned thought. It never occurred to him that the people in the van were there to protect some very high-level Patriots out at the Prosser Farm.

Meeting the occupants of the van provided Brian with one final test so he could be reassured that this was safe. He wanted to meet the EPU agents to make sure they seemed OK to him. If they didn't, he would tell the van to go back. Ned was right: there was no taking this decision back, so Brian knew he'd better get this right.

Brian motioned for Carly to come out of the van. She obliged and walked up to Brian with her hands up.

She looked depressed. She expected the worst.

"I'd like to meet your friends," Brian said.

Carly started to jump up again, but remembered she had a lot of guns pointed at her, so sudden movements were a bad idea. She knew this was good news. Brian wouldn't want to see the agents if he were sending the van away.

Carly took Brian to the van. She was skipping. She couldn't contain herself.

"You're going to love Brad, you know, Russ's dad," Carly said, talking a mile a minute. "And Jerry. He's great, too. A former Marine. And Mike. He played football for the Huskies," meaning the University of Washington Huskies. "Oh, and Chrissy. She's great. Awesome with kids. Somehow manages to keep them calm even when there are people with guns all around."

This was the first time Brian got a good look at the van. It was a stretch white van with government license plates.

Carly opened the driver's side. There was a man in a suit. Brian hadn't seen anyone in a suit for months. The driver seemed overdressed for going to a farm.

"This is Jerry," Carly said.

"Pleased to meet you, sir," Jerry said. From appearances, he seemed like a decent guy, though Brian couldn't really tell the difference in just a few seconds.

"What's with the dress up clothes?" Brian asked. The directness of his question seemed a little rude, but he was entitled to cut to the chase and see if these people were going to murder him and his family. Polite chitchat needed to yield to something more important.

"Oh," Jerry laughed, "I'm used to being dressed up on protection details. Besides, we still have our EPU credentials, so we wanted to look the part if any Limas stopped us."

Jerry paused and then pointed to the back of the van. "We all brought suits with us for when Governor Trenton is in office."

Wow. That sounded weird. "Governor Trenton"? "In office"?

Why would assassins dress up for a messy slaughter of women and children? Blood doesn't come out of clothes. Why destroy a perfectly good suit to kill some people? Brian couldn't believe he was thinking these things.

Carly opened the van's sliding side door. There were two men and a woman in the back seat.

"This is Mike, Chrissy, and Russ's dad, Brad," Carly said. They all shook Brian's hand.

All three were also in suits. They all had a distinctive pin on their lapels, which was likely a way for EPU agents to identify each other. They looked like Secret Service agents.

Behind them, were stacks and stacks of things; many were in protective cases.

"Whatcha got back there?" Brian asked.

"Communications gear," Brad said. "We will be able to keep you and the Think Farm in contact." Brad pointed at a different spot in the back of the van. "Lots of weapons. Mike's a sniper. We have a ton of clothes, too. We need to look the part in a wide variety of settings."

"You guys know you're going to a farm, right?" Brian said. They had passed the test. They could come out.

"Roger that," Brad said. "But it's hard to get these guys out of a suit. They feel comfortable in them. It's what they're used to."

"That will change after they're constantly stepping in cow crap," Brian said. He felt that he had earned the qualifications of "farm boy" after his several months out there.

"OK, you guys can come in," Brian said. Carly started clapping.

Brian looked at all of them and said, "Understand that we don't really know who you are and we're entrusting our lives to you. Don't be offended if people are a little suspicious of you. Oh, and I told my kids to kill you if I tell them to. I'm serious." He was lying, but wanted to leave them with the proper impression.

They nodded. They'd never had to prove themselves to the people they were protecting before, though this was a very different situation than normal.

"You got room in there for me so I can guide you in?" Brian asked. Carly hopped into the back so Brian could ride in the passenger seat.

"Okay, let's go," he said. He had no idea if he was about to die in a few minutes or have the greatest adventure of his life.

Guess we'll see, he said to himself.

Chapter 226

"Embahla"

(Late October)

People were increasingly coming to the gate at Pierce Point and wanting in. FCard food was dwindling. It was becoming more and more common for shipments to the stores to be "late," or not arrive at all. There were glitches with the FCard network system. The government blamed Patriot hackers, though it was probably Loyalist incompetence or corruption. People had heard that Pierce Point had food. And a medical clinic. Word traveled fast. So why weren't there hordes of people at the gate?

The problem that the gate visitors faced, and what was saving Pierce Point from being overrun, was that it was so hard to get there. It was a ten mile walk from Frederickson. There weren't many people coming that far, especially when Frederickson had a somewhat adequate supply of food. The supply was adequate enough to make a ten-mile walk into the unknown a bad decision.

Occasionally, a few people from Frederickson, hearing that Pierce Point had a medical clinic, would come to the gate and say they had a sick person in Frederickson and ask Pierce Point's medical personnel to go back into town with them. That request was easy to turn down. Well, not easy, but understandable.

Hungry people were different. "Spare a little food?" was harder to say no to than going into town to provide medical care. At first, in the summer, the gate guards would give people a little food and some water and then tell them to move along. But now there was less food in Pierce Point, so the guards stopped providing it.

The exception was kids. The guards always gave them some food. Everyone still got water, but that wasn't in short supply. There was a big creek right at the gate so people could drink from that. There weren't so many people using the creek that it was contaminating the water. Yet.

Al was doing a great job of managing the people coming in and out of Pierce Point. He was screening people who had relatives there or, in a few cases, owned property and were just now making it out to Pierce Point. He was also screening some people with skills. He managed to get two engineers, a radio operator with equipment, and another EMT. All were let into Pierce Point, along with their families, and put to work.

Several people appeared at the gate with loads of valuables. Gold, silver, cash, FCards, alcohol, cigars. Al assumed these were stolen. He couldn't be sure; some people seemed like they had legitimately traded for the gold and silver and now wanted a place to stay in exchange for it, but there was no way of telling if the person was a criminal and got the loot that way. Al was not about to let criminals into Pierce Point, so he turned them away.

There were increasing numbers of insane people walking down the road from Frederickson. It wasn't clear if they were off their meds or whether they had cracked under all the pressure of post-Collapse life. The guards persuaded them to move along. Occasionally, it took pointing a rifle at them and using harsh language.

Al produced a few soldiers for the 17th, or the "rental team," as he thought it was. He found a former Army logistics soldier from a chemical warfare unit. Al hoped that there was no more need for chemical warfare specialists, but a soldier was a soldier and should have basic skills they needed out there. Al got the soldier's information and learned that he was in the 23rd Chemical Battalion at Ft. Lewis. He provided this information to Grant who passed it along to Ted, who radioed HQ. They verified that the soldier was, indeed, AWOL from the 23rd Chemical Battalion.

Vetting walk-ons to the 17th was time consuming, but vital. The 17th had to take all the precautions it could. One spy sending in the GPS coordinates of Marion Farm would mean a visit from a Lima attack helicopter that could kill a hundred troops in fifteen seconds. This was one of the biggest threats to the unit and merited some of the biggest precautions.

Boston Harbor was loaded with FUSA military intelligence soldiers, who were known as the "MI guys." Instead of spending a lot of time and resources trying to spy on the enemy (who was right out in the open), the MI guys worked primarily on vetting recruits. Boston Harbor had one of the few copies of the very top secret Oath Keepers membership list and it was invaluable for this work.

Boston Harbor could only usually vet the walk-ons who claimed to be former military. Civilians, and even law enforcement, were a different story; Boston Harbor had almost no way to verify if they were who they said they were.

The non-military people walking up to the Pierce Point gate—

and that was the vast majority of the walk-ons—could be anybody. The Limas would undoubtedly try to infiltrate guerrilla units. They'd be crazy not to; this was standard counterinsurgency strategy. Then again, the Limas had their hands full trying to keep the population fed and under control; maybe spy-versus-spy games were a luxury for them.

The Pierce Point gate walk-ons were told they were joining a rental team. This was mainly done to lessen the odds of a walk-on who was a spy getting too much information. They were told that the authorities thought the rental team was illegal so they had to be prepared to be living outside the law and they couldn't leave the compound once they got there. They all agreed. They just wanted a job. They fully knew they were joining an outlaw group, but not one as outlaw as a guerrilla unit. There was "outlaw," and then there was "treason." The Limas didn't care much about outlaw security contractors, but full-on guerrilla fighters were another matter.

At this point, the walk-ons couldn't be trusted with the information about the true nature of what was going on at the Marion Farm. This was very dishonest—asking men and women to join something they weren't fully informed about—but Ted and Grant didn't want to risk telling these strangers about the 17th. It is said that truth is the first casualty in war. Grant was learning exactly what that meant.

Once the walk-ons were in the unit, their vetting had only begun. Just because they had passed Al and Grant's initial screening, or the vetting by Boston Harbor, didn't mean that they were good to go. Ensuring the loyalty of personnel took much more time and planning than Grant had expected it would. He had, somewhat naively, thought that Patriots would just swarm to the unit because of the righteousness of their cause, Ted would put a rifle in their hand, and that would be it. But it was more complicated in real life.

One walk-on posed the biggest security concern. He was Kevin Olson, a former cop from Lakewood, which was near Ft. Lewis. Olson was single, but said he had a girlfriend back in Lakewood. He was about thirty and in great shape. He appeared as someone who could make a good soldier.

Al had screened Olson as best as he could. Olson said that he had left his police department at the beginning of the Collapse when he refused to follow an order to confiscate guns. Or so he said. There was no way to tell if Olson was telling the truth. Olson had a cop ID card (but not his badge, which he said had been taken from him when he left the force). So half of his story, the part about being a cop, seemed to be true. The other half, the part about being a Patriot, could not be verified.

Al asked him why he never joined Oath Keepers. Olson said that he didn't want to risk his job. In the run up to the Collapse, police departments were laying off cops left and right. Any little thing, like being in Oath Keepers, would be used to get you fired, Olson said. He said he generally supported Oath Keepers, but hadn't been "political." His father and grandfather had been police officers and he wanted to be one, too. He just wanted his country back so life could be normal. He didn't really care about politics.

Olson's claim that he refused to follow illegal orders was also impossible to verify. Grant interviewed Olson at the fire station by the gate. Olson didn't know it, but Grant had Al sitting in the next room, out of sight, with the door open so he could hear everything Olson told Grant. This way, Al could verify if Olson gave the exact same account of the story about refusing the illegal order.

Olson told Grant the story about the day after May Day when he was told at roll call that due to all the "terrorist" violence, civil unrest, and crime—and the "vigilantism" in response to it—his department would begin to confiscate firearms. At first, they would take firearms whenever they saw them, like during a traffic stop. Phase two would consist of going house-to-house and rounding up guns.

Olson said there was an audible gasp in the briefing room when his lieutenant was explaining the second phase. The cops, including Olson, knew they were dead if they tried to round up guns. They might last a couple of days out there on the streets. By that point, May2nd, cops across the state were routinely getting shot trying to take guns. And not by clean cut NRA members. They were being murdered by the gangs. Well, at least the gangs that were not protected by the police.

On top of all this, returning vets and others profiled as possible "terrorists" by Homeland Security—which included people with NRA and Don't Tread on Me stickers on their vehicles—were reluctantly shooting cops at checkpoints. The vets and others with "right-wing" stickers knew the cops had targeted them and they would rather die in a shootout than get taken in, or "black bagged," as they called it. That term referred to the authorities putting a black bag over someone's head and taking them away. To Olson's knowledge, there were not any "black bag" operations going on, just checkpoints to make the public think everything was safe. But, those checkpoints were leading to dozens of cops getting shot. It was a bloody, ironic mess.

Olson told Grant that the Lakewood police quickly realized that an order to round up guns or manning a checkpoint was a death sentence. Everyone knew it. Losing his job didn't seem so bad by comparison. Besides, he could join one of the many "security contractor" firms his former cop buddies were hastily forming.

During roll call, Olson said, one of his sergeants, Tom Hurley, stood up and said he would not follow the order. The lieutenant, knowing this would probably happen, fired Hurley on the spot and asked for his badge and gun. Sgt. Hurley was not surprised. He had expected it. Hurley complied, handing his gun and badge to the lieutenant. Sgt. Hurley saluted the lieutenant and walked out of the room.

Olson said he and about a quarter of his shift did the same. Olson got up, took off his badge, unholstered his pistol, and formed a line with the other officers who were refusing the illegal orders. When Olson got up to the lieutenant, he saluted and handed over his gun and badge. Olson then walked out of the building and called his dad, apologizing that he had broken the family tradition of being a cop. His dad told him he did the right thing.

Grant thought Olson was either telling the truth or was a very good liar. Olson made eye contact with Grant the whole time, didn't tense up, and didn't use his hands or arms to subconsciously shield himself from Grant. He depicted all signs of truthfulness, but a Lima spy would be a very good liar, so Olson's truthful body language didn't seal the deal with Grant.

Grant thanked Olson and told him he could go back outside. A minute later, Al came in.

"He told me the exact same version," Al said. "Right down to the name of the sergeant and calling his dad."

That gave Grant an idea. He asked Olson to return and Al went back into the next room.

"Do you have your phone?" Grant asked Olson.

"Yes, sir," Olson replied and got his phone out. "Haven't used it much lately. The system is usually down."

Grant looked at the recent calls. They were mostly to "Dad" and "Sherisha"; no obvious calls to the Limas like a Homeland Security/local police "Fusion Center." And the calls only went back to May 15.

"So they don't go back to May 2nd, huh?" Grant asked Olson. "I wanted to see if you had an outgoing call to your dad on that day."

Olson smiled. He appreciated some good police work, even if it was being used against him.

"Sorry, I can't go back that far on this phone," Olson said.

"OK," Grant said. "Worth a try."

Grant sat back and thought. He could not verify Olson's story, but Olson seemed either truthful or was a professional liar. Grant decided to take a risk with him. He would have some good skills for the unit.

"Welcome to the rental team," Grant said to Olson, who smiled. He needed a job. And was hungry.

Grant kept thinking about whether he could trust Olson. There was a solution. Of sorts.

Embahla. That was the term Ted had previously told Grant about. This was a word in a native language of one of the countries Ted had been in for people who are still being tested for loyalty. Ted would have a special program for embahlas at Marion Farm. Embahlas would never be given information that, if it got out, could harm the unit. Different trusted members of the unit would strike up conversations with the embahlas and see if their stories changed. For example, Olson would be asked several times by different people in casual conversations to tell his story about handing over his gun and badge. The trusted soldiers would tell Ted and Sap what the answers were. They were looking for a change in the story. Ted assigned a solider, Don, the Air Force RED HORSE guy, to be the internal intelligence man.

Don kept track of the embahlas. He even assigned a trusted solider to buddy up with each embahla. A spy would likely be a loner who didn't want to get close to the people he was trying to kill. In contrast, a genuine Patriot soldier would naturally want to buddy up with fellow Patriots. Don was issued the very limited liquor they had out at the Marion Farm. He used the liquor to get the embahlas drunk at least once and see what they said when their tongues were loosened.

So far, all of the embahlas were checking out. They still didn't get near the communications information. Their bunks and unused clothing were secretly searched when they weren't around. They were not allowed to leave Marion Farm under any circumstances. That way, they couldn't communicate with the Limas and couldn't conveniently be absent if a strike was about to annihilate the farm. If the Limas had people infiltrating Marion Farm who had undetectable communications and who were willing to die in the resulting strike, then so be it. The 17th didn't have a countermeasure for that. It was one of the many risks they took operating a guerrilla unit.

Chapter 227

Crazy-Ass Idea

(November 10)

Because it was November, Grant thought about the Pilgrims back in the Massachusetts colony. They were hungry, in constant danger, and cut off from all they knew as normal. They, like the people at Pierce Point, were heading into a bad winter. What did they do? They scratched together the best of what they had and put on a feast to give thanks.

That gave Grant an idea. Things were getting a little worse each day at Pierce Point. People weren't starving, but the "summer picnic" was over. Some people were running out of food. There were constant pleas at each Grange meeting to start distributing the food in the semi-trailer.

Grant, Rich, and a core group of others fought off the requests for the semi food each time. Not until things were absolutely dire, they kept saying. Even though a semi of food was an amazing amount of food, it would be gone in two weeks if the five hundred or so people in Pierce Point were relying on it. Then people would be back in the same situation. Not only would it run out quickly, but tapping the semi also presented the problem of distributing the food in exactly equal portions; that would cause fighting. The whole topic of opening up the semi was a problem they didn't need out there until it was absolutely necessary.

Only a small portion of the people at Pierce Point were clamoring to get free stuff. Maybe ten percent insisted on opening up the semi, with people softly supporting them making up another ten percent. Though only about twenty percent wanted to dip into the reserves, that small group was loud.

It was interesting. These demanding people had never been to Grange meetings all summer, yet they were showing up regularly now. Almost none of them volunteered at the Grange. They couldn't be bothered to participate in the community's decision making back in the summer. It was different now, when they wanted something.

Needed something was more like it. They were desperate and showed up for the first time to plead for what they needed. Just like the old days, Grant realized. Goof off all the time, need something, and then go beg the community for it. It will be given to you. People will feel sorry for you. You'll get whatever you want. Cry a little and say, "It's for the children."

But that didn't work anymore. Now there wasn't a bunch of free government money to dole out. There wasn't much of anything.

Grant was trying to avoid a full-on political fight over opening up the semi, but the constant cries to distribute the semi food were getting louder and louder. Finally, Grant said what needed to be said.

"You people," Grant loudly exclaimed at a Grange meeting, "wanting to open up the semi had all summer to prepare for the winter. Gardens, hunting, fishing, canning, smoking, drying, freezing. What the hell were you doing all summer? Ralph Ramirez, the 'Ag. Director,' and his volunteers were available all summer to help you start gardens. Didn't Ralph and his folks coordinate people working on farms and then getting food in return? You all could have worked for a farm and you'd have some food now."

It was silent. This issue had been brewing for a long time. "Wasn't there beef and even llama," Grant continued, "available for barter at the Winston farm? Weren't there a zillion hunting parties that went out from every neighborhood and shared the meat? Didn't everyone go fishing and then smoke the fish? Clams, oysters? Picking berries? Making jam and canning vegetables in neighborhood canning parties? Storing up FCard food from Frederickson? What about starting a little business, like the kids mowing lawns with push mowers, and buying food with your earnings?"

Grant paused and yelled, "What the hell were you doing all summer?" The unprepared people became furious when they were confronted with this question. They had various excuses. They didn't know how to garden or hunt. Fair enough, but there were plenty of people teaching these skills. Most people hadn't gardened in years or ever, yet gardens sprung up almost overnight during the summer. Need seeds? Ralph and his volunteers had a seed bank. Don't know how to hunt? Tag along with a rifle and don't talk in the woods. Shoot at suitable animals. Someone will help you butcher the game.

There were some people who had a legitimate reason for not preparing over the summer, like the elderly and people with disabilities, but they were taken care of by neighbors' charity and the Grange. That was not an issue. And they weren't the ones who were angered by Grant's question. The ones who hated to hear that were the able-bodied who, for whatever reason, didn't prepare for the winter.

They were the grasshoppers who played all summer while the ants prepared for the winter.

Grant tried to think of why people wouldn't get off their asses and prepare over the summer for the approaching winter. Most of the unprepared were people, often younger people, who had never had a job. Or even worked … at anything. They never had any chores around the house, never had a part-time job in high school, and never had a job after they graduated. They were like so many other Americans. They just sort of floated along and always seemed to have money for fast food and video games. They never thought about how to feed themselves; food just appeared. They had attention spans measured in milliseconds. They couldn't spend more than a few minutes in a garden or hunting without quitting. They were useless. And American society had allowed them to be that way.

That didn't get them sympathy with Grant or the majority of Pierce Point residents. It meant the lazy needed to adapt or … die. It was harsh, but true. Adapt or die. Well, "die" might be too strong of a word. Adapt or "don't try to take the food I prepared," was more the sentiment.

Grant was glad that the majority of Pierce Point residents had the same attitude toward the unprepared. Over the course of the summer, the majority worked hard at preparing and saw the shitbags sitting around. They told lazy people to get working and saw them still sitting around. They personally tried to get specific people to prepare who didn't. Now, many of the people telling others to prepare had a personal experience to throw back at the lazy. Like, "Remember around July Fourth when I tried to give you seeds and you said you wanted to hang out with your friends instead?" Lots of lifelong friendships and even some families were torn apart by this.

So, politically speaking, there was a big problem out at Pierce Point, but the majority of people were solid. Grant was not concerned that the twenty percent or so of people wanting to open up the semi would win. He was not happy about a significant minority of people being so at odds with the majority, but at least the good guys had the votes.

Then again, the twenty percent were fairly well armed. Chip had quietly beefed up the guards at the Grange where the semi-trailer was located. As the winter approached, it was beefed up again. There were constant rumors that some group of people would try to take the food. So far, the rumors had not materialized.

It was against this backdrop that Grant had his big idea: a

Thanksgiving dinner at the Grange for the whole community. For everyone—even the slackers. It would be the last free meal. One free meal was a lot less of a big deal than the months of free meals they wanted. Plus, the majority could tell the slackers: "We gave you a free Thanksgiving dinner. We gave you something. Now shut up and start working for your meals."

But there was a bigger purpose for the Thanksgiving dinner. It would give everyone hope. If they could have a Thanksgiving dinner under these conditions, anything was possible. Anything.

Thanksgiving would allow them to reflect on how grateful they were for how good they had it in Pierce Point compared to the rest of the country. It would be a big community-wide celebration; a feast.

There was just one problem.

The food. Where would they get all the food, especially the turkey, stuffing, and cranberries? America was heading into a winter of possible starvation and Grant was planning a Thanksgiving dinner for about five hundred people? Had he lost touch with reality?

Grant knew what to do. He walked out of the Grange where he was pacing around, mulling over his big idea and found Chip.

"Chip," Grant said, "I have a crazy-ass idea."

Chapter 228

Throwing Some Turkey Around

(November 10)

"I'm listening," Chip said. He always loved it when Grant approached him with one of his "crazy-ass" ideas. They were usually pretty good. Sometimes not, but always entertaining.

"Thanksgiving is in about two weeks," Grant stated. "How much would it kick ass to have a Thanksgiving dinner for everyone at the Grange and one at Marion Farm. Turkey, gravy, the whole nine yards. Mashed potatoes. Hell, maybe even some pumpkin' pie, brother."

Chip just looked at Grant like he was kidding or crazy.

"Well, it would kick ass, except there isn't any frickin' turkey to be found within a fifty-mile radius," Chip said.

"Here's my crazy-ass idea," Grant said as he motioned for Chip to come closer and hear his secret.

Chip approached. This better be good, he thought. Chip thought about how great Thanksgiving dinner would be. He realized how much the community needed it. A Thanksgiving dinner might bring people back together after all of the increasing bickering. It would be the most memorable Thanksgiving of their lifetimes. It would be exactly what everyone needed. But Chip didn't want to be disappointed by some stupid joke Grant was probably about to tell, so he got himself ready to be disappointed.

"Got any extra ARs?" Grant asked Chip.

Aha. That was how to buy the turkey.

"Um," Chip said, "we kinda need all the ARs we can round up for the little thing going on at the Marion Farm." Chip rolled his eyes at Grant and said, "Maybe you've heard about what's going on out there, Lieutenant."

"But do you have any extras?" Grant asked, undeterred by Chip's logic.

Chip thought about it. He had two ARs in his personal stash. They were old A2s with carry handles and iron sights. They worked fine, but were pretty basic. Chip had been holding onto them for some reason. He didn't know why. He was just holding onto them.

"Where do we buy turkey, especially with ARs as cash?" Chip asked.

"I dunno," Grant said as he shrugged.

Chip laughed. "Remember the last time you said to me 'I dunno'?" he asked.

Grant shook his head.

"When Rich asked you," Chip said with a smile, "Why you knew to go get Gideon's semi and have him drive it into here, you said, 'I dunno'." Chip grinned and asked, "Remember that?"

"Oh, yeah," Grant said. "Well, this is the same thing. I don't know where to get the turkey. But I know we will."

That was logical enough for Chip. The more he thought about it, the more he wanted to have a Thanksgiving dinner out there. Chip never had a family around for Thanksgiving. He usually dreaded the holiday. Now he had a family. Finally. And, damn it, he was going to have a Thanksgiving dinner with his new family.

Chip thought about it. He could only think of one reason not to do it. "What does Ted think about this?" Chip asked.

"I dunno," Grant said with a grin, realizing he was using that trademark phrase again. "I was going to bring a couple of the turkeys to Marion Farm for the unit to have a Thanksgiving dinner, too." Grant thought for the first time that maybe ARs would be better used fighting the coming war than paying for a single meal. Grant was embarrassed that he was just now realizing this.

"If Ted is OK with diverting two ARs for turkeys — if we can even find any turkeys — then I'll donate them," Chip said, not really believing that he was saying something as stupid as that.

Grant smiled. Now he just had to convince Ted. That might be hard.

A couple ARs was a big deal. Oh well. Grant was one step closer to his Thanksgiving dinner. Chip had just agreed to donate two extremely valuable items.

"Thanks, man," Grant said. "Really. Thanks."

Chip just nodded. "No problem. I love turkey."

Grant headed over to Marion Farm. The 17th guards let him in.

"To what do we owe a rare daytime visit, Lieutenant?" One of the guards asked.

"Top secret," Grant said with a smile.

The guard radioed, "Giraffe 7 here to see Green 1." Ted would be waiting for him.

"Thanks," Grant told the guard as he dipped his head as if he were tipping his hat. No saluting out in the field. Especially when saluting would let an observer know that the two men were in a military unit.

Grant walked down the road toward the farmhouse. Ted was there and came up to see him.

"What's up?" Ted asked, assuming something must be important if Grant was coming to the farm during the day.

"I've got a big political problem brewing at Pierce Point and I need your OK on something to solve it," Grant said, "and this will do some great morale boosting for the unit here."

Ted was naturally curious. He wanted to say yes to something that solved a political problem and boosted morale. He just didn't quite know why Grant needed his permission.

"I'm opposed to it," Ted said after hearing Grant's proposal. "Two ARs is a big deal. That's two soldiers I can't field."

Ted thought and then said something that might be offensive to Grant, but he didn't care. "Grant, we're in the war business, not the catering business."

Grant was a bit taken aback. Ted had a point, but that "catering business" jab was kind of lame. Grant stiffed his posture and got a serious look on his face.

"I'm the commanding officer out here," he said in his command voice, which was something he rarely had to use. "Those guns are Chip's, not the unit's."

Grant stared Ted right in the eyes and said, "I need to pull a rabbit out of my hat for the folks in Pierce Point. A political rabbit. We might have a little civil war of our own out there with all the slackers wanting to open up the semi. And my men—yes, my men—here in the 17th deserve a fucking Thanksgiving dinner."

Ted was surprised—and impressed—with Grant's strong stance. Ted saluted Grant and said, "Yes, sir."

Grant was stunned. Did Ted just salute him? And call him "sir"? And agree to do what he said?

Grant meekly replied, "Huh? Seriously?"

Ted laughed. "Yes, sir. We'll have a Thanksgiving dinner."

Grant and Ted broke out into laughter. Grant had been doing such a good job of being in command, except for that last "Huh? Seriously?" But he was learning.

Besides, Ted realized what a great idea the Thanksgiving dinner was, at least for the unit. It would be fantastic and bring them even closer together. Ted didn't know the details about the political situation in Pierce Point, but he knew Grant was running that place like a finely tuned watch. If Grant said he needed to throw some turkey around, that's what needed to happen.

"One question, Lieutenant," Ted said. "Where do we get the turkey? And, for what, a couple hundred people?"

"Six hundred, probably. About five hundred at Pierce Point and about a hundred here," Grant said.

Ted shrugged and asked, "Where do we get the turkey?"

"I dunno," Grant said, using his favorite phrase. Grant shrugged.

"I can't exactly order some from HQ," Ted said.

"We'll have the FCard crew that goes into town each day ask around," Grant said. "I bet the gangs can get us turkey. A couple hundred pounds of it. Seriously. They can get anything people want. And they can probably use a couple of ARs." Grant and Ted didn't want to think about how the gangs would use ARs. That was somebody else's problem. That sounded cruel, but it was the truth. They didn't really like thinking about themselves doing business with the gangs, either, but they needed turkeys and had a couple of ARs. That's just how it was.

The FCard crew was run by the Pierce Point gate guards, so Dan was in charge of that. Grant would go talk to him. As they were walking back to Grant's car, the "Tacura," Ted said, "We could really use a morale boost out here, Grant."

This was the first Grant had heard about morale being a problem. "Really?" Grant asked, very concerned.

"Well, morale is fine," Ted said. "Everyone is glad to be here instead of out there," Ted said motioning toward Frederickson and Olympia. "But we're a new unit thrown together with people from all different branches. And civilians, too. We need a bonding experience. Thanksgiving dinner would be a good one."

Chapter 229

And Cranberries, Too

November 11

The free market was an amazing thing. Even the partially-free, corrupt market during a time of lawlessness. A person could get just about anything if they had the money or ammo or gold or whatever.

Even a hundred turkeys. Rich, who loved Grant's idea about a Thanksgiving dinner, went into town on the FCard run the next day and inquired with Bennington where a person could get some turkey.

Bennington thought Rich was kidding, or maybe that "turkey" was a code word for heroin or child prostitutes. Bennington was surrounded by depravity and evil all day long, so he assumed everyone was a drug addicted child molester. When he realized Rich really wanted poultry, Bennington knew that he needed to get out of his job. He was starting to lose touch with normal things and thought patterns.

"How much you need?" He asked Rich.

"A hundred," Rich said. They had figured six hundred people. At least fifteen pounds of meat on each turkey. That's fifteen hundred pounds for six hundred people, or over two pounds per person. There would be lots of leftovers.

"A hundred damned turkeys?" Bennington asked. This seemed far more absurd than the guy Bennington talked to earlier that morning who asked him where he could get kiddie porn.

"Yep, a hundred turkeys," Rich said. "Is that going to be a problem?" As he said that, Rich realized for the first time how outlandish Grant's idea really was.

Bennington shrugged and said, "Depends on how much you're willing to pay."

"An AR," Rich said. "You know, one we captured from those damned teabaggers and we need to turn in to the legitimate authorities," Rich said with a smile.

"Of course," Bennington said as he was thinking where the hell to get turkeys, let alone that many. "I'll check around and let you know tomorrow. You'll come into town, right?"

"Yep," Rich said. "I'll be here."

Bennington left and Rich went about the business of trying to get all the FCard food they could. He could see that Martin's, the grocery store in town, was running low on just about everything. Someone in line said that the truck didn't make it yesterday and wouldn't be here today, either. They used to come every day.

The shelves were halfway bare. It was starting to look like right after the Collapse when everyone rushed into the store and stripped the shelves bare. Not quite to that level now, but maybe heading there.

Rich and the "Marine looking" FCard crew got all they could. Some of the FCards that worked the day before were not working today. Rich knew the government stores would be bare soon. By Christmas, for sure. There was no way this could be sustained.

Next, they went to the gang gas station and got some diesel for the little school bus Winters had given them. They paid for the diesel with some cash, FCards, and a little silver. They had collected this gas money from the people getting their FCard food. The price of diesel was going up, too. It was pretty obvious that the government was having severe difficulties getting food and fuel out to the people. Rich knew this was not going to end well. He was so thankful he was in Pierce Point.

The next day, Rich got both ARs, some mags, and ammo from Chip. Rich would hide the second AR and the magazines and ammo, so hopefully he could get the turkeys for just one AR. It was worth a try.

Rich met Bennington at the city gate. The Blue Ribbon Boys were looking worse and worse. They were skinny, cold, and tired. This was unlike Pierce Point's guards, who were well fed, warm, rested and, most importantly, wanted to be there. Rich realized that the Blue Ribbon Boys might scare unarmed civilians, but his guys could take them in about fifteen seconds.

Bennington was smiling, which was rare. "Found you some birds," he said to Rich.

"How many?" Rich asked.

"Eighty-nine," Bennington said. "Winters called some people in Olympia and found some at the … well, it doesn't matter where they came from." There was no use telling Rich which government agency was corrupt and selling its food to the highest bidder.

Rich smiled. "There were turkeys being grown this year? I thought the whole country was on orders to only grow wheat and corn, that kind of thing."

"Oh we are," Bennington said. "These are frozen from last year. They're still good, though."

"Okay," Rich said. "I have the AR."

Bennington shook his head. "One won't do it. Do you know how hard it is to find turkeys — especially that many — this time of year, when a whole lot of people are hungry?"

Rich wondered what the cost would be. He might not have enough ARs. He had done "pre-Collapse pricing" on the turkeys.

"Pre-Collapse" pricing was the way post-Collapse barter prices were being calculated. People started with the pre-Collapse cost in dollars of the two items. In this case, the pre-Collapse price of a hundred turkeys was about $2,500 or $25 a piece during a Thanksgiving sale. Then Rich looked at what the pre-Collapse price of two ARs was. They were about $1,000 each for a total of $2,000. So eighty-nine turkeys were worth about $2,200 and two ARs were worth $2,000. Throw in some magazines and you'd be in the same neighborhood.

Post-Collapse actual prices depended on much more than just their pre-Collapse dollar prices, however. Supply and demand were everything. If there were a lot of turkeys or ARs, that would affect prices. A scarcity of turkeys or ARs would, too. A burning need someone had for turkeys or ARs would also affect pricing.

Rich knew that Bennington had done the pre-Collapse pricing calculations. It all depended on how much Winters could get for the ARs.

"Three ARs or two with all the fixings," Bennington said. He had, indeed, done the pre-Collapse pricing.

"I got two ARs," Rich said. "That'll have to do."

"No turkey for you," Bennington said. He started to get in his car.

"Oh, wait," Rich said. "I just may have some magazines and five hundred rounds of 5.56." Rich smiled.

Bennington knew Winters wanted a full case of ammo, but a half case was OK. Winters had no use for these turkeys. What was he going to do with them? Feed people? What a waste that would be. Those ARs, especially the ammo, were worth a lot to the gangs. Winters could only steal so much ammo from the Feds before they'd start to get pissed.

"Deal," Bennington said as he got on the radio and called for the truck with the turkeys. "Cash and carry. You haul 'em."

Rich nodded. He went and got the ARs and the fixings. Pretty soon, a county public works truck showed up with a bunch of turkeys in the back. They all loaded the turkeys into the little school bus.

Bennington motioned for Rich and his crew to come over to the county truck.

"Bonus," Bennington said. In the cab of the truck were four cases of canned cranberries. "Compliments of the good Commissioner Winters."

"Awesome," Rich said. The cranberries truly surprised him. It wasn't much per person with six hundred people, but a little taste of cranberries would make this seem like a real Thanksgiving.

They loaded the cranberries in the bus and headed back to Pierce Point. The whole ride back Rich kept thinking what an amazing story this would be someday. Going to town to get turkeys in exchange for AR-15s. Right that very instant he was living the things that would be stories he'd tell his grandkids. That is, if he lived to have grandkids.

Chapter 230

Dinner for a Few Hundred

(November 12)

"What the hell you got there?" one of the gate guards asked Rich, as the little school bus pulled into Pierce Point. All of the seats and the aisles were filled with white round orbs covered in frost. They looked like giant snowballs with a plastic coating.

"What are you doing two Thursdays from now?" Rich asked the guard.

"Nothin'," the guard said. He thought for a second. "Hey, that's Thanksgiving, right?"

Rich figured the news of the Thanksgiving dinner could get out now that they actually had the turkeys. The best way to get the news out at Pierce Point was to tell someone and let the rumor mill work its magic.

"You like white or dark meat?" Rich asked the guard and motioned for him to come into the bus and look for himself.

"Shit!" the guard yelled after seeing the turkeys. "No way. No frickin' way," he continued. "Wow. We need this. We really need this. Where'd you get this?"

"OPSEC, son," Rich said. "Just enjoy it on Thanksgiving."

This was a good sign, Rich thought. People really were primed to have something special—and something that reminded them of the good old days—happen out there. He was getting really excited about Thanksgiving just by watching the guard's reaction. Grant's "crazy-ass" idea was a pretty good one, even if it cost two ARs and all the fixings.

Rich and the bus headed to the Grange like they always did to drop off the FCard food they brought in from town.

Chip was the first one to smile as they pulled into the Grange. He couldn't wait to see what the small fortune he had donated had gotten them. Eighty-nine turkeys in a small school bus is quite a sight, not to mention the cases of cranberries. What a nice touch. Chip knew that a few hundred people would always remember this Thanksgiving as the best one of their lives. The very best.

He got Kathy McClintock, the chief Grange kitchen lady, out to see the haul. Grant and Rich had talked to her and asked if the Grange could cook up a hundred or so turkeys and serve them. She said yes, but thought they were kidding.

The logistics to pull off such a meal would be pretty complicated. They decided it would be easiest to offload all the frozen turkeys to a dozen or so families who would put them in their freezers. The Grange had some refrigerator and freezer space, but not nearly enough to also store food for the daily meal-card people, which was now up to about two hundred a day. Kathy, who was a very typical looking grandmother, had a running list of people in the community who had extra refrigerator and freezer space. She could remember exactly who had what Grange food at their place. These were trusted active Grange people who wouldn't steal the food. Off-site storage in lots of people's freezers and refrigerators was just-in-time inventory for the Grange—except it didn't rely on the internet, semi-trucks, safe passage on thousands of miles of interstate, or access to diesel. So it actually worked.

The second part of the plan was to build a giant wood-fire rotisserie. Some of the metal fabricators, including Paul, would sketch out the plans for one and get the materials together.

The plan was to roast them in twenty-four hour shifts. When they were done, they'd carve them up and have the off-site refrigerators and freezers store the meat. They would also store the bones and innards for soup making later. Not a scrap of these turkeys was going to go to waste. Not everyone would have just-roasted turkey; most would have warmed up meat, but Kathy doubted that anyone would complain.

The fixings—gravy, potatoes, stuffing—would be supplied by potluck. Kathy devised a simple method of assigning side dishes. She used the alphabet. If someone's last name began with A through E, they brought potatoes. E through J, brought stuffing, and so on. People who didn't have the ingredients for their assigned item could trade their assignment with another family who did.

There was one special item: pumpkin pie. Kathy was going to put the word out that she needed pumpkins. Several people had grown them in their gardens that year and canned them. Kathy would coordinate all the ingredients for the pies—not an easy feat—and bake them at the Grange. She knew this would take several days without more than a few hours of sleep. But she was in heaven. Cooking a meal so memorable for so many people was what she lived for.

The Grange didn't have enough dishes, so they would use paper plates. People had lots of them lying around and were willing to pool them together. They didn't have any plastic utensils, so people were asked to bring their own silverware.

Drew helped, too, using the list of residents to figure out how many people would be coming. The dinner was announced at a Grange meeting and a special edition of the *Pierce Point Truth*. Drew oversaw his crew of administrative helpers who kept track of RSVPs and helped coordinate who was bringing what. Thanksgiving dinner was a reason for people who hadn't previously participated in the census to be counted. Drew had been able to keep a very good rough count of people since he'd started the census, but now, with a free Thanksgiving dinner on the line, people were coming forward. The final tally of Pierce Point's population was five hundred forty-one people. Four hundred eighty-seven sent their RSVPs for the Thanksgiving dinner; an amazingly high percentage. Everyone wanted to be part of this experience, and it wasn't just for the free food. They wanted the most memorable Thanksgiving of their lives, and to have a little bit of "normal" back, even if it was only for a few hours.

The final part of the plan was getting people there. Many people lived a mile or two away and could walk, even if they were carrying food. A committee coordinated all the rides for those that needed them.

Seats were limited at the Grange, so people would eat in shifts. It would have been great if everyone could have eaten at once, but that wasn't possible. At first, the idea was to assign a morning, afternoon, or evening spot based on the first letter in a person's last name. However, people wanted to have dinner with their friends and neighbors. Therefore, people could sign up for a slot as long as the numbers roughly balanced out into each of the three slots. Few people wanted the morning spot, so those who didn't respond got that one. The natural leaders for a given area, the "block captains" as they became known, went around and made sure people in their area knew what spot they had. It took a tremendous amount of administrative work to feed five hundred people in a little Grange hall. But it was worth every damned moment of effort.

Everyone — every single person — was excited for the Thanksgiving dinner. It gave people confidence in their leaders and — more importantly — in their neighbors. They knew that people were looking out for them. The dinner caused people to knock on each other's doors and see which of the spots they had for the dinner, to borrow ingredients for their side dishes, and to arrange for rides. People in Pierce Point were close to their neighbors already, but the

Thanksgiving dinner made them even closer.

The political decision was made by the residents — at Grant's suggestion — that the Thanksgiving dinner would be open to all. Just like the first Thanksgiving at Plymouth Rock. But this dinner would be the last freebie for people who didn't work for the community.

The news that Thanksgiving would be the one and only freebie got a few of the slackers to sign up for jobs and get a meal card. The ones who didn't were too far gone to worry about. They were totally on their own after getting numerous chances to pitch in and be fed.

On top of this excitement and planning for the Pierce Point dinner, Ted and Grant were busy planning a secret Thanksgiving dinner for the 17th, too. It was easier to plan this one because it was a military unit and a leader just gave orders and people followed them. But still, there were a lot of logistics to feeding all those people in secret.

They devised a plan for Kathy McClintoch and her crew to roast all of the eighty-nine turkeys at the Grange and Chip would bring the ones for the 17th out to the Marion Farm. Kathy would be told that between ten and fifteen turkeys and a corresponding amount of fixings were going to the "rental team."

The 17th had limited access to the ingredients for proper Thanksgiving side dishes. They had mashed potato mix — plenty of that because it was an FCard staple — and even had some stuffing. A few months ago, Carl, Stan, Tom, and Travis had stolen a bunch of food back in Olympia. In the summer, no one wanted stuffing mix, so it was just sitting out at a government facility. The 17th had been eating stuffing non-stop all summer and fall. People were actually tired of it, but that was OK. The 17th was eating better than most people in the country.

To provide the most authentic Thanksgiving meal, Grant and Ted made sure the Grange would provide side dishes other than potatoes and stuffing. Chip would bring cranberries and the ultra-coveted pumpkin pie to the "rental team."

The Thanksgiving meal planning at the 17th raised morale there, too. Soldiers were talking to each other about Thanksgiving traditions from their families back before all this started. But the fact that, even in this bleak world of rainy Washington State in the middle of a pending war, life was going on like normal. They would have a Thanksgiving dinner. There was hope. Things hadn't gone completely down the crapper. Not completely.

People were talking about how much better Thanksgiving

would be next year. This would all be over in a few months and things would be back to normal next year. They hoped.

Since so many Thanksgiving traditions had been interrupted by the Collapse, people had a clean slate to start plenty of new ones. And they did.

Families started their own new traditions. For example, Grant and Lisa allowed the kids (who were now teenagers) to try some wine that day. A neighbor had made some homemade wine from berries. It was amazing. Grant was afraid the kids would like it too much. As a community, Pierce Point also started its own tradition. The Wednesday night before Thanksgiving, they held a Thanksgiving service at the church. It was not very "religious" at all. Non-believers and people who hadn't been to church in a while were welcomed and they felt comfortable there. There was no sermon, but a very appropriate prayer thanking God for all they had. The bulk of the service was people standing up and telling everyone what they were thankful for. It was amazing and heartwarming. Many couples who hadn't told each other how thankful they were for each other stood in front of everyone and told the whole community how much their spouse meant to them. There were lots of tears. Happy tears. Thankful tears.

Grant was in the front row, so he was one of the first to get up and talk. He thanked the community for being so squared away. "Lots of amazing things are happening out here at Pierce Point," Grant said. "You know what they are. Many of them have made your lives better. They've sure made my life and my family's life better. And for that I am amazingly thankful. Thankful like I've never been in my whole life."

Grant paused and looked around. All those faces. All those people who he hadn't known at all back in May. Now he knew almost every one of them. Closely. That person over there had helped him. Grant had helped that person. And so on.

"We can't lose this," Grant said, his voice quivering. "We can't lose this — what we have right now. The whole community working together. We will make it through this together. We will die if we don't keep this up. Sorry to get heavy, but the only reason we're alive now and are going to make it is that we are doing this together. I am so thankful for the people here at Pierce Point. I am so thankful that God put me and my family here with you people."

In the remarks that followed, many thanked Grant, Lisa, Rich, Dan, the Team, the gate guards, the kitchen ladies, and everyone else for all they'd done. But when people were thanking Grant, he would look at them and remember all things that person had done for the community. For the canning jars, for the smoked salmon, for the gas, for the moped, for taking in a kid who had lost her parents, for volunteering for guard duty or working in the Grange kitchen. He was thankful for the person who was thanking him.

Pierce Point was solid. They were cemented together. Cemented.

When the service was officially over, people stayed and hugged and continued to thank each other. The Matsons stayed an hour after the service. Grant was amazed at how many people thanked Lisa. He was usually out in the field and didn't see all that Lisa and the medical team did. They treated people on a regular basis. They reduced pain. They told people that whatever it is they had was not as serious as the person thought. They provided comfort.

Grant was very proud of Lisa, and not just because of all the good doctor things she did. She had gotten over her normalcy bias. She had gone from not wanting to go out to the cabin to gladly living out there and helping people. Now the people at Pierce Point, who were a little too "rural" for the old Lisa's liking, were her friends and patients. She had come a very long way.

When they got home, Grant tucked in Cole and asked him what he was thankful for. Grant didn't expect much of an answer, but he always asked Cole questions to continually improve his talking skills.

"I'm thankful for you and Mom, Sissy, and Grandma and Grandpa," Cole said. That was nice, but not as great as what Cole said next.

"And I'm thankful that we're here," Cole said. "Our old house was dangerous. Bad people were there. Like the mean lady who hit me. People are not bad out here. I feel safe here, Dad."

Grant was overcome with joy. This was some of the best talking he'd ever heard from Cole. Even though he couldn't say much and many people thought he was stupid, Cole was a smart kid. He knew lots of things, he just couldn't say them. Cole knew that Olympia was dangerous and that Pierce Point was a much better place to be. He knew more than most adults back in Olympia. But most of all, Grant melted when he heard Cole say, "I feel safe here, Dad." That was Grant's job: to make things safe. And he was succeeding. He had lots of help, but he was pulling it off.

Grant cried. Cole sprang up in bed and asked, "Are you okay, Dad?"

"Oh, yes," Grant said. "I'm fine. I just am so thankful that you are out here and know that you're safe. It's my job to make you safe."

"I know," Cole said in a matter of fact tone. "Thank you, Dad."

Grant melted again.

He went to bed and told Lisa how thankful he was for her.

She looked at him and said, "I'm thankful for you, too. You know, for everything that's happened." She smiled.

Grant was speechless. He literally could not speak. Lisa's "I'm thankful" was as close to a gushing thank-you as he'd get from her. That was okay. What she just said was heartfelt. It was just her way. He'd still marry her all over again.

They both fell asleep instantly.

Chapter 231

Thanksgiving

(Thanksgiving Day)

Grant got up early. He looked at the clock and it was 4:17 a.m. He felt fantastic. Rested and relaxed. That "thank you" last night from Lisa was the culmination of months of hard work out there. Finally, he knew that she was fully okay with being out there. Finally.

Maybe now she won't leave me when she finds out I've joined the unit and I'm going into combat, Grant thought. Yeah, that's it. She's thankful for me, he thought. Maybe she'll cut me some breaks. Maybe.

Then Grant started thinking about it again. He hadn't been thinking about this topic constantly like he had weeks before. He realized he had worn out this mental loop in his head. He had been through this a million times. He came to the same conclusion he had the million previous times.

Lisa would still leave him, Grant realized. If anything, her happiness at all he'd done would just mean she would be more disappointed when he left to fight some stupid war over politics. "Disappointed" wasn't the right word. She would feel betrayed because he had been lying to her constantly for months, telling her he was just working on things at the Grange and wouldn't go play army.

Stop thinking about this, Grant told himself. Stop.

He was getting better at stopping the worry and the over analysis loop in his mind. That ability had developed out at Pierce Point. Back in peace time, when his worries were over little things, he couldn't turn off the worrying very well. But now he could. He had to focus on things that directly related to living one more day. Directly related to it. He found it easier to turn off side thoughts and get down to what counted.

Grant got dressed as quietly as possible. Lisa was still out cold. She worked very hard at the medical clinic, and she knew that Thanksgiving would be a day off. She knew she didn't have to set her alarm and that always let her sleep more soundly.

Grant put on his pistol belt, like always. The weight felt so natural on him. He couldn't imagine not having his pistol. And he needed it. There were a million likely scenarios where he'd have to use it, when he least expected it. Even at something joyous, like Thanksgiving.

Grant put on his "uniform": a long sleeved Mossy Oak hunting camouflage shirt and his trusty 5.11 pants. He continued to wear hunting shirts and jackets on purpose. He had — of course — a political reason to do so. He wanted the people at Pierce Point, most of whom had hunting clothes, to feel comfortable around him. He didn't want them to think of him as a "commando wannabe" in military clothes. Although, Grant had to admit, when he went out to Marion Farm, he tried not to wear "duck hunter" clothes. Out there, Grant wore solid colored shirts in earth tones. When he wore those, he looked exactly like a military contractor, which was intentional.

Grant's 5.11 pants were holding up fabulously. He only had two pairs, but that was all he needed. He hadn't worn sweat pants or jeans the whole time since he bugged out to Pierce Point. His 5.11s were the ones with unobtrusive knee pads sewn right in. People made a lot of jokes about the knee pads but, after having to kneel for twenty minutes pointing a rifle at something during training, the jokes usually stopped. Grant would get the last laugh when those people got a rock jammed into their kneecap and limped around for a few hours. Having built-in knee pads was indispensable.

Grant got his AR and tactical vest. He couldn't go anywhere without them because he never knew if the Team would get called out to a big fire fight, or if some crazed jackass would try to kill him at the Grange. Or if the gate was attacked and he had to rush down there with whatever he had on himself to endure a four-hour gunfight.

What a change in a short period of time. "Can't go out of the house without an AR and kit" would have been an absurd thought before the Collapse. Now, leaving the house without them seemed absurd.

Grant tiptoed to the front door of the cabin. He got his slip-on Romeo boots from the shoe rack. Those hillbilly slippers were another thing that worked perfectly during the Collapse. Rugged as hell, water proof, comfortable to walk in, and easy on and off. He couldn't have better general purpose footwear than those.

Grant quietly opened the door and went outside. It was raining. No surprise. It was November in Western Washington. He was wearing his old reliable dark green and black Gore Tex jacket.

As Grant walked over toward the night cabin where the moped was kept under cover, he noticed that the lights were on in the yellow cabin. It looked like the Team was stirring in there, getting ready for work. Things just kind of ran on their own now at Pierce Point. Grant didn't know everything going on, and didn't need to. Stuff just got done. The place was running itself.

Grant walked up to the guard shack. There was Gideon, awake and alert, standing in the shack and staying dry. That guy was awesome. He took his job very seriously.

Gideon was so thankful to be here in Pierce Point instead of...anywhere else. The people at Pierce Point had been so decent to him. Well, he did give them a semi-truck of food, so that probably made them a little nicer. But, as a black man, he had been worried about living out here in the country with all these hillbillies. It turned out that they were fine, and they weren't as solidly white as he'd thought. There were plenty of Hispanics, some Indians from the nearby reservation, and a few Asians. Gideon had a home out here. And a family.

"Hey, Grant, you're up early," Gideon said. "Something up?"

"It's Thanksgiving, man," Grant said. "Be sure and come by the Grange about mid-morning. Seriously. You're coming, right? I mean, mid-morning is late night for you." Gideon always worked nights.

"Oh, I'll be there," Gideon said. "I've been thinking about that turkey dinner ever since I heard about it." Gideon had a huge smile. This meant more than a great turkey dinner to him. He had a family. He had a home. He had a Thanksgiving dinner to share with his new family. It meant everything.

"I'm going out to watch the dinner preparations get underway," Grant said. Gideon was one of the very few who knew what was going on at the Marion Farm. He was on guard duty when Ted and Sap originally came to the yellow cabin for the meetings. So Grant could actually talk about the Marion Farm with someone outside of the Team. Finally. What a relief.

"After I make sure things are rolling at the Grange," Grant said with a wink, "I'm heading out to the farm to wish a happy Thanksgiving to the rental team." Gideon was one of the indispensable assets that Rich and Dan said needed to stay with Pierce Point instead of joining the 17th. Grant supported that decision wholeheartedly. He wanted his family guarded and Gideon was superb at it. Besides, Gideon, the former Army MP, had no desire to join up with some irregular force. Looking for a fight with the Loyalist regular forces seemed like a big risk to him. On top of all that, Gideon had done all the good he needed to do by driving that semi of food into Pierce Point and giving it away. He'd done his good deed for the day — for a lifetime, actually. No one even thought of trying to talk Gideon into joining the unit.

"Turkey, stuffing, gravy ..." Gideon said. "You cracker asses got any sweet potato pie?"

"Doubt it," Grant said. "But, hey, it's a potluck, so who knows what people will bring. People seem kinda appreciative toward you for some reason, Gideon. I bet you'll get first crack at any sweet potato pie."

Gideon laughed. He wanted to talk to Grant about Thanksgivings back home, but as he started to get into a conversation, he stopped himself. He didn't talk much out on guard duty. It was a habit from his MP days. Talking just distracts you and lets any attackers know where you are—and that you're distracted. So he merely said, "See you at the dinner, man." He could talk to Grant then.

Grant got on one of the mopeds and headed toward the Grange. That thing was still on the same gallon of gas from three weeks ago.

Riding a moped in the rain was no fun. Grant got out the military poncho from the little storage compartment on the moped. That worked pretty well. It fit over his slung AR and kept him pretty much dry. He wouldn't arrive at the Grange soaked, although things like being wet and a little cold were no longer the big bugaboo they had been before the Collapse. You got wet, cold, dirty, sweaty, thirsty, and hungry doing things. You just did. It wasn't some horrible thing to be avoided at all costs like before the Collapse. People were tougher now. Way, way tougher. And wondering how they had ever been so soft.

The ride to the Grange was uneventful. It was dark out, so there was nothing really to see. Grant was almost at the Grange. He slowed down as he approached and flashed his headlight to the guards. The light stayed on automatically, so he had to put his hand over the light and then remove it to simulate flashing. The flashing light let the guards know that he was a friendly. They shouldered their rifles toward him, but did not aim directly at him. It was standard practice. They could squeeze off enough rounds to take out a suicide bomber. That was very unlikely, but their job was to keep the number of suicide bombings or other attacks at exactly zero.

Grant parked his moped in the nearly empty parking lot. It used to be, before the Collapse, that a nearly empty parking lot meant that there weren't many people in a building. Not anymore. Almost no one drove their own car or truck. They carpooled or, more likely, walked or rode a bike. So a few vehicles in the parking lot could now mean a packed building.

Grant got under cover from the rain and took off his poncho. He shook it off and found one of the nails in the wall of the outside of the building that people put up for drying jackets.

From the entrance to the Grange, Grant could see the rotisserie off to the left side of the building. It had been going non-stop for a couple of days. A big bed of wood coals roasted the turkeys and would give them a slight smoke flavor. It smelled fantastic.

The rotisserie was massive; a steel flat box that looked about the size of a full size mattress. It was full of turkeys. It was enclosed with a metal cover to partially keep in the heat. The rotisserie slowly spun around with the help of a big electric motor.

Thank God, literally, that the electricity had stayed on for the most part during the Collapse. Grant thought about the survival novels he'd read like *Lights Out* and *One Second After* where a nuclear weapon, an EMP, wiped out all the electrical circuits and left America without any electricity. What an "end of the world as we know it" disaster. Everything ran on electricity. Like the freezers and refrigerators that allowed them to keep the turkeys for eventual roasting.

Grant noted the stunning contrast between the conditions outside and inside. Outside, it was cold, dark, and rainy. Miserable. But inside the Grange, it was warm, light, and dry. And the smells. The smells of Thanksgiving came pouring out of the door the second he opened it.

Turkey, stuffing, gravy, potatoes. Grant hadn't smelled those smells in … a year. He assumed he would never smell those smells again. There is power in a sight or a sound, but smell is often underrated. A smell can communicate just as much as a sight or sound — sometimes more. And smells are linked to memories. You remember a smell and, when you smell it again, it transports you back to the earlier time you smelled it.

That was certainly going on with Grant. He was transported back to his house in Olympia with a big Thanksgiving dinner with his family. To wearing sweat pants and watching football as the turkey cooked. To a lazy day when eating and visiting was all he had to do.

There were fifteen to twenty people in the Grange working hard cooking and organizing. Kathy McClintoch saw him and smiled. "We're not serving until about noon and only then if your last name starts with A through J," Kathy said with a laugh. "You'll have to wait out in the rain."

"Can I help with anything?" Grant asked.

Kathy shook her head. She had everything under full control. She had this thing so fully organized it was mindboggling. She'd spent a week working up the plan for cooking so much with such limited conditions before she even knew if dinner would happen. She'd been cooking since yesterday morning, with only a one-hour nap. The coffee, which was in very limited supply nowadays, kept her going.

Kathy pulled Grant aside to say something that others couldn't hear.

"Rich is coming by at 5:00 with a truck to take ten cut up turkeys and all the fixings to the rental team," she whispered with a smile.

Kathy was smiling because all the food was cooked and ready to transport. She'd overseen all of that. Yes, she was proud. She was thrilled that the brave men (and maybe some women) on the rental team out there volunteering for a dangerous job would have a nice Thanksgiving dinner.

Kathy took Grant into the kitchen and showed him the three extra refrigerators they had plugged in and sitting outside, under cover from the rain. There were also coolers. About a dozen big ones. All filled with turkey and side dishes. Amazing. It wasn't just that they had all this food when things were so scarce. It was the organization it took to cook it and store it for transportation. *People will work together after the war and do amazing things. You will be a part of it.*

Grant got chills. He hadn't heard from the outside thought in a while. Grant soaked it all in. Whenever he heard the outside thought, he would pause and just experience the moment. He looked at all the food and let his mind be amazed at how incredible this all was. If we can do this together, he thought, what else can we accomplish?

Rebuild. That's what we can do together, Grant thought. He smiled. He knew how this was going to end. Well. That's how it was going to end. After a bunch of pain and misery.

Grant was excited for the future. That's right: excited for the future. He hadn't felt that way in a few years. Now he wanted to get the war over with and start the rebuilding. He couldn't wait to have a thousand amazing experiences like this Thanksgiving.

"Is everything okay?" Kathy asked.

"Yeah, sure, why?" Grant asked.

"You got real quiet all the sudden and just started staring off into space," she said. "Is this not enough food?"

Grant laughed. "Oh, no, it's plenty. I was just … well, I was just so thankful."

"There will be a lot of that today," Kathy said. "That's why we're doing all this." Yes, that's right, Grant thought. That was exactly why they were doing this.

Some vehicle headlights were coming up to them. Someone was parking off to the side of the building near them. Kathy walked over and looked.

"It's Rich," she said. Grant looked at his watch. It was 4:58 a.m.

Grant heard men jumping out of the truck. The gravel they landed on made that distinctive crunch sound. He heard familiar voices. It was the Team. That must be who was going to take the food to the "rental team."

"Over here, guys," Kathy said. The Team huddled under the cover of the eaves of the Grange building.

"Whoa," Ryan said, pointing at all the food.

"You are kidding me," Wes said with his North Carolina drawl. "Y'all cooked that? Overnight?"

Kathy just nodded with a giant grin. This was better than cooking for a wedding. This was the best cooking she'd ever done. The day was already magic. And it wasn't even 5:00 a.m. yet.

"Holy …" Pow said, and then caught himself before he swore in front of Kathy. "Toledo," he said.

"Can you weak girly men pick up these heavy coolers of food and get them in the truck?" Grant asked. "Or does a wussy lawyer have to do all the work here?"

They started loading the food into the back of Rich's truck. They all had ARs and kit, except for Rich, who just had his pistol. But the Team had become accustomed to loading things with their ARs slung on them. They had those awesome SKT slings that cinched up tightly against their bodies and didn't let their rifles flop around. A quick tug of a small release strap and the sling opened up into the regular length for aiming.

Loading took a while because there was a tremendous amount of food. When they were done loading, there wasn't any room in the back of the truck for the guys to ride.

"Someone find us another truck for you guys to ride in," Grant said.

"Aye, aye, Lieutenant," Ryan said—and then realized what he'd just said.

"Lieutenant?" Kathy asked. "When did they start calling you that?" Kathy was sharp. Nothing got past her.

"It's just a joke," Ryan said. "We tell Grant that the only reason he gets any breaks is that he 'outranks' us."

"Oh," Kathy said. That didn't seem like a very funny joke, but oh well.

A second truck came around and they all got into it. Grant rode in the cab of Rich's truck. Grant was glad to be in the warm truck cab. Rich had the radio going to that country music station he liked. They were playing Christmas songs, even though it was only Thanksgiving. Apparently the Limas wanted to get the people thinking positive thoughts and remembering the good times of holidays past. Grant couldn't fault them. That's what Grant was doing, too.

After a while, Rich said, "This is the first time in a couple years I've been hopeful, Grant. The first time since…" Rich thought. "I don't know when. Since before I left the Sheriff's Department."

Grant just said, "Yep." He wanted to hear what Rich had to say.

"Truth is," Rich said, "up until a couple days ago, I didn't think we'd make it through the winter. Oh, sure, most of us, like the people in this truck, would. But I didn't think the community would make it through together as an intact group. I figured there'd be arguing over food, especially the semi. Then the arguing would turn to shouting. Then pushing. Then shoving. Then shooting."

"Yep," is all Grant said.

"But people are really coming together for this Thanksgiving," Rich said. "Who'd have thought a meal could do that?" Rich thought about what he'd just said. The Pilgrims, that's who, he thought to himself. There was something about the power of a big meal and a tradition that could do this.

"Grant, it's weird," Rich said. "I feel like we're one of the only functioning communities. Like we're an island in a sea of craziness. Why us? Why are we making it while others aren't?" Grant could tell Rich was feeling guilty about their apparent success.

"Dunno, man," is all Grant could say. Well, actually, he could talk for hours about why Pierce Point was making it while others weren't, but now wasn't the time for that.

Rich got quiet. They both seemed to be fixated on the windshield wipers and the song on the radio as they rode silently to the turn off to Marion Farm.

Behind them, the truck with the rest of the Team flashed its headlights, which meant Scotty had called into the farm guards on his radio and told them they were coming. This was another example of how things that used to take planning and discussion now just happened.

The Marion Farm guards knew that Thanksgiving dinner was coming, but were still amazed when they saw a truck bed full of coolers and food. In the light from the guards' flashlights, they could see steam from some of the coolers with warm turkey.

"Unbelievable," the guard said as he saw, and smelled, the turkey. It was unbelievable, especially when people had been eating lots of cornbread, beans, and biscuits lately. And didn't really expect to each much better than that—ever.

Chapter 232

Band of Brothers

(Thanksgiving Day)

Grant felt like Santa Claus as they drove the turkey down the road toward the farmhouse. He was bringing a sleigh full of goodies made by happy elves. Grant felt so glad that these guys and gals, who had been working their asses off for months, would have a memorable day and a big meal.

The lights were on in the farmhouse even though it was only 5:15 a.m. They drove up to it and started to unload the food. Some of the soldiers on KP (kitchen duty) came out to help. Their eyes were as big as saucers when they saw all of the food.

Franny, a Navy submarine cook from the nearby Bangor sub base who went AWOL and joined the 17th, came out with his apron on and a big smile.

Petty Officer John "Franny" Francis was a huge asset. Sub crews had the best cooks. There is a lot to know when feeding a hundred people in semi-primitive conditions, and a great cook makes a huge difference, in morale and by getting the very most out of the food that a unit has. Franny knew how to stretch food supplies. There wasn't a huge extra stock of food on a cramped submarine. Nothing went to waste in Franny's kitchen.

Ted got Franny by basically trading him for two infantrymen. Back at Boston Harbor during the planning phase, another unit had two cooks, Franny being the second one. The other unit, the 14th Irregulars based on Anderson Island, needed trained infantrymen. Ted realized what a huge find a submarine cook would be and, knowing that he had plenty of regular military men and the Team, he traded Franny for the two infantrymen. Franny was happy to go wherever he was needed.

Franny started to organize the effort to get the Thanksgiving food inside and ready to start eating. The plan was for a Thanksgiving breakfast. That wasn't the old tradition, but they were starting new ones out here. Thanksgiving needed to be a breakfast because Grant and the Team had to go back and do a second Thanksgiving at the Grange.

Rich went back while the Team, the KP detail, and a few extra soldiers got everything in order. They would have the meal in the equipment shed because it was the only place big enough to hold everyone.

The unit didn't have enough regular plates and silverware for everyone to eat at once; normally, they ate in shifts so they could get away with having half as many dishes as they had soldiers. So, at Franny's suggestion, Grant brought out plenty of paper plates and plastic utensils to make up for the lack of regular dishes and silverware.

The prep work for the meal went on at full speed. At about 8:00 a.m., the light was coming up, and soldiers started arriving at the equipment shed. Coffee was brewing. That was a luxury. The 17th had managed to steal some coffee months ago when Stan, Carl, Tom, and Travis went on one of their "liberation" missions.

Normally, the unit only had coffee on Sunday mornings during the optional chapel service that Pastor Pete came out and provided. Ted and Grant wanted to encourage attendance at the chapel; a rare cup of coffee was an extremely effective incentive to attend, but today was special. Very special. Coffee for everyone. Hell, there was even creamer and — treasure of all treasures — sugar. A basic cup of coffee with creamer and sugar tasted like a milkshake to the soldiers who hadn't had any sugar in months.

Grant made sure to talk to as many soldiers as possible that morning. He'd met them all when they first came to the unit, but that might have been the only time he'd talked to them. He was trying to remember their names, but was candid with them that, with his day job taking up so many hours, he couldn't spend as much time out at Marion Farm as he'd like. They understood.

As Grant talked to the soldiers, he marveled at how lucky they were. They had a stunning 105 soldiers out there. Over half were recently AWOL active duty. Of these, twelve were infantrymen from Ft. Lewis. Another dozen were Air Force and Navy who came out in the first wave and got the base set up. Another thirty-two were military and ex-military of all branches and specialties. There were lots of support troops in this category: supply, communications, vehicle maintenance, administration. They didn't have their former sophisticated military equipment out at Marion Farm to work on like they did back then, but all the support troops knew military discipline and were adapting well to their new roles as irregular fighters. There were the four walk-ons, including Nick, the much-valued combat medic, and Olson, the former cop. There was the Team and eight of the really good Pierce Point gate guards.

Rounding out the unit were thirty-five civilians sent out by HQ. They had an amazing set of backgrounds and skills, but no previous military experience. It was a mix of former construction guys and computer guys and gals, and plenty of former retail workers. The one thing they had in common was that they no longer had their old jobs and they were Patriots. More importantly, they had no families. The 17th was their new family.

For the most part, the civilians were adapting well. Ted, Sap, and Grant worked very hard at this. It would be easy for the military people to form a clique, especially the more elite ones, such as the infantrymen. The civilians could do the same, perhaps forming up around the college-educated civilians, so Ted and Sap made sure that military and civilian personnel were mixed together on things like KP duty. Obviously, some tasks, like guard duty, required more military skills (although the Pierce Point civilian guards did a great job of guarding). But most didn't. Ted and Grant told the squad leaders — the men and one woman who were in charge of a squad of ten soldiers — that military personnel and civilians were to mix into one cohesive unit.

While combining the military and civilian people was the goal, basic military discipline and customs were to be followed by all. This meant the civilians needed to adapt and become "military." While Marion Farm wasn't West Point with its rigorous military protocols, a civilian couldn't respond to a squad leader by saying, "I'm on it, dude," either. With lots of work, and the good examples set by Ted, Sap, Grant, and the squad leaders, the civilians saw how they needed to act. In the end, the 17th found the balance between being a squared away and disciplined unit without being a bunch of uptight screaming West Point assholes.

One minor distinction between military personnel and civilians remained, however, and that was the clothing. For the most part, the military people wore military fatigues, usually the ones they brought with them from their former units. The civilians, for the most part, wore hunting clothes. The Team was a third category: tactical clothing. They looked like a SWAT team; neither military nor hunters.

The civilians appreciated that "one of theirs," Grant, was the commanding officer. The military people appreciated that "one of theirs," Ted, was in day-to-day command.

Training was the main way the unit bonded; it integrated

everyone in the unit because they all had to know the same things.

The main training subjects were firearms and unit movements. That matched the 17th Irregulars' mission: to go in behind the regular units and occupy a city, which was increasingly obviously going to be Olympia. Soldiers in the 17th needed to know how to move toward their objective and defend themselves along the way. They needed to know how to enter a recently taken city. They would then need to know how to set up defensive positions. Then they would need to get out into the population and make a show of force and deal with any threats from remaining Limas or gangs. Finally, they would need to know how to help with the civil affairs program, which was the last training priority.

Firearm training was the main focus because it would be a part of everything they would do. At a minimum, they would have to defend themselves, and probably go on the offensive.

The support troops, and most of the civilians, were only minimally familiar with ARs. The infantrymen, the couple of Marines, and the Team showed everyone how to safely handle an AR and, for the ones without ARs, how to handle an AK.

The unit primarily used ARs because it was what they had. They got most of theirs from Chip's guns store and the remainder from HQ.

While every member of the unit had a rifle, only about a third of them had pistols. Everyone was on their own for pistols. There were a wide variety of pistols; lots of Glocks. Ted and Sap had their military-issued Beretta M9s. Nick, the medic, was an exception to the rule and was issued a pistol because he really needed one. He got Bobby's spare Glock in .357 Sig.

There weren't enough ARs for everyone, but there were enough AKs to make up the difference. The 17th was better off than some irregular units, who had to use civilian guns.

The 17th was short fourteen ARs, so the fourteen troops least likely to fight—guys like Franny—were given AKs. This wasn't because AKs were inferior, but because ammo resupply to the fighting squads meant that only one standardized kind of ammo and magazine should be used, if possible. But, in the event of a "battlefield pick up" — where a soldier couldn't use his rifle for some reason and needed to pick one up off the ground—everyone was trained on AKs, in addition to ARs. There were a fair number of AKs out there, especially with the gangs, so a battlefield pick up of an AK was a fairly likely possibility.

Ammo was at an extreme premium. HQ sent lots of ammo—

pallets of it—donated by defecting troops and stole lots more. It was all 5.56 ammo for ARs. However, it was likely that the hundred plus soldiers of the 17th would use an incredible amount of ammo. There was no way to go into an enemy city without having piles and piles of ammo. There would be no helicopters resupplying them; what few helicopters the Patriots had were devoted to other duties. The 17th might have to be in a hostile city for a month and shoot it out all the time. They had to carry in everything they needed, which meant that each irregular unit had to have five hundred rounds per soldier. HQ sent enough 5.56 for the ARs, but not enough 7.62 x 39 or 5.45 x 39 for the AKs. Chip and the Team donated most of the AK ammo. The troops with AKs would just have less ammo. Usually they only had a few magazines.

With ammo at such a premium, training with live rounds was hard. There were two ARs in .22—one of which was the Smith & Wesson M&P15-22 Grant donated—and these were used for the support troops and the civilians to train on. Even .22 ammo was at a premium; it was literally currency. It was like shooting dollar bills.

Much of the training was done without shooting. The 17th constantly practiced moving as a unit and communicating between squad members. They primarily used voice commands and standard infantry hand signs because they had so few radios. They practiced this over and over again. Ted and Sap provided an overview of explosives training with some dummy training explosives, but they knew that the irregulars would not be blowing up buildings; the training was just an overview of explosives. Quite honestly, it was mainly for morale, to make the irregulars feel comfortable that they could handle situations involving explosives.

First aid was another topic of instruction. Many soldiers, especially the former regular military, knew this topic well. Nick, the medic, gave these classes.

Rounding out each day of training was lots of basic work around the farm. There were always heavy things to move, but no equipment to move them, which meant work details. There was cooking and cleaning; lots and lots of cleaning to keep things sanitary. And there was guard duty.

From all this training and the work details, people were bonding. Grant sat back and watched as the people who really didn't have a reason to talk to each other a few weeks ago were now joking with one another. They were totally at ease with each other. There were some quiet guys, but there always were in any unit.

All the hard work of training and the stress of knowing they were going into combat soon would be forgotten today; it was a day of celebration, a day for everyone to celebrate what they had to be thankful for. By about 9:00 a.m., everyone was in the large equipment shed. Most were jacked up on coffee for the first time in a long time. People were talking a mile a minute. They were relaxed and thankful. Really, really thankful.

Franny rang the metal triangle that was the meal call. It was one of those metal triangles like in the cowboy movies.

Pastor Pete, who was trusted enough to know about the actual activities out at the farm and had become the unit's chaplain, came out and was ready to say a few words before the meal.

Grant started off by getting everyone's attention. The squad leaders made sure their squads quieted down to hear from their commanding officer.

"What can I say?" Grant started off with. "What can I say? Here we are. A group of strangers a few months ago. Most of us were wondering what the hell an 'irregular unit' was and why the hell we'd volunteered for this. Now we know, don't we?"

"Yeah!" and "Hooah!" people shouted.

"We're here to ..." Grant paused. Everyone expected a speech about fighting for liberty. Nope. Not today, Grant thought. Not today.

"We're here to be thankful," Grant said. "For all we have. For a place out here that's safe. For supplies. For HQ. For comms. For a medic. For food. For water. But for something much better than all of that: for each other. We have what a lot of people don't: a family. Not your normal kind of family with weird uncles and annoying cousins. A family of people who've got your back. Who will die for you. And you'll die for them — although we'll do our best to not give you that opportunity."

That got some laughs. But it was true.

"You guys have what most people never will," Grant continued. "You have a band of brothers." Grant felt bad using the name of a movie instead of something original, but the term fit so well.

"I'm not leaving out the ladies," Grant added. There were six women in the unit. No fraternization problems. Yet.

"By 'brothers,'" Grant continued, "I mean people you'll never, ever forget as long as you live. People who will take a bullet for you and vice versa. People you can count on to run through fire to save you if you're hit. Remember these days, ladies and gentlemen. Remember them. Savor every memory out here. Every one of your fellow soldiers.

Remember and savor them. You'll be telling stories about these days for the rest of your lives. Your kids and grandkids and great grandkids will retell the stories."

Grant paused and looked at the amazing spread of food. Turkey, stuffing, potatoes and gravy. Even butter. Oh, wow, there was butter for the rolls. Grant hadn't had any for months. It was so creamy, so sweet, and made whatever it was on taste so much better. Butter made foods taste "normal" again.

But the star of the show wasn't butter. It was the pumpkin pies. Kathy even got some cream from one of the Pierce Point dairy cows and Franny whipped it up.

With the amazing spread of food on the tables and the whole unit there (except a skeleton crew of guards), it was time for Grant to say something to kick off the feast.

"Today is Thanksgiving," Grant said. "This will be the most memorable Thanksgiving of your lives. I know it will be for me. Sit down. Eat. Eat some more. Talk to the guy next to you. Get up. Sit down and talk to another person. Enjoy this time with your band of brothers."

Applause. Lots of nodding.

"Now Pastor Pete will say something," Grant said.

"I can't add much," Pastor Pete said. "Just be thankful. 'Be joyful always, pray at all times, and be thankful in all circumstances.' First Thessalonians 5:16. 'Be thankful in all circumstances.' Thankful you're not out there. Thankful we're going to fix this mess. Thankful that we can. But, like Lt. Matson said, be thankful for each other. This unit isn't anything without each and every one of you. Now let's eat."

And they did. It was a joyous time. Everyone was smiling. People were laughing. Squad leaders were handing out turkey wishbones for breaking for good luck. Everyone was telling stories about their Thanksgiving traditions back home. Several stories about past football games played on Thanksgiving were being told. People were talking about their family's special Thanksgiving recipes. Oh, and crazy uncles. Everyone seemed to have a story about a crazy uncle who came over for Thanksgiving and did something off the wall.

The big hit of the meal was the sliver of pumpkin pie — with whipped cream! — everyone got. People were slowly eating each bite. Savoring it. Closing their eyes as they ate it and grinning.

Grant lost count of how many people said, "I'll never forget this Thanksgiving" and "I'll never forget all of you." He knew that the story of this Thanksgiving would be told for decades to come. It was legendary.

By now it was 10:30 a.m. and time for Grant, the Team, and Pastor Pete to get back to the Grange for the Pierce Point Thanksgiving. "Tough duty," Grant joked. "We've got another feast to attend — work, work, work," he said with a smile.

Grant signaled to Scotty, who got on his radio and called in to Rich to come and get them. They couldn't get a ride from just anyone, only someone who could know they were out with the "rental team" at the farm.

"I don't want to leave," Ryan said. The rest of the Team nodded. "This is amazing," he said. He had been in combat. He knew how important this kind of bonding was. He just kept looking around the room and nodding with a smile on his face. He had been in a band of brothers in the Marine Corps in Afghanistan and knew what it felt like. He was feeling it a second time out at Marion Farm.

The band of brothers made this whole shitty job of killing people and getting killed tolerable. Men (and some women) were wired that way, and had been since men began fighting each other, which had been as long as there had been men.

Chapter 233

Different, But Normal

(Thanksgiving Day)

As they approached the Grange, they saw over a hundred people standing in the parking lot. Most were holding coolers or other food items. It had stopped raining about an hour earlier, so it wasn't miserable to be standing outside.

There were so many people that Rich had to park a few hundred feet from the Grange. Rich, Pastor Pete, and Grant got out to hear cheering and applause.

As Rich, Pastor Pete, and Grant were walking toward the crowd, people started yelling out their thanks for the meal. Not for the food, although that was nice. They were thanking Grant for thinking of having a big Thanksgiving dinner. For Rich going into town and somehow coming back with turkeys. For organizing this. For making this the most memorable Thanksgiving they would ever have. Smiles, laughs, high-fives, and pats on the back. Grant felt like a million bucks.

As they walked into the Grange, there were more smiles and cheers. The place was packed. Rifles had been placed against the wall in the entryway. Grant took his rifle and kit off, which he never did. But, just like he didn't wear a rifle to church, he didn't want to have a rifle here. That wouldn't help Thanksgiving feel "normal." He wanted this to be a community feast; taking off the rifles would foster that feeling. So he did. The Team, seeing him do it, followed suit. Most people in the Grange had never seen the Team without their rifles and kit.

The smells. Not just the turkey, stuffing, and potatoes and gravy smells. Now the smells of all the food people brought was mixed in. There was fresh bread, desserts, all kinds of foods. Coffee, too. And sweet potato pie. Betty—the hippie chick organic gardener who had been ahead of her time and to whom rednecks now flocked to for gardening advice—had managed to grow some small sweet potatoes and made the pie. There was Gideon talking to her. Guess who was getting a big ole' slice of that pie? A man who earned it.

Grant and Rich couldn't just sit down and eat so they went into the kitchen to see if Kathy needed anything. She just shook her head and kept telling people where food went, where the plates were, and the million other things it took to feed five hundred people in one day — with no grocery stores, almost no transportation, and no big dining facilities.

"This is just the first shift," Drew said as he came up to Grant. There was Eileen, Lisa, and the kids. They were eating. Except Lisa. She had people talking to her about their medical needs. She was used to it by now. At some point, she would need to eat some before it got cold. Grant decided to help her do just that. He sat down next to her said, "Go ahead and eat, dear." The person next to her realized she was impeding Lisa's meal and politely excused herself. Mission accomplished.

Lisa smiled when she saw Grant. "This was a really cool thing to do," she said. "Remember when we had Thanksgiving at our house and you put too much water into the stuffing?" Lisa and Grant talked about their Thanksgiving memories as they ate. About when the kids were little and they had to drive to distant relatives' houses for Thanksgiving and one time Grant fell asleep at the wheel driving home. Today's feast was entirely different than a "normal" Thanksgiving but ... it was entirely normal to have Thanksgiving. So it was different, but normal, which was exactly what Grant was trying to accomplish.

Different, but normal. That's how life was out there now. Thank God for normal. Even if it was different.

Manda was talking to Cole, asking him what he was thankful for. "Mom and Dad and Sissy," he said. "And Grandma and Grandpa, too." Grant couldn't ask for any better answer, especially from a kid who wasn't supposed to be able to talk very well. Grant and Lisa looked at each other. They communicated with each other with just a glance: They were thankful for what Cole had just said.

Manda was scooting over, with Jordan right behind her. He looked even more grown up than the last time Grant had seen him. He was sporting a beard. Of sorts. It wasn't thick, but he was seventeen. It showed that he had grown up in a hurry during the Collapse and was trying to look like a man.

Grant whispered to Lisa, "Bringing a boy over for Thanksgiving dinner. You know what that means?" Lisa laughed. They had this joke about bringing a boyfriend or girlfriend over for Thanksgiving. It always meant they would get married. They had seen that in their own Taylor family Thanksgivings. Grant had known that when Lisa invited him to Thanksgiving back in college that they would end up getting married. They watched as cousins at the big Taylor family Thanksgivings brought guests over and then got married.

Grant was proud of Manda. Being on the path to getting married at this very early age was not what Grant had envisioned for her, but he was okay with it.

The whole college, job, kids in your early thirties thing was just what people did at the time; it wasn't set in stone that that was how human beings were supposed to live. In fact, throughout history and in every part of the world, it was the opposite. America in the late 1900s and early 2000s was an anomaly. Things were returning to normal now; to how the rest of the world did it and had always done it. Different (for Americans) but normal (for the rest of the world).

"Welcome to Thanksgiving, Jordan," Grant said, breaking the tension. Manda was still worried that her dad was being overprotective. Grant wasn't. He accepted and even welcomed Jordan. He just didn't want his daughter to make any rash, teenager puppy-love decisions. He had to admit, however, that Jordan was a very fine boyfriend for her out here.

Accepting Jordan meant accepting that America was done for and would be for some time. Accepting Jordan meant Grant had given up on America returning quickly to the college, job, kids in your early thirties world. Even if this were over today, the rebuilding would take … a generation? More?

Manda was the rebuilding generation. If her generation worked hard at rebuilding, maybe her kids could go back to the college, job, kids in your early thirties thing. Maybe. If that made sense to Manda's kids' generation. It might not. That was their decision.

So the very real prospect of his daughter getting married as a teenager was the point of no return. After that happened, things would never be (pre-Collapse) "normal."

Mark Colson came up to Grant. He looked concerned. "Have you seen Paul?" he asked.

"Nope," Grant said. "Why?"

"We can't get him on the radio," Mark said. "He was supposed to be here for Thanksgiving."

"He probably has his radio off," Grant said. Mark seemed really freaked out.

"Since last night?" Mark said. "He hasn't responded since then." This was serious. Grant excused himself from the table. He hated to end the great family Thanksgiving dinner, but this was important. Lisa understood.

Grant got Scotty, who had the ham radio. Scotty went outside where he could hear the radio. A few minutes later, Scotty came back. He was pale.

Chapter 234

Purple Heart

(Thanksgiving Day)

Scotty was in shock. He motioned for Grant to come over.

"Paul is missing," Scotty whispered to Grant. "The Chief found his boat drifting without Paul in it. The Chief is looking for him." Scotty looked very seriously at Grant. "It doesn't look good."

Oh God. The perfect, happy memorable Thanksgiving had just been shattered. It was memorable, all right. They would remember losing their first man that day. On Thanksgiving of all days. How would Mark and Tammy—and poor, sweet little Missy, Paul's daughter—ever face Thanksgiving again?

"What do we do?" Scotty asked Grant who didn't have any good answers.

"Go and try to find him," was all Grant could say. He knew it would probably be futile. Paul had probably fallen into the water. He didn't wear a life jacket, despite the Chief's constant barking at him to put one on. Paul didn't think a life jacket looked "tactical." After a while, the Chief just gave up on it. There's another victim in all this, Grant thought: the Chief. He would feel guilty the rest of his life for not somehow making Paul wear the life jacket.

"Should we tell Mark?" Scotty asked.

"I think we have to," Grant said. He was dreading this, but he knew he would be doing this a lot in the coming months.

Grant got Mark and took him outside, to the back of the Grange so no one else would hear.

"We're going to go and look for Paul," Grant said. "The Chief found his boat."

"Good!" Mark said. "Why did he have his radio off for so long?"

This was going to hurt. "Paul wasn't in the boat," Grant whispered.

Mark looked at Grant and tried to figure out what Grant was saying. How could Paul not be in the boat?

Then it hit Mark. Paul was gone. Forever.

"No!" Mark yelled. He would not accept that Paul was gone.

"He's on a beach somewhere," Mark said it like he knew it was true. "He made it to shore! Let's go pick him up."

"Sure," Grant said, wondering if maybe Mark knew something he didn't. "Did you come in your truck?"

Mark nodded. He couldn't speak. He just wanted to get down to the water to go find Paul.

"Bring it out back here," Grant said.

"Get the Team," Grant said to Scotty. "Make sure they do it discretely. If they run out, people will know something's up and they'll worry the whole time. I don't want to blow this Thanksgiving for everyone."

Scotty nodded. He calmly went back into the Grange and whispered to Pow, who nodded and whispered to the other guys. One by one, they discretely got up and excused themselves. The Team Chicks were upset that they finally had a nice meal with their guys and now they were leaving, but they had come to know that if the Team had to go and do something, it was important.

Scotty realized that they couldn't leave their rifles there. They had felt naked without them slung across their chests. He went into the entryway and stealthily grabbed their rifles and kit and loaded them into Mark's truck, which was waiting in the back.

Grant went over to Lisa, who had figured something was wrong, and said, "Sorry, honey, gotta go."

Lisa understood. "Glad we got a little Thanksgiving together, at least," she said. He kissed her. At that moment he realized how thankful he was that his family was safe and sound. None of them were missing. Thank God.

When the Team assembled around Mark's truck out behind the Grange, Grant said, "Sorry guys. I know you were enjoying Thanksgiving, but something obviously very important has come up."

"No problem," Bobby said. "Band of brothers, dude. Band of brothers. Paul's a brother. You go out and try to save your brother." The guys nodded.

"Yeah," Ryan said after a while. "Paul would do the same for me. It's how this works."

Ryan paused some more and thought about what he'd gone through with his unit in Afghanistan. "It's the only way it works," he said. Ryan looked the guys in the eyes and said, "If I don't know you guys will come out and look for me, then I don't want to go out there." Everyone understood the deal: I'll die trying to save you. And you'll do the same for me. There was no stronger bond.

Grant realized that Mark was waiting on them to go find his son. "Let's go," Grant said and got into the cab of the truck. Mark was fighting to control himself, almost having spasms. He was so amped to go and find Paul.

Mark threw the truck in gear and sped out of the parking lot. They went flying down the road toward the beach. Way too fast; the guys in the back of the truck had a hard time staying in the truck bed. It was wet, but they ended up lying down on the wet bed just to avoid being flung out.

Grant didn't say anything to Mark. In fact, he was getting very nervous riding with Mark. Mark was driving so fast it was frightening. It was the most scared Grant had been in quite some time, and that was saying something. Finally, as Mark was taking up both lanes of the road and overcorrecting the steering wheel, Grant said, "Slow down, man. We need to get there in one piece."

Grant wasn't sure if Mark heard him. Mark was in a trance of some kind. He eased up on the gas just as they were cresting a hill. The guys in the back were lifted up and slammed down as the speeding truck flew over the hill.

"Slow down!" Grant yelled. He was really concerned now. Mark had lost his mind.

Mark still didn't respond. They quickly came to Over Road. There were two taps on the roof of the cab. Mark looked perplexed.

"Slow down," Grant said, knowing what the two taps meant. "Scotty has something to tell us." Mark slowed down. Grant rolled down the window and stuck his head out so Scotty could talk to him.

"Boat launch," Scotty said. That's where the Chief must be. Pierce Point had a boat launch in the middle of the waterfront cabins. The Chief normally didn't use it for operations that needed to be kept secret because there were too many eyes around. But there was no secret that they were looking for one of their people.

Grant told Mark to go to the boat launch and he roared off toward it.

"Slow the hell down, Mark," Grant said. He was really worried about getting in a wreck. What a way to die, he thought. Make it this far and die in a car wreck because a freaked out guy was driving like a crazy man.

Mark seemed to be coming in and out of his trance. He must have heard Grant because he drove to the boat launch somewhat normally.

There was the Chief in his boat. The tide was out so he was far away, too far to shout to. There were two other boats there. Why weren't they at Thanksgiving dinner? Then Grant remembered that they were at the first of three shifts of Thanksgiving dinner. A third boat was coming into the boat launch area. Some people were running toward the boat launch. They had binoculars and CB radios.

The Chief motioned for one of the people who were running up to get into his boat. She did. Once she was in the boat, the Chief jumped out and came ashore. He wanted to make sure someone was in his boat before he got out of it so it wouldn't drift. He didn't have time to anchor. They had to go look for Paul.

By the time the Chief got to shore, there was a small crowd of searchers. The Chief had done a thousand rescues before when he was in the Coast Guard, but this one was different. It wasn't some drunken jackass boater. It was Paul.

"Okay," the Chief said. "We're using CB channel 7. I want teams to form up, each one with a radio. I want one person with a CB to stay behind and brief the others coming here." The Chief proceeded to tell people where Paul likely was when he last called in a radio check, which was last night at midnight. The Chief described which way the current and tide were going then. With Mark there, the Chief was careful to talk about where to find Paul and pick him up. He didn't use the word "body" to describe Paul, even though the Chief knew the odds of Paul falling into the water last night and still being alive were very slim.

"I found his boat this morning and it was here," the Chief said, indicating a point on his nautical chart of Peterson Inlet, the body of water surrounding Pierce Point. "That is consistent with the current and tide I mentioned. So we'll focus on this area and go get him off the beach." The Chief was being vague: was getting him off the beach rescuing him or picking up his body?

The Chief looked at Grant and, because there was a crowd of people who didn't know about Marion Farm, said to him, "Let our friends know we're out on the water." That was a good idea. They didn't want the pickets and sentries at Marion Farm to shoot them, thinking they were a Loyalist recon or landing party. Grant motioned to Scotty who went out of hearing distance of the crowd and called it in to the farm.

By now, more people had come running up to the boat launch to help. One of them brought a gas can, which was worth its weight in gold.

"How many radios we got?" the Chief asked. Grant was

realizing how valuable CB radios were. Sure, ham radios were better and had better range, especially when you hit a radio repeater and could talk to people far away, but CBs were so common. That meant lots of people had them. They were perfect for situations like this. Grant had always meant to get a CB radio as part of his preparations before the Collapse, but never got around to it. At least other people had.

Grant was also wishing right then that he had gotten his ham radio license — the test was easy — and a handheld ham radio. The radio was about the half the cost of a gun and Grant had plenty of guns. "Shoot, move, and communicate" was the military phrase for what it took to operate as a unit. Grant had the shooting down and was pretty decent at moving, but without the communications, the shooting and moving weren't enough to stay alive, let alone win.

"I want a member of the Team on each search team," the Chief said. He didn't need to say it, but the Team was armed and there were still pirate threats on the water. The primary mission was finding Paul, but there was always a chance they'd have to fight off some pirates. There hadn't been any pirate attacks yet, but Murphy's Law meant it would happen when they were searching for Paul.

A member of the Team went over to each of the search teams forming up. By now, two more boats had arrived which totaled five boats, including the Chief's.

The Chief pointed to Grant and said, "You're on my team." Grant nodded.

"Mark, you're riding with me," the Chief said to Mark who also nodded.

"That's it," the Chief said. "Let's go find Paul." The teams started walking, and then wading, out to their boats. When Grant got into his boat, the Chief said to him, "You're doing comms," and pointed to the CB in the small cabin of his boat.

Grant nodded.

"Get me a radio check," the Chief said.

Grant got on CB channel 7 and asked each of the search teams to check in. Grant assigned each boat a code name — Team 1, Team 2, etc. — not to be secretive but to keep things straight. It was clearer to use "Team 2" than "Jimmy Bob's boat."

Mark just stood there the whole time, not saying a word. He was in that trance again.

The Chief was in agony, too, but just not showing it. He was replaying in his mind how many times he could have forced Paul to wear a life jacket, but didn't.

"Here," the Chief said to Grant and Mark and handed them each a life jacket, which they put on.

The boats headed out, toward the part of the inlet where the Chief thought Paul most likely was. The Chief was watching the other boats and making sure they were covering their assigned sector. He was very good at this.

They spent the next four hours looking for Paul. They landed a beach team and had people walking the beach. Grant and Mark stayed in the Chief's boat.

No one talked. There was radio traffic and occasional questions about where to send a team, but no conversation; just silence. Mark continued in his trance. It was spooky. His mind had shut down.

A boat came out with some fuel. It was getting dark and was starting to rain. "We'll gas up and head back," the Chief said.

"No," Mark said, the first words he'd spoken all day.

The Chief was ready for this. It happened all the time during a search. Loved ones would refuse to suspend a search. Sometimes they got violent.

"We'll keep a beach team out tonight," the Chief said. "But it's too dangerous to have these amateur boaters out here at night. I'll stay out because I do this all the time, but no other boats."

"You're not trying!" Mark screamed. All the emotion that he'd been bottling up during the day finally came flying out of him.

The Chief took a few moments before speaking. "We'll have this vessel and a beach team out. We'll find him," he said.

"We'll find him now," Mark said with an almost childlike gushing optimism. "Just a few more minutes and we'll find him."

The Chief had been in this situation before where loved ones tried to negotiate with the searchers for more searching, even when searching was endangering the searchers.

"Two more minutes and then the other boats go back," the Chief said.

"Five," Mark shouted.

"Two," the Chief said firmly. "I am in command of this search. Understand?"

Mark was stunned by the Chief's firmness. Mark was snapping back into reality.

"Okay," Mark said sheepishly. He felt a bit embarrassed that he had insisted on searching in the soon-to-be dark.

"Can your guys do an all-night beach patrol?" the Chief asked

Grant.

"Yes," Grant said. "They'll need jackets." They had light rain jackets on, but it would get cold. It would be miserable outdoors tonight once the rain picked up.

"They have basic flashlights on them in their kit," Grant said. "They could use their head lamps and their spare batteries." The Team had not geared up for an all-night search.

Then it hit Grant. The whole Team couldn't be out on a beach. What if there was a SWAT situation in Pierce Point or an attack on the gate while they were stranded on a beach?

"I'd rather not have the whole Team on the beach in case a situation arises in Pierce Point requiring them," Grant said.

Mark exploded. "You don't want to find Paul! You're not even trying!"

Grant was genuinely scared of Mark right then. He was so erratic and not himself that Grant couldn't predict what he might do. For the first time ever around his longtime friend, Grant was glad he was armed. He feared Mark might try to attack him. Mark, the jolly guy who had Grant over to countless barbeques, who would give someone the shirt off his back, who welcomed Grant to Pierce Point when he first got the cabin. That Mark was now scaring Grant. A switch had gone off in Mark's brain. He was not himself.

"Pipe down," the Chief said to Mark. "You're making it harder to find Paul. Shut the hell up. Now."

Mark did. Then he started crying. It was stressful enough for the Chief and Grant looking for Paul, but a crying man made it worse.

"Call half your Team in," the Chief said. Mark continued crying. Grant got on the radio and made contact with each member of the Team. They were all on different boats or at different parts of the beach. He told them half of them would go back to Pierce Point and get together with the Crew and be on ready reserve for any trouble.

"Negative," Wes said on the radio in his southern drawl. "I'm stayin' on the beach."

"Me too," Bobby said over the radio.

"Yep," said Pow.

"Not leaving," said Scotty.

Ryan chimed in. "Band of brothers, dude."

Mark stopped crying and was staring at the CB radio in hope.

Grant was shocked. The Team was telling him no? Not following his direction? Then Grant realized that this was actually a good thing. The Team was refusing to abandon a brother. Grant smiled.

"The Crew and the gate guards can handle anything that might happen," Grant said to the Chief. He hoped the CB frequencies they were using weren't being monitored by the Limas, who would now know Pierce Point wasn't at full strength. Oh well. There had been no evidence so far that the Limas were monitoring the frequencies, let alone that they had the forces lying around to try to take down Pierce Point. They were busy selling booze, cigarettes, and stolen guns. "Alcohol, tobacco, and firearms," Grant laughed to himself, used to be a government agency. Now it's pretty much what the government did.

Grant was proud of his guys. They were staying out all night in the rain to look for Paul. He couldn't ask for anything more. Grant would join them.

Grant and the Chief planned for getting the Team regrouped and then onto the beach. He was also working on getting jackets, headlamps and some food to the guys, dividing up the beach areas for both of the two-man teams, and making sure each two-man team had a radio and knew the frequencies they'd be communicating on. Grant, the fifth member of the Team, would stay on the boat with the Chief, but he'd still get rained on, so he was sharing the misery with the Team. And it was always dangerous being out on a boat in the dark. As Paul had seemingly found out.

"Mark, we've got it covered," the Chief said. "You go back. We'll keep you updated on the radio." The Chief expected Mark to insist on staying on the boat, but he was in that trance again. He just mumbled. The Chief called in and had a boat sent out to pick up Mark and bring out the supplies the Team needed for the overnight search. Mark left the boat without saying a word.

After eating some dinner—MREs, which didn't quite compare to Thanksgiving dinner—they were ready to go back and try to find Paul. They all knew that they were looking for a body. Mark was the only one who seemed to disagree.

During a lull in the search at about 11:00 p.m., Grant said, "Hey, Chief, we should award Paul a Purple Heart."

The Chief nodded. "Some people will say this wasn't 'combat,' though," he said.

"Yep," Grant said. "But the whole United States is basically a combat zone now. Very low intensity, but it is. Paul was doing something dangerous. He wasn't shot by a bad guy, but he died while serving." Grant had always thought that military accidents never got the respect they deserved. It seemed like only those people getting killed or injured in direct combat made a sacrifice that "counted" when, in reality, all of it counted.

The Chief was starting to get emotional. He had been occupied all day with the search and hadn't let his emotional guard down. He loved Paul, who had become the son the Chief never had. They had spent hundreds of hours on the water together. They had done dangerous things together. He had watched Paul go from a fat kid with no self-esteem to an in-shape confident warrior.

"The worst thing," the Chief said, choking back tears, "is that Paul was finally comfortable with himself. He lost all that weight. He finally knew he was good at something. He had Green Berets telling him how good he was at navigating the tides and currents. He built that steel gate. He had found his purpose."

Right then and there Grant decided that they would write Paul's name on the gate as a reminder of all he'd done for Pierce Point. He'd create a permanent monument.

"And little Missy, too," the Chief said. "What a poor, sweet, little angel. Lost her mom to the drugs. And now she's lost her dad. She didn't do anything wrong." There was a tear running down the Chief's face.

"For what?" the Chief asked. "What did Paul die for?"

Grant didn't have any eloquent answers. "Freedom" or "liberty" just didn't cut it. Not now. It definitely wasn't time for a political speech. Grant felt obligated to say something positive to help the Chief get through this.

"He'll be immortalized," Grant said. "People in Pierce Point, who never even knew he existed or maybe just knew him as the fat guy who played video games all the time, now know Paul Colson as a hero. That's something. It's not a good trade for dying, but it's something."

"Not a good trade," the Chief said. "Not a good trade at all." After a while he said, "But it's something."

The Team spent the rest of the night searching. This, too, was dangerous. The driftwood logs on the beach were as slick as snot in the rain. Stepping on one could easily lead to a face plant into a log. It wasn't as dangerous as rushing into a house full of armed drug addicts, but it was still pretty dangerous. They had to watch the tide to make sure they didn't go around a log sticking out in to the water, have the tide come in, and end up stranded. The Chief's boat could always come in to get them, but they'd lose valuable time sitting around on a part of the beach they'd already searched.

They combed the beach in the area Paul most likely was and

fanned out to the other beaches. They covered the beaches surrounding the whole inlet. They even went over to the other side where the houses weren't part of Pierce Point. They were concerned they'd be shot by homeowners, so they turned off their headlamps and moved very slowly.

There was no sign of Paul. They had been operating under the theory that Paul had fallen overboard somehow and, without a life jacket, had drowned, but he would float and should wash up on a beach if that were the case. There had been two complete tide cycles since he was last on the radio. That probably would have washed him up.

Was Paul taken from his boat? By pirates? Or Limas? Did he board a boat trying to help someone who then took off with him? If he boarded a boat, he would have radioed. If pirates, Limas, or friendlies approached his boat, he would have radioed that in. Did he have the wrong frequency on his radio and radioed all this in but no one ever heard it? Grant and the Chief talked about all the possible scenarios throughout the night.

Around midnight, Grant took off his tactical vest and reached in the inside pocket that had his emergency caffeine pills. He took one, which would make it possible to stay up all night. He ended up taking a second one at about 3:00 a.m. He offered one to the Chief, who was happy to take one due to the lack of coffee in that situation.

Soon, the sun started coming up, which meant it was about 8:00 a.m. The Team wouldn't admit it, but they were exhausted. Walking the beach in the dark with kit and a rifle, and shivering in the rain all night, took its toll. The Chief and Grant were tired and cold, too. Everyone was famished.

"Time to pack it in," the Chief said. Grant could only muster a nod. The Chief radioed to the Team that they would be picked up. They were too tired to insist that they stay out looking. They all knew the odds of finding Paul alive were down to about zero. Even if he made it to the beach alive, he had been in the cold and rain for over twenty-four hours.

There was barely enough room in the Chief's boat for the whole Team. They went back to the boat launch, which had become the command post for the search. There was a small crowd there. It was raining so people had set a covered area up. When they pulled up to the boat launch, no one said a word. They all knew Paul had not been found. As the Team went under the covered area, people brought them food. People were thanking them, but it wasn't jubilant thanks, it was more like solemn thanks. They wolfed down their breakfasts and got another one. They got in someone's truck and went back to their cabins and slept.

The community organized daylight search parties for that day. They didn't send out a night search party. The odds of finding Paul alive were too low to risk more accidents. That made sense to everyone.

Except one person.

Chapter 235

"Lil' Sissy"

(November 29)

"There he is! There's Paul!" Mark yelled.

Tammy started crying. Again. She left the room.

Mark was looking out his window toward the water. It had been days since Paul went missing. Mark would sit there with his binoculars and think he saw Paul several times a day, but no one would go and try to rescue him. He would scream and insist that someone go out and get Paul and bring him back.

He came to believe that there was a plot by the Chief and Grant and the others to make people believe that Paul had been lost, but he was still alive.

At first, people thought Mark had temporarily snapped, which was understandable. But he didn't come out of it and then it got worse. The details of the "plot" to hide the fact that Paul was alive became more and more bizarre.

Tammy, who had just lost a son, now also had the tragedy of her husband going insane. She had lost her husband too, in a sense. That boating accident had claimed two lives. Tammy was holding it together pretty well, but after days of Mark's insanity, she couldn't take it any longer. She and Missy started staying at a friend's house.

Grant and the others were afraid that Mark would become violent. He hadn't so far, but if he really believed there was a plot to keep his son from him, he might try to hurt people. Gideon, whose guard shack was between Mark's house and the other cabins on Over Road, was told he could shoot Mark if Mark came out of his house with a weapon.

This forced a very difficult decision for the community. Should Mark be committed to the mental ward? He no longer left his house so he was not at the Grange meetings. They decided at one of those meetings to take Mark—forcibly if necessary—and commit him. After taking him, they would have the formality of a commitment trial, but everyone knew the outcome.

The decision was made to have the Team take Mark in. They didn't want to do it; Mark was their friend, but they knew that it had to be done. One day, the Team went over to Mark's house to give him an "update" on the search for Paul. (The search had long been abandoned.) When they got in, Wes and Ryan charged toward Mark at full speed and knocked him to the ground. The other guys fought the kicks and punches and, after accidently breaking Mark's arm, put some zip ties on his arms and legs. They let him scream and flail around for about forty-five minutes until he tired himself out. It was horrible to watch a good man be hog tied and scream like a lunatic. Mark kept screaming for Paul to come and help him. It was the worst forty-five minutes the Team had experienced in their lives; far worse than the raid on the meth house. This was just watching the punishment of a damaged man who used to be such a wonderful person.

When Mark finally stopped flailing, Tim gave him a shot, which put him out. They took Mark to the mental ward. While he was still out, Lisa set his arm in a splint and put on a makeshift cast. It was a minor fracture. That afternoon, Grant held a five-minute trial. They empanelled a jury and Bobby described what had happened earlier that day, which was enough evidence. Mark would be committed. He would get regular medical care, but they had no mental illness medications for him; not that he actually had a mental illness. Mark would either snap out of this or would be insane for the rest of his life. It was unbelievably sad. A second life essentially lost from the accident.

There was a third life lost too: Missy. She had lost her dad, Paul, and now her grandpa. She thought her grandpa was mad at her for her dad being gone. She assumed that must be why grandpa was always yelling and screaming.

Missy quit talking. She would sit by herself for hours. She had shut down. She quit eating. Tammy had to force her to eat. One time, in total desperation, Tammy pinned Missy down and tried to shove food down her throat. That's when Tammy knew this wasn't working. Her little granddaughter might starve herself to death.

A fourth victim was Tammy. She was handling the tragedy better than Mark, but that wasn't saying much. She busied herself with all she needed to do for Mark and Missy, and at her job, which she still was doing. She visited Mark, as horribly difficult as that was. She would spend all the time she could with the silent Missy, which was also horrible.

Cole started coming over to see Missy. He could tell that she was sad and would just hang around with her. He wouldn't talk to her and she wouldn't talk to him; they would just be in the same room together for hours without talking. They could think their own thoughts and not be bothered.

Cole helped Missy. He would occasionally break his silence and tell her when it was time to eat. She would eat with him. He started calling Missy "Lil' Sissy." After Cole got Missy eating on a regular basis, he would roll a ball to her. She would roll it back. Then they'd roll it back and forth. Cole would ask Missy to play, which she would, though not always. Sometimes she just wanted to sit there silently all day, which was OK with Cole. He didn't mind the quiet.

It didn't take very long for Cole and Missy to become like brother and sister. They had their own language worked out. No one else could understand them, but they understood each other. Grant would hug Cole every time he found out how much Cole was helping Missy and say, "You're a good, good boy, Cole." Cole would say, "I know, Dad. I want Lil' Sissy to be happy. She's my friend."

Tammy would cry every time she saw how Cole was helping Missy. They would be tears of happiness. Her wonderful little granddaughter might not be lost forever. An autistic boy may have saved her.

Cole was doing even better now that he knew he was helping Missy and that no one else could. He had an important purpose. He was needed. He wasn't the "kid who didn't talk much" who needed help himself. He was helping someone else. Cole's confidence and comfort with himself went way up. He realized that he was different than other people because of his talking. But he also had a skill no one else had. He was the only one who could help Missy.

Cole was very proud of himself. All the grownups told him what a great job he was doing. He would talk at dinner about what he and "Lil' Sissy" did that day. It was unheard of for Cole to talk about his day at the dinner table. Not anymore.

Paul's death and Cole helping Missy was a good example of how things were during the Collapse. It was ninety-nine percent horrible, and one percent good, but the one percent good made up for a lot of the ninety-nine percent horrible.

Blessed, Grant thought. The people of Pierce Point were blessed to have each other around. All those people out there — many of whom, like Cole, were the weak and needed help themselves — were helping each other. They would survive this nightmare by the blessings of having each other.

Chapter 236

"Lt. Matson"

(November 30)

Tony Atkins was cutting trees down at Marion Farm with a chainsaw. He hadn't used one of them in quite a while; probably since he was in high school. He was twenty-six years old with black hair and a thin build. He had his whole life ahead of him.

Tony had been a computer technician for the cable company in Olympia until about a year ago when people quit paying their cable bills and he got laid off.

Tony was a "gun guy" and had always been a Patriot. He had a "Don't Tread on Me" sticker on his truck before the Collapse. That sticker had gotten him a lot of crap after the pre-May Day terrorist attacks, which were — of course — blamed on "Timothy McVeigh types." There was never any proof the attacks were from "right wingers," but the media persisted in speculating that "militia tea party" people had done it. Most people believed the media back before the Collapse, which meant that having a "Don't Tread on Me" sticker caused many to think Tony was a terrorist.

As a result of that sticker, right before the Collapse, Tony got reassigned from his computer job because he was now a "security risk." His new job was going out and being an on-site troubleshooter. Crime was through the roof and the company prohibited him from carrying a weapon even though he had a concealed pistol license. He would have liked to quit, but he had one of the only remaining semi-decent jobs that were available.

In the end, he never had to decide whether to quit because he got laid off. Some of Tony's co-workers — without "Don't Tread on Me" stickers — held onto their jobs for another few weeks, but eventually they got laid off, too.

A few days after he got laid off, Tony's truck was vandalized, which was when he decided to take the sticker off. He decided to lay low and try to ride out the Collapse, though that became impossible.

Tony soon got in touch with some friends who were also Patriots. Before he knew it, he was at Boston Harbor being vetted to join an irregular unit. He ended up with the 17th.

He was glad to be in the unit, which was very squared away. Like many of the members of the 17th, Tony had no formal military training, but he quickly learned everything he needed to know. They were just irregular troops; they didn't need to be commandos.

Tony had grown up in Lewis County, a rural area to the south of Olympia. Growing up out there, he'd learned how to use a chainsaw. He was cutting firewood at the Marion Farm. They had a big woodstove in the barn. That was all the heat they had, but luckily Washington State winters weren't bitterly cold.

One cool morning at the farm, Tony was cutting a tree and suddenly, the saw jumped up and hit his leg. There was an explosion of red mist and he heard the most horrifying noise: the blade hitting what sounded like bones.

Tony wondered what was going on. He looked down at his left leg and saw it hanging there by some muscle. He could see his leg bone. A split, woozy, second later, Tony realized that he had cut his leg. Then the pain hit. It was the worst thing he'd ever felt. Then everything went black.

The other soldier cutting wood heard Tony scream, came running over and quickly applied direct pressure while someone got Nick, who rushed over and applied a tourniquet. Tony was going in and out of consciousness at this point. He was delirious.

Nick realized that he needed some real medical attention or Tony would die. Ted and Nick had planned for an injury that was so severe that they needed to go to the Pierce Point medical clinic. It would risk their cover, but saving a soldier was worth it. Besides, the "rental team" story was widely known out at Pierce Point. They would just play along with the "rental team" story and get their "rental team" member some medical help. Everything would work out fine. That was the plan.

Tony was rushed to the medical clinic at the Grange. Nick had stopped the bleeding, which was good because Tony was perilously close to dying from blood loss. Nick didn't have the equipment to amputate, which he hoped wouldn't be necessary, but it likely would be. At least it was something they could do at Pierce Point. They had saws and rubbing alcohol.

It was raining and almost dark. Not night-time dark—it was 2:00 p.m.—but dark gray and pouring rain. It was typical late-November weather in Washington State. It was hard to see in the rain and low-light conditions.

When a strange truck came speeding toward the Grange, Chip

and the guards scrambled to defensive positions. They clicked off their safeties. A couple more yards and they would open up. They had sticks with fluorescent surveyors' tape set up fifty yards from the parking lot boundaries. If a strange vehicle crossed the fifty-yard line without stopping, the guards were authorized to open up. Shoot the driver and then concentrate on the engine block.

Nick was in the bed of the truck with Tony. Don, the RED HORSE guy, was driving dangerously fast.

Don, who had never been there before, could start to see the Grange and the guard shack. He had been speeding, which was a good thing since Tony was on the verge of bleeding out. But then, in an instant, it flashed through his mind that the Grange would be guarded. He realized he was quickly approaching the guard shack. The next instant his mind said, "Friendly fire." He went from full speed to sudden stop in an instant.

When he stopped, they were at about one hundred fifty yards and closing. Chip put his hand up, which was the signal for don't fire. When his arm dropped down, that meant shoot to kill. Knowing that this was not a drill, Chip started to let his arm go down. He tasted the adrenaline on his tongue. Someone was trying to ram the Grange. Whoever was in that truck was about to die; they'd sort out the details later. Everyone in Pierce Point knew not to charge up to the Grange. Everyone knew what the flags at the fifty-yard line meant.

Suddenly, the truck's headlights flashed on and off, which puzzled Chip. Were the lights a signal? He kept his arm up.

As he was flashing the headlights, Don saw the guards pointing rifles at the truck. He thought, for a split second, that he was going to die by friendly fire. How embarrassing. Of all the ways to go.

Nick jumped up from the bed of the truck and, with his hands up, screamed "Medical emergency. We need help." He kept his hands way up and then yelled, "Cornhuskers suck!"

Chip yelled to the guards, "Lower your weapons. They're friendlies." He turned around and made sure every one of the guards were no longer pointing a rifle at the truck.

"Come on in!" Chip yelled and motioned for the driver to pull forward. Don did. He, too, could taste the adrenaline on his tongue. He had almost been shot.

Nick came running up and said, "We have an injury on the rental team." Nick had been told to keep the "rental team" cover story going no matter what, even though Chip knew exactly where Nick and the truck had come from.

"Cornhuskers suck" was a code phrase Ted had worked out with Chip. The two were longtime friends and Ted was from Oklahoma. Ted, a University of Oklahoma football fan, hated the rival powerhouse team, the Nebraska Cornhuskers. Ted told Nick the Cornhusker code phrase when they planned for getting a wounded or ill soldier to the Grange. As Ted was fond of saying, "We have a plan for everything."

Chip signaled and one of the guards ran into the Grange to get the medical team ready to go. He waived the other guards toward the truck to help move the injured person into the Grange. By now, people were pouring out of the Grange to see what was going on.

The guards ran up to the bed of the truck and looked inside of it. Tony was a mess. There was blood everywhere. The bed of the truck was coated with a thick crimson red liquid. The rain was diluting it and carrying it away in little streams.

Tony was going in and out of consciousness and occasionally screaming. He had a tourniquet on, but his lower leg was being held onto the upper leg by a splint made out of branches. It was primitive.

They rushed Tony into the Grange. The medical team, led by Lisa, started to work on him. They kicked everyone out, except for Nick.

Pretty soon, the guards and the bystanders started looking at Don. He was in Air Force fatigues. Only about a third of the soldiers in the 17th wore military fatigues. Ted encouraged those who had military fatigues to wear them. This "military look" emphasized to the unit, especially the former civilians, that the 17th was, indeed, a military unit. An irregular one, but a military unit nonetheless. Looking and feeling like a military unit highly increased the likelihood that they would act like one. Instead of like a gang or mercenaries.

Don usually had a name tape that said "Wash. State Guard" where the "U.S. Air Force" name tape should have been. The plan was that if anyone from the unit had to leave the farm, they would remove the "Wash. State Guard" tape. The guards at Marion Farm would make sure anyone leaving the farm did so.

Don was glad that the Marion Farm guards remembered to grab his "Wash. State Guard" name tape. Thank goodness. It would have been hard to explain to the Pierce Point people why a "rental team" had "Wash. State Guard" on their uniforms.

Don had never seen these Pierce Point people before. He realized that they had never seen him, either. He was a stranger in a military uniform. It was time to start the cover story.

"Hi, everyone," Don said casually. "I'm with some contractors around here. We don't really talk about what we're doing, so I'd appreciate it if you don't mention that I exist."

More stares. Chip came up and said to the onlookers. "This guy doesn't exist. He and his guys are making Pierce Point a bunch of money, which means more food. That goes away if people know they exist. Did you enjoy that turkey dinner? Ever wonder where the money came from? Want another turkey dinner? Then don't blow this cash cow. Got it?" People nodded a little. They trusted Chip, so if he said things were okay and these guys didn't exist, then they didn't exist.

Don realized that the more he stood there on display, the more people would see him. "I'll wait in the truck," he said.

"Good idea," Chip said. He had been thinking the same thing.

Now that things were secure, Chip went into the Grange.

Then he heard something terrifying.

"Lt. Matson! Lt. Matson!" Tony was screaming.

No one in the Grange, except Chip and Nick, was supposed to know that Grant was a lieutenant. Grant was only supposed to be "Judge Matson."

"Lt. Matson!" Tony screamed again.

Chip looked at Lisa. She shot back a scowl at him. Her face seemed to be saying, "So, my husband is a lieutenant in something? He never fucking told *me*."

Chip gave Lisa a puzzled look, as if to say, "I have no idea what that delirious guy is saying." Lisa wasn't persuaded. She had heard little things that there might be a Green Beret unit or some crazy thing like that out on a farm in Pierce Point and that the "rental team" was their cover story.

Now it all made sense. Grant being away all the time with "the Team." Grant acting weird all the time like he was hiding something from her. And Grant had basically stopped talking about how to prevent the government from doing what it was doing. Lisa had thought that he had come to a conclusion about what to do to stop the government, but just wasn't talking about it. "Lt. Matson" explained everything.

Lisa refocused her attention on saving the patient. Nick had done an amazing job of stopping the bleeding, but the leg had to go. Unfortunately, they didn't really have any proper amputation equipment. And they had very little pain killers.

They decided to use a hand saw. It was grisly. Lisa had never done that before. None of the nurses or EMTs had, either. They gave

Tony as much pain meds as they had, waited for them to take effect and … started sawing.

The sound of the blade cutting into flesh and through bone made people throw up. Even Tim, the EMT, who had seen it all. Lisa kept sawing, trying to avoid any further damage. Tony had gone unconscious as soon as the pain meds entered his system. The tourniquets were holding. The leg was off. Now they were cleaning up.

Lisa didn't notice it, but the medical team was coming and going from the clinic room to throw up. When everything was done, she collected her thoughts and then she went outside and threw up. She went back into the Grange, smelled the blood and others' vomit, and ran back outside and threw up again.

But something even worse was in store for Lisa that day.

Chapter 237

Todd and Chloe

(November 30)

Todd's wife, Chloe, was crying again. There is one sound men are genetically hardwired to pay attention to: their wife crying. No man could ignore it. Crying meant things were horribly wrong, and it was a man's job to fix it.

Except Todd couldn't fix it. Chloe was crying again because everything was horrible. Food was getting scarce in their very upscale Bellevue neighborhood outside of Seattle. Crime was terrible. Their girls, ages eight and six, were scared of everything and just sat in the house all day worrying. Everything they knew from just a few months ago had changed. Just a little while ago, they lived in a happy and comfortable upper-income neighborhood. Now they lived somewhere that looked and seemed a lot more like Detroit.

"What is it, honey?" Todd asked. He knew this would begin an hour-long rant about all kinds of things outside of his control, but he felt obliged to help her get it out of her system.

"Thanksgiving," Chloe said as she put away the breakfast dishes. "That was the worst Thanksgiving ever. A can of chicken? For Thanksgiving? Toast instead of stuffing? No trip to Hawaii like we've been doing since the girls were old enough to fly." She put her face in her hands and started sobbing.

Todd looked around his magnificent two-million dollar home. He would trade all of it to make Chloe stop crying if he could.

Todd drifted in and out of paying attention as Chloe went down the list of all the things that were wrong. Todd had heard it dozens of times. He heard it at least once a day, whenever the girls weren't within hearing distance. He was starting to dread when the girls weren't around because he knew the cry fest would start. He wasn't mad at her and didn't think she was overreacting. He just wanted his wife to be happy.

That's what caused all of this, Todd realized: trying to make her happy. He had slowly come to realize that, which was making the ordeal that much harder on him. This situation could have been entirely preventable if he had just been willing to do things that made her temporarily mad on occasion. But, no, he couldn't do that. He had to make her happy.

He thought about all the things he'd done since they first met to make her happy. He got the MBA because she wanted him to. He got his job at the auto parts company and worked hard to climb the corporate ladder. They got a really nice house they couldn't really afford. They had new cars every few years ... that they couldn't really afford. They went on fancy vacations because she wanted to. They put the girls in an extremely expensive private school. Todd made great money, but not enough for all that. It didn't really matter though, because all of it made Chloe happy. He was proud to be able to make her happy. He prided himself on it.

Pride. That was it, he realized as he stood there listening to her cry. Pride was what drove him to try to make her so happy, which led to the current hell they were living in.

Pride was what led him to believe that they didn't need to have a plan for the bad times everyone could see were coming to America. He had inklings about it and even suggested to Chloe that they get a cabin. She didn't want to go "camping" as she put it. She wanted new furniture for their mini palace in Bellevue. He went along with it and she was happy.

Not having a gun also made Chloe happy. He remembered talking with Steve Briggs, the manager of his company's store in Forks, about a week after the Collapse. Steve told Todd that he needed a gun. "Chloe won't like it," Todd had answered. That was the end of it. If Chloe didn't want it, it wouldn't happen.

"Dianna was raped!" Chloe screamed, as Todd drifted back into paying attention to her crying. Dianna was one of Chloe's yoga friends who lived a few streets away. "In the middle of the day," Chloe added. "No one could stop it. What's wrong with everyone? Why is this happening?"

"It will get better, honey," Todd said, trying his best to believe it. "Things always get better."

"The girls haven't been to school in months," Chloe continued. "They're falling behind academically. They'll never get into a good college now." Todd wondered if there would even be colleges after this disaster. He didn't say anything.

"If I eat any more mashed potatoes from that horrible mix," Chloe said, "I'm going to puke. And that awful cornbread mix? It's so gross. The girls aren't eating that crap and are starting to lose weight." She was right about the girls. Todd was scared that a nutritional deficiency was happening right when they were growing and developing.

Suddenly Chloe stopped crying. She looked up at Todd and softly asked, "Why didn't you do anything?"

Todd had no idea what she was talking about. "Huh?" he asked.

She started crying again and asked, "Why didn't you get that cabin?"

He couldn't believe what he was hearing. "You didn't want it," he said, realizing that he shouldn't be so honest.

She screamed, "You should have got it, anyway!" She was furious. "You should have just done it. We'd be safe out there, away from all of this, if you had just been a man and done it. You should have taken care of us!"

Those words stung Todd. He felt all the blood drain out of him. He felt shameful and defeated. It hurt so much because he knew she was right.

His first thought was to argue with her and explain how she had told him not to do everything he had suggested.

"Why didn't you get a gun?" she yelled. "We need one now."

He didn't tell her that he had suggested it, but she had told him no. A few weeks after the Collapse, he tried to buy a gun, but all he could find was a rusty 16 gauge shotgun with one box of shells. The guy was asking $10,000 in FCards for it. Todd had over a million dollars ... in his bank account, but that was before it was confiscated and converted into a few thousand dollars' worth of an FCard balance. Now all he had was mashed potato mix that his wife and girls hated.

"Ken and Kim got a place in the country, a bunch of food for it, and some gold and silver," Chloe went on, referring to a couple in their neighborhood. "They're probably fine. You know why?"

Todd was afraid to hear what was coming.

"Because he was a man!" she screamed and then stormed out of the room.

Todd just sat there. He was surprised with himself for not being mad at her for screaming at him to do things she had told him not do. He closed his eyes in shame and realized that she was right. He should have been a man and taken steps to protect his family when he saw a threat to them. It would have been so easy a few months ago. Now it was too late.

Or was it?

What if they could get out of Bellevue and go stay with Ken and Kim? Maybe he could redeem himself with Chloe and get her and the girls into a safer place.

He started to feverishly think about how he could take them out to wherever it was Ken and Kim were hiding out. Lake Chelan, he seemed to remember Ken mentioning. That was about three hours from Bellevue.

Why hadn't he thought of this earlier? He asked himself. Duh, he thought: because Chloe would have screamed at him about not abandoning their beautiful house. She was the one who would look for any little sign of things getting better and start talking about how everything would be fine soon. He assumed suggesting they leave would have made her mad.

Well, he thought to himself, now that Chloe was open to the idea of leaving, and was even demanding that he "be a man," maybe he should revisit the issue.

Todd started to approach the idea of leaving Bellevue like the smart MBA that he was. He started to come up with a plan. He first defined the objective, which was getting the family out of Bellevue and to Ken and Kim's. What would it cost? It would cost their beautiful home, he realized. While there were no roving gangs in their posh and secure neighborhood, there was no way they could be gone for long before their stuff would be gone. It wouldn't be gangs, he realized; it would be his neighbors "borrowing" things. They would probably return some things if they came back home, but things would be taken.

Todd looked at his home again. It was so beautiful. So perfect. But there was no way to keep things like they were. It was like Chloe: so beautiful and perfect, but no way for things to be like they'd been. Everything had changed and it was time to act accordingly. About six months after the Collapse, but better late than never, he told himself.

"Constantly reassess the situation," he remembered from MBA school. He was reassessing things now. About time, he thought.

He was starting to feel much better. He could solve this problem now that he had permission from Chloe. He hated thinking about his wife giving him "permission" to save them, but he was being honest with himself. For a change.

And quite a change it was. Todd found himself acting like he was a military officer planning a mission. He needed a map, because that is what military planners start with, he thought. And because the GPS in his BMW wasn't working anymore.

He went online – the internet still worked for things that

weren't "political" – and pulled up a highway map. The web page displayed an error message. He tried other web sites to find a map. All of the sites were taken down. Then he got nervous; if he were trying to access restricted web sites, the authorities would be alerted. They couldn't do anything about it because there weren't enough of them, but he'd get on some list. He didn't want that.

He wondered why maps had been taken off the internet. Of course, he realized, because the government didn't want people to leave the cities where they could be controlled. So people couldn't do exactly what he was trying to do.

Todd really needed a map. Planning an escape without a map was impossible. He ran into the garage. He checked the glove box in his car. Yes! He had an old paper map in there. Thank God.

He took the map into the kitchen. At first he was afraid Chloe would catch him looking at it, but then he realized that he had her approval now.

He unfolded the map and quickly found Lake Chelan, which was in the very middle of Washington State, right in the middle of the Cascade Mountains. They would need to get out of Bellevue and through I-405, which went through the heart of the suburbs, and then get onto I-90 and go east into the Cascade Mountains. How hard could it be?

Todd spent the next few hours making lists. To-do lists, packing lists, and lists of things he needed others to do, like having his neighbors watch the house while they were gone. He ended up with a pile of lists by lunchtime.

Chloe came into the kitchen to find something for lunch. She knew all they had were those awful mashed potatoes and cornbread, but she was hoping she'd find something that she'd overlooked in the past.

Todd decided that now was the time to tell her about the plan he'd been working on all morning.

"I listened to you, Chlo'," he said. "I'm going to get us out of here."

Chloe's eyes lit up. She'd wanted to hear that for weeks now. Todd was finally manning up.

He was gauging her reaction, and the look of relief on her face was what he was hoping to see.

He proceeded to tell Chloe about his plan as if he were making a presentation to the board of directors at his company. He was very thorough.

"Impressive lists, honey," she said at the end of the presentation. "Thank you. I'm very proud of you. I didn't mean those things I said this morning."

Todd smiled and hugged her. He knew that she did, indeed, mean those things, but he was very glad she said them. Now they had a plan. Something he should have done months ago. For the first time since early May, Todd felt relieved.

When the girls came back from the neighbors where they were taking online elementary school classes, Todd and Chloe told them the plan.

"Will there be bears there?" his youngest asked. "I'm scared of bears."

"No, silly," his oldest said. "There aren't any real bears in the woods anymore. Right, Dad?"

"Right," Todd said. "The bears are all hibernating in caves now that it's winter." Then he made a snoring sound. The girls and Chloe burst out laughing. They hadn't joked around in so long. Todd really missed it.

"You girls go back to studying and go to bed early," Todd said. "We're leaving early in the morning."

"Will there be real food at the cabin?" his oldest asked.

"Oh, yes," Chloe answered because she assumed things were much better out in the country. "The yogurts you like, juice boxes, carrot sticks, and the organic mac and cheese with the bunny shapes." That about summed up all the girls ate before the Collapse. After she said those foods would be available, she wondered if that were true. Oh well. The girls needed to have some hope.

The girls jumped up and down and started running around the house. Todd and Chloe were glad to see that, which, like the joking around about snoring bears, hadn't happened in a very long time.

"Things will work out," Todd said. "I got a late start on this, but I'm going to make up for lost time."

Chloe started crying; happy tears this time. She hugged him and they kissed, something else that hadn't happened in weeks.

Todd finished his lists and coordinated with Chloe on the packing. They had to take all the girls' favorite things and didn't want to forget any of them.

Hours later, Todd and Chloe crashed onto their bed and slept soundly, yet another thing that hadn't happened in a long, long time.

Their alarm clock jolted them awake the next morning at 4:00 a.m. sharp. It was time to start getting out of there.

Chloe woke the girls and made them eat some cornbread. "That'll be the last of that forever!" she said to them. They clapped and got into Chloe's Range Rover. They were ready to go.

"Let's go out to the woods!" Todd said as they pulled out of the garage into the darkness of their neighborhood. As they left, Chloe looked at her magnificent house. A tear rolled down her cheek, but she wiped it off before Todd could see it. She didn't want him distracted from what he needed to do. She should have been thinking that way months ago, she admitted.

They drove a few blocks to the entrance of the subdivision. They slowed down for the guards, who were surprised to see anyone driving that early. The residents chipped in to hire them, paying them in gold and silver and other items that could be bartered.

When Todd stopped the Range Rover and rolled down his window, his youngest yelled, "Hello, police helpers!" to the guards. Todd and Chloe had told the girls that the men with guns were "police helpers."

"Can I help you, sir?" the first guard asked. He kept his AR-15 hidden under his jacket because, in this upscale neighborhood, the residents didn't like seeing guns. He was in his thirties and very clean cut. He had been on the Bellevue police department before most of his fellow officers quit reporting for work back in May.

"We're leaving to see my parents," Todd said. He hated lying in front of the girls, but they had worked that out the night before: Daddy is going to tell some fibs when we leave to go the cabin in the woods. It's okay for Daddy to do this, Todd explained, and he would explain why when they got there. Todd had no intention of explaining, but figured that the girls would forget all about it by then.

"Where's that?" The guard asked.

"Wenatchee," Todd said. That was near Lake Chelan, but Todd didn't want the neighborhood to know they were going to Lake Chelan because they'd figure out it was to Ken and Kim's.

"Sir, have you been out of the neighborhood recently?" The guard asked.

That was an odd question, Todd thought. "Nope," he answered. "It's been a couple of weeks. I haven't been out much because gas is hard to come by."

"That's an understatement," the guard said. "Do you have a full tank and gas cans to get to Wenatchee?"

"We have almost a full tank," Todd said. He'd filled up Chloe's Range Rover a few weeks ago by selling his mom's formal silverware.

He hadn't told Chloe. "That's enough to get to Wenatchee."

"Maybe it was," the guard said. He saw the little girls in the back of the SUV and decided not to be too candid with young, impressionable ears. He didn't want to scare them. "But now things take a lot longer than before ... all this." He couldn't bring himself to say "Collapse."

"Oh," Todd said. "Like how long will it take? A couple extra hours?"

"Please step outside the vehicle, sir," the guard said like a cop. Old habits die hard.

"Is everything okay?" Chloe asked the guard as she leaned over toward the driver's side window to talk to him.

"Oh, yes ma'am," the guard said. "I just need a word with him," he said pointing toward Todd. To calm things down, he motioned for Todd to roll down the rear windows, which he did.

"Good morning, young ladies," he said to the girls. "Who's having fun this morning?"

The girls said in unison, "I am!" He gave them a thumbs up.

Todd got out of the Range Rover and went up to the guard, who motioned for him to come over to the makeshift guard station where the other two guards were.

When Todd got over to the station, the guard said, "Do you know what you're doing, sir?"

"Oh, yeah," Todd said casually. "I'm going to Wenatchee." It was no big deal. He'd gone there dozens of times to golf before the Collapse.

"Sir, do you know what's out there?" One of the guards asked in a very concerned voice. "It's rough. Things get bad in about a mile. From there to the city limits is really bad, especially in the dark like it is now. And it's extremely bad farther out."

Todd had heard rumors of this but hadn't wanted to verify them before he left. Things felt so right making a plan and getting Chloe on board that he didn't want bad news to burst his bubble.

"Like what?" Todd said. "Some robberies or what?"

The guards looked at each other and tried to not roll their eyes.

"No, sir," one of them said. "It's way worse."

"Like what?" Todd asked. He was starting to realize that he should have done his due diligence, as they say in the corporate world. Maybe he was being too hopeful with the easy drive he planned out.

"Well, car jackings, especially of nice vehicles like yours," one of the guards said. "Sir, this is a delicate topic, but needs to be said:

your wife and even your little girls are in extreme danger in a carjacking." He waited to see if Todd understood what he was talking about.

Todd stood there looking at them. He had an inkling of what they were suggesting, but didn't want to think it or say it out loud.

"Rape," a guard said. "And your girls, in addition to being raped, will be sold."

Todd felt blood pulse through his veins and he was suddenly boiling hot. He was starting to get dizzy.

"What?" he asked. "C'mon."

"A beautiful woman, pretty girls, and a Ranger Rover?" The third guard said. He held his hands up to gesture, "Figure it out."

"Are you guys serious?" Todd asked, realizing now what a fool he was to think things would be fine.

All three guards nodded slowly. They didn't enjoy breaking this to people.

"Are you armed, sir?" The second guard asked.

"No," Todd said. "That's illegal, right?"

Once again the guards tried not to roll their eyes. "There's illegal and then there's 'illegal,'" the first guard said. "No one cares if you're armed. So are you?"

"No," Todd said, sheepishly, realizing what an idiot he was.

The second guard shook his head and said, "I cannot recommend you leave the neighborhood, sir. I simply cannot."

Todd stood there. He felt like all the air had left his lungs but he was gasping for air. He was deflated.

Finally, the third guard said, "We can arrange for you to get where you need to go."

Todd jumped at the suggestion. "Yes!" he said, remembering from his business experience to not seem too anxious about any potential deal.

"Okay," the first guard said. "But it won't be cheap."

Oh, that's what's going on, the businessman in Todd realized. At first he was furious, but then he thought about it. He needed what was for sale. Kind of like the huge markups his company used to charge on auto parts when people really needed them, he thought with a chuckle. Supply and demand.

Chapter 238

The Republic of Texas

November 30

"Friday afternoon traffic sucks," Maj. Bill Owens muttered as he saw the red brake lights coming on ahead of him on the packed interstate outside San Antonio, Texas. Then he laughed at himself. He was extremely fortunate to be stuck in traffic.

That was because traffic meant people had gas and felt safe enough to drive. He was in some of the only traffic in the United States – or whatever the country was called these days.

Man, I am lucky, he thought. He started thinking about how he was living compared to other people, like his friend from law school, Grant Matson in Washington State. He wondered how Grant was doing. He'd seen some Intel reports showing that Seattle and its surrounding areas were firmly in Lima hands. Well, as "firm" as the Limas could control things, which was actually closer to "soft."

Bill was a military lawyer in the Texas State Guard and based at Joint Base San Antonio. The state of Texas had "requisitioned" the base from the FUSA, the Former United States of America. In fact, the last MPs at the base who hadn't gone AWOL in early May had pretty much handed it over to the Patriot army, the Texas Guard, and then promptly asked to enlist in the Guard. Bill would never forget the first time he saw the Texas flag flying on the base instead of the stars and stripes. It was scary, yet gratifying at the same time. Just like so many of the changes that took place over the last few months.

Texas, and the rest of the states bordering Mexico, had it the worst in the first phase of the Collapse. Millions of refugees streamed across the border to escape the Mexican civil war – more accurately, a gigantic drug war – right before the U.S. collapsed. Refugees, most of them totally innocent women and children, were doing whatever they could to survive. The feds came in to provide relief and completely botched it. This led some of the Mexicans to resent the feds and they took it out on them. And on civilian native Texans, many of whom were Hispanic. It was a bloody mess.

Along with the refugee crisis came all the other crises. Highways jammed, no gasoline, food shortages, crime waves, authoritarian government, and medical facilities shut down. The rest of the country experienced this, too, but Texas got the first taste of it because of the refugees.

Eventually, many of the refugees went back to Mexico because the gangs were too weak to keep going after the drug lords killed several hundred thousand of each other's followers. So, to many people's surprise, after a few weeks, Mexico actually calmed down and became somewhat more stable than Texas.

But Bill and his wife, Sandy, were well prepared. They saw this coming years ago, as did many in their neighborhood. They actually had a little extra food to give out to refugees. They also had a very strong neighborhood protection system – everyone had guns, lots of guns, in Texas – so they only had isolated instances of crime, at least in their area.

After a while, though, they went through their stored food. Luckily, Texas was known for its farmland, oil reserves, ocean access, and manufacturing facilities. It even controlled its own electrical grid. It took months of adjustment and hard work, but Texas was pulling together to keep people fed and even put some gas in the tanks of key employees, like Bill. He stayed on base during the week, but got to go home on the weekends, which was why he was in Friday afternoon traffic.

Patriot delegations from other states would come to Joint Base San Antonio and Bill would answer their questions. The delegation would ask him why Texas was relatively well off now. "'Cause we're Texans!" Bill would say. Then he would give the real answer.

"We got rid of the feds right off the bat." He described how, on the very first day of the Collapse, Texas state and local officials refused to assist the feds. Some, like the San Antonio police department, went further and started to repossess the state and local vehicles FEMA had commandeered during the refugee crisis.

"The feds couldn't do anything without state and local help," Bill would tell the delegations. "Oh, sure, they'd go to federal courts and get court orders and waive them around, but..." Bill would say with a shrug, "we weren't afraid of court orders. That's what saved us." Most other states agonized over their supposed legal obligation to follow federal laws and orders from federal bureaucrats, losing critical days and weeks while their states disintegrated into chaos and violence. By then it was too late. In those parts of the country, things had become so broken that the only entity powerful enough to step in and take control was a coalition of FUSA military, Department of

Homeland Security thugs, and a few allied state and local police units: the Limas.

Except in Texas. Being a fed or Loyalist was unpopular, at best, and dangerous, at worst. Quite simply, the majority of Texas, led by many of their elected officials, would not tolerate it anymore. They were sick of taxes, mandates, regulations, and ineptitude. And Texas had what other states lacked: a history of, and respect for, being an independent state. School kids in Texas knew that their state was a Republic, not just a state. Decades of the "Don't Mess With Texas" sentiment took hold and actually gave otherwise-scared citizens the courage to tell the feds, "No." Bill would never forget the meeting he was in with a federal military officer when the general in charge of the Texas Guard told the Lima officer, "You may leave now, Colonel." That summed up the Texas spirit: no yelling or screaming, no waving of rifles. Just, "You may leave now." Backed up by millions of rifles.

There was one exception: Houston. The greater Houston area was the only place controlled by the Limas. It was the only part of the state where the stars and stripes still flew. It became the refuge for all the Loyalists and most of the recent Mexican refugees who stayed in the U.S.

However, as predicted by many, including Bill, now Houston was facing a new refugee problem: people trying to leave the gangs in Houston. The Texas Guard did its best to let decent people return to the free areas of Texas, but criminals, or those who seemed like criminals, were dealt with harshly on the border of the Republic and Houston.

"How come there wasn't a big civil war?" was a common question Bill would get from the delegations. The visitors knew the answer, but couldn't really believe it; they wanted to hear some secret "inside" scoop that explained it. There was no inside scoop.

"The Limas didn't, and still don't, have the troops and supplies," Bill would answer. That was true, but unbelievable. Everyone, even Patriots, had assumed the massive U.S. military could crush anything in its path. They were right – if it were the old U.S. military. But it wasn't. Most of the troops went AWOL and the just-in-time inventory system for crucial parts went down like it did for civilians. So, without technicians and spare parts, the mighty U.S. military wasn't very mighty anymore.

That didn't mean the FUSA was powerless. It still had thousands of loyal troops with low-tech weapons, like rifles, machine guns, grenades, and rocket launchers. The Patriots had the same thing, and in similar numbers, from defecting troops. There were numerous intense firefights on the borders of free states and within states divided between free and Loyalist areas. Bill had personal knowledge of this from his time at the Oklahoma front.

About a month after the May Day collapse, the Limas massed in Oklahoma and tried to push into Texas. Thousands of troops on both sides were engaged in vicious small arms fighting. The Limas had to retreat when they couldn't be resupplied. The supplies were coming, but were being stolen by corrupt Limas. And the Texans had a steady stream of volunteers and supplies coming up to the front.

Perhaps most importantly, the Limas did not have the support of the general population in Oklahoma. Most Oklahomans would not supply the Limas or give them vital intelligence. Instead, most Oklahomans gave supplies and intelligence to the Patriots behind the lines. These Oklahoma Patriots, well supplied and having excellent intelligence, conducted devastating guerilla raids on the Limas. At the same time, the well supplied and much more motivated Texans pushed up from the south to cross the Red River and liberate Oklahoma.

Oklahoma was an example of how the Limas operated. They used the Department of Homeland Security as their main force. Most of the Lima military units were young kids in the National Guard who were poorly trained and equipped and, most of all, didn't want to be there.

DHS was different. It sought out people who enjoyed hurting others. Bullies, sociopaths, and psychopaths were welcomed. "Think of a power-tripping TSA agent driving a tank," Bill would say to the delegations. DHS was above the law – the perfect place for people who wanted to abuse people and get away with it.

Another feature of DHS that made it such a nasty thug force was the culture in the agency. DHS viewed everyone as a "terrorist" out to get them. They protected their own. They even created secure DHS compounds for their families to live in. To do this, they had to evict the residents in an area and take their homes.

Hiding family members in compounds was unsustainable, however. The Patriots, who were generally humane and honorable, were forced to target DHS family members. The Patriots tried, whenever possible, to hold the family members hostage instead of killing them, but sometimes they couldn't take them alive. This hardened the resolve of the DHS troops.

Adding to the "us versus them" mentality of the agency, DHS troops knew that they could not leave their units. They would be shot by the internal security forces in the agency or, if they made it outside of the DHS compounds and into the general population, they would be killed by the residents. DHS was hated. There was no forgiveness for them. So almost all DHS troops, despite their family members being kidnapped or killed, had to stick with their units. They made a decision to join DHS – the money, the cool gear, the glory, being above the law – and now they had to suffer the consequences. They picked sides and had to live, or die, with it.

In Oklahoma, the Lima push started by massing DHS forces in Oklahoma City and Tulsa and fanning out from there. DHS, aided by the remaining Lima elements of local police forces who had been receiving free DHS equipment, training, and indoctrination, started rounding up Patriots. They intimidated National Guard units and local elected officials. DHS also stole everything they could find. Citing "emergency powers," they took all the food and gasoline they could.

At this point in the Collapse, DHS was the strongest force in most areas. They got what they wanted – for about two weeks. Then the Patriots organized and fought back. DHS got cocky from their two weeks of running roughshod over the population. They forgot that they needed the support of the people if they were to be an effective occupying army.

The Patriot counterattack culminated in the spectacular raid on the Tulsa DHS compound. Over a thousand DHS troops and, unfortunately, their family members, died. So did a roughly equal number of Patriots.

With DHS's back broken in Oklahoma, the Limas could no longer control the general population. The people turned on the few remaining federal military, DHS troops, and Loyalist police. Now the Limas in Oklahoma were fighting for their lives and couldn't mount an assault on Texas.

"So, while there wasn't a 'big' civil war," Bill would tell the delegations, "there were plenty of brave men and women who fought hard and died." Bill had been at the front and was pressed into service guarding Lima prisoners. He was currently working on the details of a prisoner exchange with the federal forces.

"Name one thing we don't make in Texas," Bill would ask the delegations. Due to geography and a little foresight, Texas had its own energy and food, among other things. The free market took off and products started to trickle out to people.

But it wasn't a truly free market, especially at first, because the Texas Patriot officials knew that the people would shoot any company or politician ripping people off. It had happened in Abilene and Corpus Christi. So the Patriot government got out of the way and let private enterprise take off, but reminded businesses that they could not guarantee their protection if people were being cheated. That was very effective.

Texas was by no means a paradise; it was just much better off than most of the country. Most people in Texas were completely unprepared for the Collapse. Even the Lone Star State had plenty of Dorito-eating, EBT-card, couch-sitting dirt bags. It also had quite a few "drug store cowboys" who thought they were invincible because of the boots and big truck. They quickly learned otherwise.

Just-in-time inventory was a problem for Texas, like it was for the rest of the country. Almost a million people, out of almost thirty million, died from disruptions in prescription medications. About the same number died from crime, lack of proper medical treatment, and isolated cases of starvation.

Everyone in Texas realized that the life they'd lived – plenty of food, hospitals, and air-conditioning – had been an anomaly.

At this point in his commute, Bill was pulling up to the first of many neighborhood checkpoints. The Sheriff's Department, assisted by numerous volunteers for the posse, operated the first one, which was at a major intersection that led into several neighborhoods.

"Howdy," Bill said to the posse volunteer. Bill was in uniform, which always made things go more smoothly at checkpoints. "Heading here," he said as he handed his driver's license to a man with an AR-15. The man could see that he lived in one of the neighborhoods down the boulevard.

"Have a nice weekend, sir," the man said and tipped his hat at Bill. Bill saluted him to return the courtesy. Bill drove on to the next checkpoint and did the same thing.

The last checkpoint was at Bill's neighborhood. They waved him through because they recognized his truck.

As he drove up to his house, he saw his dog, Bucky, come out and bark with delight that he was home. He pulled in the garage and smelled the smell. The smell of his garage. It smelled like home.

Sandy, his wife, opened the door and smiled. She hadn't seen her man in five days. She missed him and had something nice in store for him.

"Hey, baby," she said to him as he was getting out of his truck. "Welcome home."

"So glad to be home, baby," he said as he kissed her. Let the weekend begin.

Bill had a thing: he had to get out of his uniform right when he got home and then he could talk. Sandy understood this from years of marriage and no longer wondered if he was mad when he came home and didn't talk to her.

Bill got into his "Friday clothes," at least the ones he wore in the winter: a Texas A&M t-shirt, a Texas A&M sweatshirt, and Texas A&M sweatpants. He went downstairs and smelled something delicious.

"Enchiladas, baby," Sandy said. She had started making something special for them on Fridays. Most of the time, she ate "regular Collapse food," like pancakes and oatmeal. Texas wasn't on the FCard system, of course, but money was very, very tight so people ate cheaper food.

Bill was paid fairly well in Texas dollars, the state's own currency. Texas dollars were highly sought after all across the country because they were partially backed with gold, silver, and oil. Lots and lots of oil. Texas dollars were becoming the region's reserve currency, much like the U.S. dollar had been the world reserve currency.

Besides being backed by something real, Texas dollars were valued because they were part of the fastest-growing economy in the FUSA. Businesses were flocking to Texas. The trend started before the Collapse and accelerated after it. Not only businesses were coming, but so were talented and hardworking people from all over the country. Thousands of people a month risked their lives to get to Texas from Lima-controlled areas. The federal troops couldn't keep people out of Texas – the border was too large, and the feds were spread too thin – but they could bottle people up in the cities. Once a person got out of the city, though, the only danger on the highway to Texas was all the roving criminals. And the difficulty of getting gas. But it could be done.

Sandy was a nurse, but could only find part-time work. The problem wasn't the need for nursing; it was people's ability to pay for health care. There was no more Medicare, of course, and not even any private health insurance to speak of. Health care was a strictly cash-only business. Charitable free care was usually available for emergency injuries in larger cities, but routine and preventative treatments like MRIs were only for cash payers. Access to medical care was drastically lower than it had been before the Collapse.

Sandy worked about twenty hours a week for a cash-only urgent care clinic in a strip mall. She arranged for a ride with the neighborhood carpool coordinators who made sure precious fuel was used to get as many people to work in as few vehicles as possible. Some days, when she couldn't get a ride, she couldn't go to work. She wasn't the only one this happened to. It was common and accepted by employers. They had no choice.

Sandy spent the rest of her time during the week getting groceries and, when she could, gas. The neighborhood would arrange for a truck full of residents to go to the nearest grocery store. Everyone went armed. There were not too many incidents. If trouble started, it was usually a person going crazy from a lack of medication, although robberies were not rare. There was a lot less crime now, in the winter, than there was at the beginning of the Collapse, which was largely due to the fact that most of the hardened criminals had been killed, either by armed citizens, the police, or more often, each other. The criminals who still remained were usually amateurs or very desperate people, who were far more dangerous.

Food, gas, and utilities were about all Sandy and Bill spent money on. They didn't have a house payment; foreclosure was impossible for lenders, so they just folded. Besides, all the money they loaned was in the old U.S. dollar, not the Texas dollar that everyone was using now. They no longer spent money on all the other things they did before the Collapse that cost so much. No movies, restaurants, vacation, cable TV, clothes, or a million other things. Food and gas were very expensive (utilities were not), but the money Bill and Sandy made covered it.

She opened the refrigerator and got him a cold beer, which was now officially a luxury. It was Friday, after all.

He sipped the beer and then took a couple of big gulps. It felt so magnificent to drink a beer. He now appreciated the little things that he used to take for granted.

"What's on the schedule tonight?" he asked Sandy.

"Roberto and Karmen are coming over around 7:00 and then we'll walk to the game," she said, referring to their neighbors and best friends. They lived about a half a mile from the local high school.

"If we win this one," Bill said, "we're in the state playoffs." There might be a Collapse, but there was still high school football in Texas.

Chapter 239

The Five Amigos

(November 30)

Lieutenant Commander Travis Dibble looked at the picture on his phone. Memories. It seemed like it had been a hundred years since that picture was taken. It was taken during the Army-Navy football game of his senior year at Annapolis, which had only been five years ago.

He looked at the faces. They looked so young and so fresh in their dress uniforms. They were so innocent and optimistic. The five faces were him, Steve, Zach, Vic, and Brent; the "Five Amigos" as they were known. A tight, tight group of young men who went through the most amazing experience of their lives together: surviving four years at the U.S. Naval Academy.

Where were the Five Amigos now? He wondered. He looked at the picture and thought about each man, starting from the left to right, with himself the first down the line

He was a Lieutenant Commander, the equivalent of a Major, in the Naval Department of the Washington State Guard and was actively fighting for the Patriots. The State Guard had a navy because Washington State had such a vast coastline and, quite frankly, so many FUSA naval facilities from which many sailors and naval officers defected.

Travis had been promoted quickly in the Guard. In the old Navy, the FUSA Navy, an officer with five years' experience would never have advanced to Lieutenant Commander, but this wasn't the old Navy; the Patriots needed officers, and Travis was a very good officer.

He started in the FUSA Navy in an aircraft maintenance unit. A year before the Collapse, he was transferred out to Everett, Washington, to serve on the aircraft carrier, USS Nimitz.

A native of Ohio, Travis liked Washington State. There was no humidity and he didn't even mind the rain. Then again, he didn't live too much in the state because he was usually deployed on an aircraft carrier somewhere in the Pacific.

Things were falling apart in the FUSA military even when he

was in the Academy. He noticed all the indoctrination about "terrorists" – and not the foreign ones in the Middle East. The Academy taught that terrorists were increasingly domestic: the so-called "Patriots." The upper classmen told the young guys to keep their heads down and not get involved in politics, especially not "right-wing" politics. Travis never thought much about it; he was a math and science guy and politics seemed strange. Politics was all bullshit so why worry about it?

On his first deployment, Travis started noticing the gangs. Yes, gangs in the Navy. There were parts of the ship that a white boy just didn't go onto. And there were white gangs, too. Contraband was available from them and officers didn't dare discipline gang members. This troubled Travis. He was realizing that the Navy his father served in for twenty-five years wasn't the same Navy he was in. But he did his job and was waiting for his time to be up so he could get out.

Then the Collapse hit when he and his ship were in port in Everett. A few days before May Day, they were passed the word that civil unrest was coming and they were being recalled to the ship to augment the naval security forces. They would be issued rifles and then go out and establish a one-mile perimeter around the base. "You will seize civilian firearms in the perimeter," he was told.

Travis was no right-wing wacko, but he knew that the military couldn't do that. He started to question what he was doing. As he was wondering why he was being ordered to seize firearms, the crisis was unfolding so quickly that he didn't have time to think. He was just reacting. He was trained to follow orders and did it all day long. These were just another set of orders. Unusual ones, but orders nonetheless.

Securing the base was an absurdly unorganized cluster fuck. No one knew what to do. People were issuing orders, only to have them contradicted by orders from higher-ups – and then contradicted again.

Travis knew this was going poorly when he went to get his rifle issued – an old M16 from the 1980s taken out of storage – but they didn't have anymore. He knew from the briefings that the base had plenty of rifles for the security forces and the others like him. When he asked the Marine armorer why there were no more rifles, the armorer shrugged and said, "A few are missing."

"Well, go get them, Sergeant," Travis ordered.

The armorer laughed. "I'd love to, sir, but there are some guys on this base you just don't mess with." Gangs. The Navy gangs took the rifles. This definitely wasn't his dad's Navy.

Travis was finally issued an M9 9mm pistol. That was it. He was sent out with a group of sailors, most of whom were maintenance technicians, to go clear and occupy the area around the base. Only a few of them had rifles and most hadn't shot one since basic training.

They stood outside in the cold on base all night waiting for the order to go. They finally got the order, advanced a few hundred yards and were then ordered to turn around. They spent the rest of the day milling around the base. That night, when they were tired and hungry, they were ordered out into the perimeter. Two of Travis's men didn't report for the muster, as a formation was called in the Navy, before they departed.

Out they went into the darkness, slowly advancing behind the real security forces. They could hear gunfire and had no idea if it was from their side or the civilians.

Then it hit Travis: "their side" and the "civilians" were different sides. This was not why he joined the Navy.

It got worse. Around midnight, they heard a high volume of fire. Someone shot up the Navy security forces pretty bad. Travis' men looked at each other and many of them decided this unorganized, dangerous show of force against their own citizens was a bad idea. They wanted to sleep, eat, and not be shot at by their own people. Within an hour, half of his men were gone. It was easy to hide in the darkness and confusion.

Travis envied the men who went UA, the naval term for AWOL. But he was an officer. He had a duty and was held to a higher standard. He didn't care about his career anymore; his motivation for staying was simply to not dishonor himself.

By dawn, after being awake for twenty-four hours, and slogging through alleys and getting contradictory orders every block or so, Travis had enough. He looked behind him and saw only a handful of his men left.

"I'm going to keep going," he told his last remaining petty officer, "and I won't turn around for a couple of minutes."

"Roger that, sir," the petty officer said. "Thanks."

Travis nodded and started walking. A little while later, he turned around and the last of his men were gone. Good. Now he could take off, too.

It took him several hours, but he got out of the perimeter and started walking toward his apartment a few miles away. He got there mid-afternoon, fell asleep on the couch and woke up a few hours later to the sound of sirens and gun fire.

He had no idea what to do. He was UA (AWOL) so he couldn't go back to base, but he had to do something. He couldn't just sit in his apartment. There was chaos and fighting going on. He had to have a plan. The best one he could think of was to go over to his cop friend, Justin's, apartment.

Travis rang the doorbell and after a minute or two, he heard the distinctive sound of a shotgun being racked. "Who the fuck is it?" Justin yelled through the door.

"Travis."

"Travis who?"

"Travis Dibble, dude. Open up."

Justin opened the door. He'd been sleeping in the middle of the day, just like Travis had. He looked like hell.

After cracking open a Rock Star energy drink, Justin started to talk. "We had a deal in my department," he said. "If we called for backup and no one came, we could leave. That was when we couldn't do anything more. That happened early this morning. Looting, carjackings, dumb asses cruising around looking for 'action.'" Justin stared out the window. He wasn't just tired. He was numb.

Travis told Justin about the melting away of his naval unit and asked, "What do we do now?"

"I have a friend," Justin said. An hour later, they were in Justin's truck heading to the house of an Oath Keeper buddy who was a Snohomish County Sheriff's deputy.

From there, Travis joined a Patriot naval unit. He went out on commandeered civilian boats and made contact with Patriot privateers, who were civilians with watercraft intercepting Lima and pirate ships and turning over a portion of the booty to the Patriots. He loved the work. He got to see a lot of action and had been in several firefights and open-water chases. The only downside was when he had to fight FUSA Navy vessels and personnel, which only happened once. He justified it by remembering the Navy gangs and the complete disorder and chaos from his night in the perimeter. This wasn't the American Navy he'd joined; it was a bunch of thugs and idiots on boats. He had seen plenty of Lima atrocities out on the water, which made it clear to him that he was fighting for the good guys.

Travis looked at the next person in the picture, Steve. He was from California, a surfer dude and computer whiz. He had the laidback personality and technical skills that made him the perfect officer to oversee young enlisted computer geeks. And the Navy had plenty of them. Steve was assigned to the Air Force's Space Command. At first,

147

when Travis heard of "Space Command," he thought it was some made up thing from Star Trek. No, Steve assured him, Space Command was a real military command staffed mostly by Navy and Air Force "nerds," as Steve called them, who worked on military satellites and communications.

Steve was stationed at Vandenberg Air Force Base in California. Right before the Collapse, Steve had set up a secret, encrypted email system for the Five Amigos so they could keep in contact. Last time Travis had checked that email account, Steve and his wife were at her aunt and uncle's in Idaho. That's all Travis knew about Steve's situation.

The next amigo in the picture was Zach, who was from Florida and flew helicopters. He was fluent in Spanish because his mom was from Argentina, so he ended up in various Latin American countries flying training missions for SEALs and other special operations units training Latin American forces. Zach didn't use the secure email, probably because of the sensitivity of his assignment and the primitive bases he worked out of. Zach's wife and kids were in Florida somewhere. Travis had contacted her before the Collapse. They were fine, but she hadn't heard from Zach in weeks, which was normal so she wasn't worried. Travis hadn't talked to her after the Collapse. How would Zach and other U.S. service personnel get back to America from foreign postings when a collapse was going on? Travis didn't want to think about it.

The second-to-last face was Vic. He was a good looking Italian kid from New Jersey. He was one of eight children. His father was the president of a junior college in Trenton. When relaxing with friends, Vic was very East Coast: the accent, the talking with his hands, the insistence on only the finest brands of clothing and other things, and his dislike of "camping," as he called field exercises. But he had a heart of gold. He would do anything for his friends and family. He was very smart and could read people like no one Travis had ever met.

Vic was a Public Affairs Officer assigned to the Pentagon; a very good gig for a fresh Academy grad. His job was basically public relations: getting the Navy's story out via TV and the internet. He was often the "Navy spokesperson" who explained things on camera. He was a natural at it; he even toned down his East Coast mannerisms for the camera.

Vic was the only Loyalist of the Five Amigos. In his last email on their secure email account, he explained that he was sticking with what he knew. "I'm an officer in the U.S. Navy and the United States still exists," he wrote to them. "The Navy is helping people and I'm helping the Navy by telling these stories." Vic never really got into politics because, as he explained, "In New Jersey, politics is nauseating." Besides, he noted, "My wife and daughter are here in D.C. What am I going to do?"

Travis thought about Vic's situation. Sitting in Washington, D.C., it would seem like the United States was actually in charge. That area and the rest of the East Coast looked and felt a lot like the old United States. In fact, if a person didn't know about the South and Mountain West "opting out" of the country, a person in Vic's part of the country might think things were essentially okay.

Travis, who loved Vic like a brother, thought it would be best not to tell him about his work for the Patriots out in Washington State. Travis didn't think Vic would try to get him killed – the Limas didn't have the resources to get him out on the open water even if they knew he was working for the Washington State Guard – but it was just best not to talk about it. Travis's approach to Vic was like a dear friend who has done something horrible but forgivable and somewhat understandable under the circumstances. The topic was avoided.

The last face in the picture was Brent, or "Cowboy," as they called him. He was a real-life cowboy from Wyoming who grew up on a ranch. He herded cattle and even won some junior rodeos in high school.

He was literally a rocket scientist and was aboard the U.S.S. Henry M. Jackson, a ballistic missile submarine with dozens of nuclear warheads thought to be in the Pacific. Travis hadn't heard from Brent since a few months before the Collapse, but that wasn't unusual because Brent couldn't easily check his emails while he was aboard a submarine.

Scuttlebutt had been flying around the Navy that some missile submarines had either defected to the Patriots or were "sitting it out." Travis knew that the military leader of the loose Coalition of Free States and Patriot areas of Lima states, Gen. Warrilow, claimed to have control of at least some of these subs and could order them to launch on Lima-controlled U.S. cities. There was considerable debate whether Warrilow had control of these assets, whether they were still operational, and whether any Patriot subs would actually launch on American cities. Then came the Utility Treaty, which was the agreement between the Limas and Patriots requiring the feds to keep the utilities on in exchange for Gen. Warrilow not starting a nuclear civil war. If the Limas hadn't thought Warrilow could deliver nukes on

U.S. cities, they wouldn't have made the deal. That was a bit unsettling. Travis wondered if Brent was onboard one of the Patriot subs.

Travis looked at the picture again. They were so young and so innocent. Who could have imagined back then, at something as festive as an Army-Navy game, that some of them would be on different sides in a war? But it didn't feel like they, the Five Amigos, were at war with each other. The sides they worked for were at war. It wasn't personal.

He decided to check the secret email account one more time, just to ease his mind. To his surprise, an email from Vic had arrived. The subject was "Go Navy!" and the body of it said, "Hey, bros, I know things are a little complicated now, but I can't wait to see you guys at an Army-Navy game sometime. A few years? Who knows. I'm thinking of you guys. Nothing can ever break up the Five Amigos."

Travis cried. He knew the group could never get back together, but he appreciated Vic's sentiment. The Five Amigos were like families and friends all over the country: they could never get back together like the old times, but they didn't have to hate each other.

Travis didn't reply to the email because that could have given away his position on a remote inlet on the Puget Sound. Then the alarm went off and he had to get into a boat and go out and intercept a FUSA Navy vessel. The photograph, and their innocence, still played in his mind.

Chapter 240

"Doctor" Greene

(December 1)

"No one is listening to me!" Randy Greene yelled to himself. He was sitting in his cabin, the really nice one a few down from Grant Matson's. Grant "Mr. Wonderful" Matson. Randy hated Grant. Everyone looked to Grant as the leader when he was just a piece of shit lawyer, not some survival expert. And that wife of his, Lisa "Dr. Miss Perfect" Matson.

Randy was a doctor, too; a podiatrist. Podiatrists are not medical doctors, so no one oohed and aahed over him like they did for little miss perfect Lisa. "Dr. Foxy" they called her. What a bitch. She had it so easy.

Randy, or "Dr. Greene" as he preferred to be called, took another drink of vodka. He'd been hitting it pretty hard all day. It was December 1st. He didn't know why, but the first day of a new month — another month of rain, dreariness, darkness, people realizing how hungry they would be all winter — meant he needed to do something different. Like drink and then show everyone that Mr. Wonderful and Dr. Bitchy weren't so special.

Randy had been so glad when he first met Grant a few years ago. Randy was a prepper. He could instantly tell that Grant was, too. He thought they'd have a lot in common. As time went on, however, Randy realized they didn't.

When they first met, Grant was always talking to Randy about "just do it." That was how Grant described not reading about prepping on the internet, but rather going outside and doing things. Grant also always talked about testing things. He would get a piece of gear and go test it out. He would get the least expensive gear that still did the job; he wasn't into brand names for the sake of showing his friends that he had a fancy name brand product. In fact, Grant took delight in saving money on prepping gear and putting that money back into more stored food or more ammunition.

Randy, though, liked buying things. He loved it, in fact. He worked hard and liked to go shopping. Prepping supplies were his thing. His wife — well, ex-wife — loved to shop for shoes and clothes.

Randy loved to shop at Cabela's, the giant outdoor store. He got camping gear, guns, hunting accessories, fishing gear, a nice boat, and a big pickup to haul his RV. He even had two ATVs, but he never got a chance to ride them. He later found out they required some special oil, but he never got any. So those shiny ATVs just sat in the garage of his cabin. A lot of Randy's gear stayed in its original packaging in the basement of his cabin.

But Randy had it. He was ready for when the "shit hit the fan." Randy loved to talk to Grant about how awesome it would be when people had to live on only what they had stored. He would be fine, he would tell Grant, because of all the gear he had. Grant would just say, "Uh huh, that's cool," and that was about it.

Grant never told Randy this, but he thought Randy was "living the Cabela's dream" where people bought lots of gear and pretended to live the outdoor life, but they never actually went outdoors. It was like someone who had thousands of dollars of Harleys and all the clothing, but never rode their bike. They were living an image, not a real lifestyle.

It was bad enough that Grant wasn't enthused about all of Randy's gear, but it got worse when Randy finally got out to Pierce Point after the Collapse. Grant and that cop asshole, Rich, were running the show. Everyone loved them. The people out here weren't even prepared, Randy thought. They didn't have camping gear or water purifiers or even radiation detectors. They just had their hillbilly tools and skills. And "each other" which made Randy want to puke. Hillbillies helping hillbillies. That was a survival plan? Please.

What these yokels needed was Randy's advice and guidance. His wisdom and gear. He had read a lot about survival. He knew his stuff, yet, they were ignoring him.

So it was the start of a new month, Randy thought to himself as he poured another shot of vodka. He pondered the fact that he'd have to get through another month out here.

Randy had been through so much. There was the "incident" with his wife. Then getting out to Pierce Point followed by months of being ignored. Dr. Bitchy wouldn't let Randy be out at the clinic. Well, she welcomed him out there, but insisted that she, some big shot ER doctor, would be the lead trauma doctor. She didn't realize how much podiatrists knew about medical things. He should be the lead doctor.

Randy had respect before the Collapse. People called him "Dr. Greene." Now it was just "Randy." Now no one had a use for him. He wished he would have stayed in Seattle. They probably needed podiatrists there.

Randy hadn't eaten all day. It was noon and he was almost done with a fifth of vodka. He was feeling angrier and angrier. Like when his wife … just wouldn't shut up. Now he could hear her yelling at him, which wasn't actually possible.

Randy had an idea. The way he solved the problem with his wife would be the way to solve the problem with Mr. Wonderful and Dr. Bitchy. He had to do something. He couldn't handle just sitting in his cabin all day. Not for another month. It was the first day of a new, shitty month. It was time to try something different.

Randy looked out at the water from the huge windows of his luxury cabin. The rain had stopped. He felt like going outside. He wanted to go talk to Grant. Randy took his brand new Ruger Blackhawk limited edition cowboy action revolver. There were only two thousand of these in production and he had one of them. It had never been fired. Randy laughed at that. He would put its first rounds through it today, though.

Randy took a last gulp of the vodka, which warmed him up. He was starting to feel invincible. It was time to change things up and get some respect.

He knew that John or Mary Anne or someone would probably be the day guard if he walked down Over Road. He had no beef with them. He didn't want to hurt them. They probably hated Judge Dickhead and Dr. Wonder Woman, too. They would realize that he was a hero for doing what he was about to do. Finally, he would get the thanks he deserved. And without Dr. Little Miss Perfect out there, they would beg him to be the doctor. He smiled for the first time in months.

Randy went downstairs and out the back door of his cabin toward the water. He would go down the beach and then come up the Matsons' stairs and go pay Grant a visit. If he was there. Randy didn't know, but he had a plan for that. He would tuck his Blackhawk in his pants, put a coat over it, and ask to see if Grant and Lisa were home. If they weren't, he'd ask when they were expected back. He would be patient. He'd been stewing for months in his cabin about what to do about this. He could wait a few more hours to solve this problem once and for all.

He went down to the beach. No one was around. It was a short walk to the stairs that went up to the Matson house. He crept up the stairs. He felt like he was hunting, like he was in one of the hunting DVDs he'd watched over and over.

As he got up to the deck and the door to the cabin, he paused to listen. He didn't hear anything. He took one step onto the deck. He knew that anyone inside would hear him coming, but they would think it was Grant or that accountant asshole, Drew, or whoever.

Randy decided to act like he was supposed to be there. He just walked up to the front door.

Inside, Manda heard someone coming. That's funny, she thought, she wasn't expecting anyone. She was alone. Cole was over at Missy's house and the grownups were all out doing whatever. Manda had come home to make some lunch and then go back to taking care of the little kids.

Manda heard someone try to open the door. It was locked, of course. That was the rule. The door was always locked. Someone was twisting on the handle hard.

Then came a pounding on the door. A really angry pounding. The kind of pounding no one ever wants to hear.

Chapter 241

The Redheaded Princess

(December 1)

"Who is it?" Manda asked in the toughest voice she could. She was scared. Terrified, actually.

This couldn't really be happening. Someone was probably playing a joke on her. No sane person tried to open a locked door or would pound on a door so hard.

"I need to talk to Grant and Lisa," the male voice said. "Now. Right now."

"They're not here," Manda said. She was officially scared. She could feel her heart pounding. If this was some joke, it wasn't funny. She ran into the kitchen. She wanted to be away from the door and whoever it was out there.

"Let me in!" the man screamed. "I said let me in, you little bitch." Randy could tell from the voice inside that it was the little redheaded Matson princess. He hated her, too. Everyone thought she was so wonderful. Just like her mom and dad.

"Bitch"? Manda thought. That wasn't a word someone who was joking around used Manda did what she and her dad had practiced. Her hands were shaking, but she was ready. She was surprisingly calm after taking a deep breath, just like her dad taught her. She had hoped this would never happen, but it seemed like it was happening now.

On the other side of the door, Randy drew his revolver out of his belt and smiled. He felt so warm and joyous inside. He was going to show everyone who was in charge. He had been waiting months for this.

He would just scare the redheaded princess. She'd run away screaming. That would show everyone that Mr. Invincible wasn't around to help her. He couldn't wait.

He aimed his Blackhawk at the door lock. It was a .45 Colt, so it would do a number on that lock. He cocked the hammer back. The first shot from this gun would be a doozy. He needed to make the bold statement to everyone out at Pierce Point that Dr. Greene would not be humiliated.

He squeezed the trigger.

"Boom!" The lock flew apart.

Manda flinched. It was so loud. And violent; the door just blew up around the handle. She couldn't believe what just happened. She ran to the kitchen entry so she could lean against the wall and still see what was coming through the front door. She was remarkably calm. She knew something was going to come through the front door and she was ready.

Randy used his brand new Blackhawk to ream out the remnants of the lock. It scratched up the barrel, but oh well. He had many more brand new guns. At least this one was getting some use.

In a few seconds, Randy had the door open. Finally. That little bitch had locked it and he had to get the door open. It was her fault that he had to blow the lock off and scratch up his limited edition Blackhawk.

He pushed the door open and looked into the cabin. He found her there cowering up against the wall.

Pointing something toward him.

Manda lined up the sights of her Glock 27. She took a breath and softly pressed the trigger. Again. And again. Until the man in the doorway was on the ground.

She wasn't scared anymore. The threat was down just like she had practiced.

She and her dad had practiced what to do if someone was trying to break into the house. Wait to make sure of your target, if at all possible. She had. There was a man trying to come in. Wait to see if he has a weapon, if at all possible. She had; she heard the shot. If he comes in the house, shoot. "Your Dad will never be mad at you if you do this," she remembered him saying.

She just stood there. Waiting to see if any other men were trying to come in. "Bad guys usually travel in packs," her dad had said. Nope, no more men trying to come in.

Manda stood there for ... who knows how long. Her arms were getting tired of holding the gun up, so it must have been a while.

She heard some people yelling and running toward the cabin. It was John and Mary Anne's voices.

"Oh God! It's Dr. Greene!" John said.

Randy, who was just about to die, heard John call him "Dr. Greene." Randy smiled. That's what he'd been waiting to hear. Everything went black.

Chapter 242

"Two to the chest, one to the head."

(December 1)

Manda was fine. Or so it seemed. She had been threatened and acted completely appropriately. She knew she did the right thing. She was so glad she had that Glock 27 with her all the time. Things seemed fine.

Gideon had woken in the night cabin when he heard the first shot. He called in the shots on the radio and then ran out in their direction. He knew exactly what happened when he saw Greene—who Gideon always thought was a weirdo—crumbled up at the front door. The only question was who shot him.

"Manda? That sweet little redhead?" Gideon asked when John told him who had shot Greene. Gideon shook his head. "What's this world coming to?"

By then, the radios crackled with news of a shooting on Over Road. The Team came screaming over. They fanned out looking for additional shooters, assuming this was a coordinated attack on one of Pierce Point's leaders and his family. They radioed in, and some guards from the Grange set up a roadblock at the intersection of the only road leading from the waterfront cabins. If there were more, they'd catch them, especially if they were stupid enough to try to drive away. The Chief was out on the water actively looking for any retreating boats.

Grant and Rich weren't far behind the Team. Every possible bad thought ran through Grant's mind as he and Rich zoomed to the cabin. Actually, Grant didn't remember too much of the ride there; just that they were in a hurry.

Someone told Lisa what had happened from the radio traffic. She was terrified. She jumped in a truck and raced toward the cabin. Every horrible thought went through her mind. She was sure that Cole or some other kid had found a gun and accidently shot someone. She just knew it. Guns were bad. They only led to accidents and crime. She wished all guns on the planet would go away.

Once the Team verified that Greene had acted alone, they went to his cabin. There they found the empty fifth of vodka. That explained everything: a weird guy snaps after getting extremely drunk. They radioed that in. Grant and Rich heard it on the radio in Rich's truck on their way to the cabin.

"Is that it?" Pow asked Rich. "Just, a guy gets drunk and tries to break into a house with a gun?"

"Yep," Rich said. "Happens all the time. There isn't always a motive for these things. Hey, people are under enormous pressure right now. They react differently. I'm surprised we haven't had even more of this 'going postal' shit." Rich shrugged.

Grant got to the cabin and ran in to comfort Manda. She wasn't crying. She was shaking, but was able to tell him what happened. It was about the fourth time she'd told the same story, but she felt better each time she told it. It made the events feel even more in the past tense each time she told the story.

"Just like you told me, Daddy," Manda said with a tear and a smile. "Two to the chest and one to the head." Manda wasn't really that tough. She was trying to joke her way through the awful ordeal. She wanted her dad to know that she was okay, even if that wasn't entirely accurate.

Lisa came in and hugged Manda. "Are you okay?" she kept asking.

"Yeah, Mom, I'm fine," Manda said. "That crazy man isn't, though." That was yet another attempt by Manda to sound tough so everyone would know that she was okay.

Lisa hugged her daughter so tightly it hurt Manda.

"What happened?" Lisa asked her.

"He shot open the door and I shot him back," Manda said flatly.

"You have a gun?" Lisa asked. Grant cringed. Here it came.

"Yeah, of course," Manda said and pointed to the Glock 27 sitting on the table. "I carry it all the time. Dad gave it to me."

Lisa glared at Grant. He knew she was furious.

Wait. Why the hell is she mad at me? Grant thought. I saved the day, he thought, by giving Manda the gun and training her to use it. Lisa ought to be thanking me!

"Manda did exactly what she was instructed to do and it worked out well," Grant said with some grit in his voice. "She's alive, so everything worked well."

"You let her carry a gun!" Lisa yelled. She'd just sawed a man's leg off and now this. What the hell was wrong with Grant? Did everything have to be a Wild West shootout with him? All these guns. Guns, guns, guns. Everywhere. She'd had enough of guns and killing and maiming and … everything since the Collapse. She'd had enough. She had been okay with all the guns over the past few months, but not anymore. This had to stop. All these guns and killing.

People were starting to stare at Grant and Lisa as they were having a giant fight. Grant tried to calm Lisa down, "We can talk about this later," he said. "Right now, we need to make sure Manda is okay."

"Oh, she's just fine," Lisa yelled. "She just shot someone. That makes her fine and dandy in your book, Grant." Lisa walked toward Grant with her finger pointed at him like she was going to poke him in the chest with it. "Killing people — fine and fucking dandy!" Lisa screamed. It was so rare to hear her swear. She was enraged.

"Yes, Lisa," Grant screamed, "it's fine and fucking dandy because — in case you didn't notice — our daughter is alive."

Silence. People were leaving the cabin. Better to let this fight happen in privacy.

"Manda, go outside, I need to talk to your mother," Grant said.

"No!" Manda screamed. She pointed to the doorway she needed to walk through. There was a blood-spattered body she would need to step over.

Grant motioned and the Team took Greene's body away.

After the body was gone, Manda walked out, trying not to notice the blood stains on the entryway and the deck by the door. The Team took her over to the yellow cabin.

"What the hell are you doing giving Manda a gun?" Lisa screamed when everyone was gone.

"Saving her life, Lisa," Grant said with a sarcastic sting. "What the hell's wrong with you? These are dangerous times. In case you didn't realize, there's no 911 to dial." Grant felt himself slipping into the same old argument they had when he shot the looters and wanted Lisa to leave Olympia with him and come out to the cabin. Right as he went into the old argument, he realized what a bad idea that was. Now Lisa would be arguing why she had been right in the past. The past and the present would become tangled together. They shouldn't be.

"Don't start the 911 shit with me," Lisa yelled. "You made your little point about that a while ago. Don't talk to me that way."

Lisa had a point. Now that she'd disarmed Grant with that, she decided to scream at him for what was *really* making her furious.

"*Lieutenant* Matson," Lisa screamed. "Lt. Matson, huh?"

Grant froze. Oh crap. He was done for.

"Who's that?" Grant asked. Might as well lie some more, he thought. It'd been working so far. Besides, he could literally be killed for revealing the unit to her. He could be hanged by a Patriot court martial.

Grant couldn't tell her the truth, as much as he wanted to. And he really, really wanted to. He wanted this lying to be over. He had thought things were going OK and she'd never know. But now reality hit him hard.

"Don't lie to me, you bastard!" Lisa screamed. She'd never talked to him that way before. Never. What had gotten into her?

Lisa was so furious because she realized she had been kidding herself the whole time. She had wanted to believe Grant wasn't doing some stupid Patriot shit. She wanted to believe that he was just being a judge out there. She knew better. But she just wanted a normal life — well, what passed for a "normal" life out there. She was so smart, but had fallen for this. All because she wanted a normal life.

Normal life? There would never be a normal life.

Then she started to cry. It quickly turned into the wailing — the kind of wailing Grant had seen when he left her in Olympia. Grant thought that had been the worst he'd ever see her. It now looked like there was a round two.

"Tell me! Tell me!" She yelled in between sobs. "A lieutenant in what?"

Grant just stared at her. It had been one thing to indirectly lie by saying there was a "rental team," but to lie to her when she asked a direct question. That was something different and way worse.

He looked her in the eyes. If he lied to her now, his marriage was over. She'd never forgive him. She could never trust him.

"What are you talking about?" Grant asked. "I'm a judge, not a lieutenant." He said it so convincingly that he scared himself.

Lisa instantly perked up. Maybe there had been a misunderstanding. Maybe she had just had such a horrible day that she was taking it out on Grant. Maybe he wasn't in some rebel army or whatever else it could possibly be.

"You're not?" Lisa asked. She paused and then said, "In the Army or something?" It sounded so absurd when she said it. Grant? In the Army?

"No," Grant said with a scoff. "I'm too old to join the Army and, besides, I have my hands full being the judge here. Why do you think I joined the Army?"

Lisa told Grant about Tony Atkins and the rumors she'd heard about some Green Berets living somewhere in Pierce Point.

Grant laughed. He was lying extremely well now and she was

believing him.

Grant knew with absolute certainty that his marriage was now over. She would find out when he left for combat and she'd remember how he had lied to her face. He couldn't blame her for dumping him. His lying was unforgiveable.

In an instant, Grant saw the highlights of their marriage flash before his eyes. He saw them on their first date, at their wedding, their first apartment, Manda's birth, Cole's birth, a school play Manda was in, hearing Cole's first sentence when he was in elementary school, their vacation to Hawaii, him leaving Olympia, and then her coming to the cabin. Grant's marriage had just died and he was seeing it flash before his eyes. He realized what a great life they'd had together. And it was gone.

"Listen, dear, you've had a terrible day," Grant said. He got the call on the radio about Tony Atkins and had gone to see him after the amputation. Tony was still unconscious. It looked like he'd make it through.

"Then this happened to Manda and you thought I joined the Army," Grant said in a calming voice. He continued to scare himself with how good he could lie.

Lisa was coming down from the rage she had felt. Now she was realizing that things were OK. Her daughter was safe and – she hated to admit it – Grant had been right about the gun. Her husband wasn't in the Army. She was having a very stressful day and snapped a little.

"I can't go back to the clinic for a while," she said finally. "I need a couple days here to de-stress. And Manda will need us around. There is no way this won't have an effect on her."

"Sure," Grant said. "I'll try to be around more the next few days. I'll try to take some time off."

They hugged. This time, though, Grant was holding back. He couldn't fully hug her. He was deceiving her. It didn't feel like all the other hugs after a fight. He felt like they weren't married. Like she was someone he lived with, but not his wife.

"So tell me about this Green Beret rumor," Grant said. "I need to know what people are saying about the rental team." Grant was in ultra-deception mode. He wasn't proud of it, but he had a job to do.

Lisa told him what the rumor was and who was spreading it. "I heard a man who's been at a few Grange meetings – Johansen or Johnson or something is his last name – talking to Kathy in the kitchen. He said he heard that some Green Berets were camping out near here and were training some rebel group. He said they were at a farm or something in Pierce Point. He'd snuck in and saw some guards at a farm."

Grant would need to deal with that. Not kill anyone, but do whatever could be done to stop the rumor. His immediate plan was to feed some outlandish rumors to this Johansen or Johnson person. That guy would spread the crazy rumors and that would wreck his credibility.

Grant's mind went from squelching the rumor to thinking about his now-destroyed marriage.

"Lives, fortunes, and sacred honor," Grant thought to himself. Sacrifice. This was his sacrifice, though realizing that didn't make this any easier.

Grant wasn't the only one making a sacrifice. Manda did, too. The first few hours after the shooting she was fine. That night, though, she started to come apart. She was terrified of every little noise in the cabin. She sat up all night. Grant had taken her gun away from her because she was so distraught. He didn't want Manda to think she heard a noise and start shooting. Lisa wholeheartedly agreed.

When Manda finally fell asleep, she had horrible nightmares. Greene was trying to break in the door in her dreams and when she fired her gun it wouldn't go off. Greene would laugh at her. His eyes were green lights in her dream. She was having it over and over again. Grant and Lisa were comforting her as much as possible.

The next morning, Manda couldn't eat. She just wanted to sleep, but was afraid of the nightmare. Finally, she passed out from exhaustion. Grant and Lisa stayed home from work and took care of her. Grant arranged for Jordan to get off from guard duty and to stay with them. That seemed to comfort her. Grant made sure that Jordan wore a pistol in the house. Grant did too, of course. Seeing two men with pistols made her feel safer.

"Jordan, you want to spend the night here? On the couch," Grant said. "That will make Manda feel better."

"Yes, sir," Jordan said. This wasn't exactly what he thought of when "spend the night with Manda" came to mind, but he was happy to help. He wanted Manda to feel better. He loved her.

Grant handed Jordan his tactical shotgun, a Remington 870. It was better for indoor use than Jordan's rifle. "You can lean my 870 up against the wall near the couch," Grant told Jordan. "That will be reassuring to her."

The couch was between the front door and where Manda shot Greene. There was no way to get into the house without coming through someone on the couch. Grant showed Manda this and that Jordan would have the shotgun. Grant and Jordan knew that no one would be coming through that door, which was all blown up but still on the hinges. People coming to the door of the Matson cabin were loudly saying, "Hello" as they approached. They didn't want anyone to think they were an uninvited guest.

After a week, Manda still wasn't getting any better. The nightmare was still there. She wasn't sleeping or eating. She was looking terrible. Grant and Lisa were very concerned. Their perky redhead was now depressed and scared.

"These things affect different people in different ways," Ted said when Grant finally got a chance to sneak over to the 17th for some training exercises. "Sometimes people get over it. Sometimes they don't." That's what scared Grant. What if Manda never snapped out of this?

Yet another casualty of the Collapse.

Chapter 243

Saving Lucia

(December 5)

Ten year-old Lucia Mirandez was crying at the courthouse. A man had just done something horrible to her. She didn't understand why he did it. It hurt and he was mean. She knew it was a naughty thing that he did.

She thought that maybe she did something wrong and that was her punishment. But she couldn't understand what she did wrong. She just knew that she was bad and was being punished.

Bennington was coming up to Commissioner Winters' office. He saw an adorable little Mexican girl crying. He asked her in Spanish what had happened. She just cried more and ran down the hall.

Just then, Commissioner Winters came out of his office. Julie Mathers, his receptionist, was at her desk and quietly crying, too.

Winters was angry. He yelled at Bennington, "Go get her! Now! Bring her back here!"

Bennington did as he was told. He chased after the girl down the hall. He caught her in the stairwell.

Lucia was kicking and screaming. Bennington couldn't understand why. "He hurt me," she screamed in Spanish. She had been told by her parents not to trust police officers, but she was so scared she just blurted it out.

"Who?" Bennington asked in his limited Spanish. Lucia relaxed a little, upon hearing him speak her language. He seemed like he was trying to help her.

"The old man," Lucia said. "The one with white hair."

"Where did he hurt you?" Bennington asked, fearing the answer.

Lucia pointed at her private parts.

Bennington got a sick feeling. He momentarily felt lightheaded and thought he might fall over.

"Get her!" He heard Winters yelling down the hall and coming up on them quickly.

"Come with me!" Bennington told the girl. He grabbed her by the hand and they ran out of the courthouse.

Bennington knew he was dead if he got caught disobeying Winters. He also knew there was no way he was turning this sweet little girl back over to that monster. This was too much. Bennington had watched as Winters humiliated Julie Mathers. That was bad enough, but Bennington had felt powerless to help Julie. This was different. This was a little girl and he had the power to help her. He had to try at the very least.

So far, no one had seen him running out the door with Lucia. Bennington needed a plan.

As he ran down one hall, there was a pile of blankets on the floor. There were always "supplies" in that hallway. The "supplies" were stolen booty from various raids.

Bennington looked around. Still no witnesses. The security cameras weren't recording anymore. They needed a part that hadn't come yet. The only thing rolling down the highways were food, gas, and troops. Video recorder parts for a hick county's security system were not a priority, but the video monitors were watched in live time; they just couldn't record. Bennington knew that the person watching the monitors was a doofus. He probably wouldn't see them, if he were even paying attention. Bennington took a risk. Hell, he had already risked his life by running away with the girl.

Utilizing more of his Spanish skills, he told the girl to hide in the blankets that were piled in a supply pile in the hallway and to be still. Lucia did what she was told. She had trusted this police officer and, besides, she knew she couldn't get away from the courthouse on her own. If this police officer was going to take her away and hurt her himself, she was no worse off than if the white haired man did it. But this police officer seemed to be helping her. She didn't have a choice. Bennington wrapped a blanket around the girl and picked her up in his arms.

Lucia couldn't see what was going on, but she felt the police officer lift her up and throw her over his shoulder. She felt him walking. She lay still. This must be how he was going to get her out of the courthouse. He must be trying to help her get away.

Lucia felt him stop and push on something. She assumed it was a door. The sound changed so he must have walked outside. She heard some rain. He walked a little further and she heard the little electronic sound of a car door unlocking.

She felt him shift her to another shoulder and heard a car door open. Bennington gently put her in the back seat. He was trying to say something in Spanish. She knew that she needed to stay hidden in the blankets, so she covered herself up and didn't move. He got in the car and started it up.

Lucia wondered where he was going to take her. Hopefully not back to her house. It was in the Mexican part of town and the gangs ran everything. Her mom and dad and her oldest brother had left town to go work on the big farms in Eastern Washington. She and all her brothers and sisters were staying behind with their aunt, but her aunt couldn't keep the gangs away. Yesterday, some young men from the gangs came to her house. Her aunt cried. The men took Lucia and her 12 year-old sister, Carmella. One of her brothers tried to fight the men. They just laughed and beat him until he stopped moving.

Lucia and Carmella were scared and worried about their brother. The men took them in a van to a nice house, the nicest one in the neighborhood. They didn't know exactly what the men would do to them, but they had an idea it would be bad.

But the men were nice to the girls. They gave them candy. The girls hadn't had candy in so long. They ate so much of it they got a little sick.

Then one of the older ladies in the house, who looked a lot like their aunt, gave them new dresses. Pretty dresses. They were a little big for them, but it was fine. Pretty dresses and candy. Maybe this wouldn't be so bad. But why did their brother try to fight the men and why did the men hurt him?

The older lady let them put on makeup. It was so much fun. They never had makeup at their house. The lady was so nice. Pretty soon, the girls looked so beautiful in their dresses and makeup. They felt like teenage girls.

Then Carmella went with some men in the van somewhere. That was two days ago. Lucia hadn't seen her since.

Lucia got in a car with another man and went to the courthouse. Then she met the white haired man. He was nice at first, but then he got angry. Then he hurt her. And did the naughty thing. She didn't want to think about it. She had been pretending in her mind that it hadn't happened.

The police officer's car was slowing down. He was saying something in English to some men. After a few seconds, the car was moving again. It must be one of those checkpoints that were in town.

"I'm taking you somewhere safe," Bennington said in Spanish. Then he said something in English into a radio. They drove for about ten minutes.

During the drive, Bennington was finally fully thinking about what he'd done. He had realized from the moment he grabbed the little girl and started to run that he was dead if he got caught. That part didn't bother him. He was ready to be done with this life. All he did every day was help corrupt people do terrible things. He was ready for all of this to be over.

But why sign his own death warrant over this? Over this little girl? Abby, that's why. Bennington thought about his own daughter, Abby. She was about the same age as the little Mexican girl. Abby was living with Bennington's ex-wife in Mill Creek, a suburb of Seattle. His ex-wife had remarried some EPA guy, so they were probably doing fine. They lived in the Seattle area and, given the EPA guy's position, probably had plenty of FCard credits. He was glad for them, especially for Abby.

Bennington missed Abby so much, but most cops he knew were divorced. It was a hard job. And in these times, fights over money made everything even worse.

Little Abby. Bennington kept thinking about her. He would do anything to prevent what happened to the Mexican girl from happening to his Abby. He would want someone — anyone — who could help save a girl to risk his or her life and do it. He would want someone to do for Abby what he was doing for this innocent little girl.

Bennington looked in the car mirror toward the back seat. There was that blanket not moving an inch. A girl who was being saved.

Bennington slowed down. He was at his destination.

"I called ahead for Dan," Bennington told the Pierce Point gate guard.

"He'll be right here," the guard said. Dan came running up when he saw the police car at the gate.

"What's going on?" He asked Bennington.

"I need you guys to take care of a little Mexican girl who was being raped," Bennington said. "By people in positions of authority. People who will kill me if they catch me getting her out of there." Bennington pointed to the blanket in the back seat. Dan looked at the blanket and nodded at Bennington.

"You can get up now," Bennington said in Spanish. "It's safe."

Lucia got up and saw men with guns all around her outside the car. She was scared, but the men were different than the men who had taken her. They looked like Army men or hunters.

"Ramirez!" Dan yelled. "Need you here."

Manny Ramirez, one of the guards, came running over to the

car.

Dan said, "I need a translator." Manny nodded.

"Tell this little girl that she's safe here," Dan said, "we will take care of her, that we will protect her, and that the bad men can't get her because we're good police, not the bad ones."

Manny went to the back seat and told Lucia this. She nodded. She wasn't sure she believed them, but she had no choice. So far, they had not hurt her and they were getting her away from the courthouse where the white haired man was.

"Get some females over here to help the girl," Dan yelled. "She needs them around. She's had enough men around her for a while."

Dan went to the front seat to talk to Bennington. "Thanks, man. Seriously. Thanks. We'll take good care of her. We have plenty of Mexican families here who speak her language and would love to take in a wonderful little girl like this."

Bennington was silent. Hearing "wonderful little girl" just made him feel worse about what had happened. The Mexican girl was so innocent and Winters — and who knows who else — had done such horrible things to her. Bennington started to cry.

Dan let him cry. Bennington needed to get it out. Finally, Bennington got a hold of himself.

"This didn't happen," Bennington said. "I did not come here — understand?"

"Clearly," Dan said. "You did not come here. The girl washed up on the beach and was lucky to be alive."

Bennington pointed to all the guards who saw his patrol car there. "None of these people saw a thing!" He screamed. He was in a rage against Winters and afraid for his own life at the same time.

"Yep," Dan said, realizing that Bennington needed to scream. "These people don't leave Pierce Point and we don't let them use phones or text. We have several..." Dan almost said "sensitive sightings that they can't be talking about." But he didn't. "We have several security measures in place," Dan said instead.

Bennington was getting freaked out that there were so many witnesses at Pierce Point. He had just reacted and grabbed the little girl and driven out there. He hadn't thought everything through. Now he was.

Dan could tell that Bennington was worried about the witnesses.

"Hey!" Dan yelled to the guards. "All hands, come here."

All the guards came running over to Dan at the gate.

"You didn't see this," Dan said. "Understand?"

"Yes, Sergeant!" they all yelled back.

"Who saw this?" Dan asked.

No one said a word.

"You guys keep a lot of secrets out here," Dan said. "Any one of you talks about this and the girl and the brave man in this car will die. Who wants that to happen?"

Not a word.

"The girl washed up on the beach," Dan said. "How'd the girl get here?" He yelled.

"Washed up on the beach," the guards yelled back.

Dan looked at Bennington and smiled.

Bennington was reassured. Not totally worry-free, but reassured. He knew he had taken this Winters thing to the next level. Stealing Winters' little girl meant Winters would come after him for sure. If Winters found out. And he probably would over time.

Bennington decided to go ahead with what he'd been thinking about for a long time.

Chapter 244

Better Late Than Never

(December 5)

"I need to talk to Rich," Bennington said to Dan. "Privately."

Dan nodded. "Rich is on his way."

"I need to talk to Rich out of the sight of people," Bennington said. "I'll back up and go park out on the road over there."

"Sure," Dan said and motioned for Bennington to back up from the gate.

"It's cool," Dan said, using the frequency Sniper Mike monitored. "No shoot. Repeat: No shoot."

Three clicks of the microphone came back which meant Mike heard and understood. Dan switched his radio back to the normal frequency.

By this time, Rich had come. Dan filled him in and told him Bennington wanted a private meeting away from the eyes of the gate guards.

Rich walked over to Bennington's car, which was parked on the side of the road headed toward Frederickson. Bennington was in his car. Rich walked up behind the car with his hands out to his side so that Bennington knew he was not a threat. Rich opened the passenger door and got in.

"Thanks, man," Rich said and pointed back to the gate and the girl. "That was awesome."

Bennington just nodded. He had something important to say to Rich, something that had been building for months, something that could easily get Bennington killed.

"Winters is a monster," Bennington said. "You don't know all the things he's doing. To innocent people. Like that little girl." Bennington's eyes filled with tears again. "You don't know, man."

Rich just let Bennington take his time. Whatever it was he was going to say couldn't be rushed.

"I'm going to kill him," Bennington blurted out. He looked Rich right in the eye and said, "I need your help."

Rich just nodded; he'd almost expected this conversation. He knew Bennington from before the Collapse when both of them were

Sheriff's deputies. He had spent a lot of time with him getting the medical supplies and turkey. He had a "cop's intuition" that Bennington was a good man and therefore couldn't remain loyal to Winters. Rich couldn't blame him for taking several months to come to this conclusion. Bennington had to live under Winters' thumb; he didn't have the luxury of living in Pierce Point with a gate, guards, the Team, and ultimately the 17th Irregulars to protect him.

"I should have left the force like you did," Bennington said and started to cry. He pounded his fists on the steering wheel, getting some demons out of him. Then he regained his composure.

"I should have never been a part of any of this," he continued. "Never. But it didn't seem that bad at first. I thought I was protecting people by stayin' on the force."

"You did what you could," Rich said sincerely. "That's the past. Now is the present. You're going to do something about it now. That's what counts. Welcome to the Patriots." Rich extended his hand and shook Bennington's.

Bennington smiled. That was exactly what he needed: to be welcomed to the good guys' side for a change, not lectured for doing bad things in the past.

"Better late than never," Bennington said, trying to rationalize why he'd been working for the bad guys for so long. He took a deep breath.

"So, how do we do it?" Bennington asked. Rich knew that he meant killing Winters.

At first, Rich worried that Bennington was recording the conversation in some kind of sting operation. He then quickly thought that would be pretty unlikely, although he couldn't fault himself for having that reaction.

Regardless, if this were a setup, Rich was done for, anyway, so he might as well roll with it. Rich didn't want to waste this prime opportunity to turn a police officer close to Winters into a Patriot spy... and assassin.

In the past, Rich had sensed that Grant and the Team thought perhaps he wasn't one hundred percent down with the Patriots. This came from his hesitancy to throw every Pierce Point guard and asset into the 17th Irregulars.

If they had thought this, they were dead wrong. Rich was an Oath Keeper before it was cool. He quit the Sheriff's Department in disgust over the corruption before the budget cuts had eliminated his job. Rich wanted nothing more than to end Winters' reign of corruption, but he wanted to do it in a way that created as little risk as possible for the civilians at Pierce Point. An inside job by Bennington was the way to do that.

Speaking freely, abandoning any fears about a running tape recorder, Rich and Bennington talked about how to kill Winters. It would be tricky, with all that security around him. A frontal assault was out of the question. Rich never let on about the 17th Irregulars at Marion Farm, naturally.

"An inside job," Bennington said. "As in: me."

Rich paused, acting like this was the first time he had thought about this. "How?"

"I have total access to the place," Bennington said. "I'm armed. Do the math."

"How would you get out?" Rich asked.

Bennington shrugged. He was just fine with dying. "Just walk out of there in all the confusion?"

"What about all the others in the courthouse who need to go?" Rich asked. Bennington paused for a moment and said, "Good point. We shouldn't waste this opportunity on just Winters. There are at least a dozen of his little bastards who need to be offed, too." Bennington started naming names and counting them off on his fingers. He got to fifteen.

"I've got an idea," Bennington said and immediately shared it with Rich who then smiled. It was brilliant; violent, but brilliant.

"Do you need anything from me?" Rich asked.

"Nope," Bennington said. "Just when the best time to do it would   be."

"What do you mean?" Rich asked, playing dumb.

"You know," Bennington said, "like when there's a Patriot offensive or something. You need to take out the cops and gangs in the town ahead of the march."

Maybe Bennington was setting him up, Rich thought. "What Patriot offensive?" He asked.

"Oh, I don't know of one," Bennington said. "Just if there was one, you know?"

"No, I don't know," Rich said. "How would I know?"

Bennington could tell that Rich was getting defensive.

"No big deal, man," Bennington said, putting his hands up. "I'm just saying that if you found out that there was a particularly good time for Winters and his pals to be eliminated, you should let me know. That's all."

Bennington seemed sincere to Rich, but still, Rich wasn't about to let him know that he could easily find out about any coming Patriot offensive.

"Okay," Rich said. "If I find out that there's a particularly good time, I'll let you know. I'll try to come into town and tell you personally." He was lying. On the off chance this was a set-up, the last thing Rich was going to do was go to town where it would be easy to arrest him.

"But if I can't tell you personally," Rich continued, "I'll call it in on the CB—using a code, of course."

Bennington nodded. Rich and everyone else used CB channel 9 for emergencies. Rich and Bennington developed a code. Rich would call in on 9 to get Bennington and then they would both switch to channel 11 to really talk. The CBs were easily monitored by everyone, so even talking on Channel 11 meant using a code.

"Code phrase will be," Rich said, "that I have a ruptured gall bladder."

"And when you tell me you have a ruptured gall bladder," Bennington said, "You'll then tell me when you're coming into the hospital. The date and time, right?"

Rich nodded. "The date and time I give you," Rich said to Bennington, "will be the date and time of when a hit would be optimal."

Bennington nodded. The simplest plans were the best, and this was pretty simple.

Rich could tell Bennington was drained. He had been conspiring to commit murder and had rescued a little girl from a rapist, who happened to be his boss who could kill him at the snap of a finger.

"Hey, man," Rich said, "you did two good deeds today: the girl and the gall bladder plan. Thanks."

Bennington needed that. His heart was in the right place—he had just compromised his morals for so long that it had led him to the situation he was now in. It was time for him to make amends. He was in a position to do a tremendous amount of good. To make up for all the bad things he'd gradually become involved with.

"Something big is comin'," Rich said, letting his guard down for a moment. "You're going to be part of it."

Bennington smiled.

Chapter 245

Faint Whiff of Smoke

(December 8)

Joyous. Excited. Brimming with life and energy. That's how Grant Matson felt that Sunday afternoon. He had totally put the Lisa stuff out of his mind. He was getting even better at that, which kind of scared him.

It was a cold and rainy December day in Western Washington State. However, inside the equipment shed of Marion Farm, it was warm, bright, and happy. The room buzzed with the vibe that everyone in there would soon be doing the most important things in their lives; glorious, fabulous, historic things, together.

Grant finished up his Sunday dinner. Deer steaks, mashed potatoes, and all the brownies he could eat. Anything with sugar in it had become quite rare, especially all-you-can eat sugary treats. Being full and warm and surrounded by these guys made Grant feel like a million bucks.

Ted stood up and got the room's attention. "We have some great news, ladies and gentlemen," he said and motioned for Grant to stand up. "Lt. Matson will let everyone know what it is."

Grant smiled and announced to the unit, "The 17th Irregulars are now fully formed. HQ told us today that we are officially a combat-ready unit." Everyone applauded. They had been working up to this goal. And, by headquarters continuing to send them troops and supplies to get up to full strength, they had the seal of approval from the brass. HQ wouldn't waste resources on a bunch of clowns out in the woods playing Army.

Grant was brimming with pride as he told the unit that the 17th was at full strength: 104 soldiers. They had lost two, Paul and Tony Atkins. Tony was still recovering from his amputation in the Pierce Point medical clinic. It was hard on Ted and the others in the unit to not be able to visit Tony, but they knew they couldn't because that would blow their cover. Tony understood, too. He was doing alright, given the circumstances. Grant visited him regularly and passed messages back and forth between him and the 17th.

To Grant's pleasant surprise, plenty of supplies were coming in from Boston Harbor. When Ted asked the Pierce Point leaders to host a guerilla unit, he had assured Grant that the unit would be supplied by the Patriots and would not draw on Pierce Point's resources. Grant had assumed this was half true and half a sales pitch. But HQ was keeping its part of the bargain. Plenty of food, though much of it was bland, like corn bread, pancakes, biscuits, beans, and rice, was coming in to feed the 17th.

A decent amount of ammo was also coming in. It wasn't as much as anyone would like, but ammo was an extremely valuable commodity. By early December, they were at the five hundred rounds per soldier level they needed, but they didn't have much more than that. Each soldier had a rifle and at least four magazines. The frontline troops, like the Team and the infantrymen, had more magazines. They also had pouches or tactical vests to carry them.

The 17th didn't have many grenades or other explosives. These were in extremely short supply. Besides, the 17th weren't assault troops who needed to blast their way in. Other units — regular units and special operations — would do that. The 17th were irregulars who would occupy and pacify an enemy city and get it up and running as soon as possible. Also, even if the 17th had plenty of explosives, they had no training facility to teach people how to use them. They were in a secret location; loud explosions would draw attention in Pierce Point.

Communications were going smoothly and Jim Q. was working out marvelously. There were enough handheld radios and batteries for the guard stations, most of the squad leaders, and Ted, Sap, and Grant. They had just enough.

Medical supplies were a little thin, mainly because HQ diverted the usual supplies from the 17th to units that didn't have a clinic a few miles away. Luckily, the 17th Irregulars had the unique luxury of being able to use Pierce Point's medical clinic for emergencies.

Morale was high. The men and women of the unit knew they were doing something important. They knew they were better off than almost everyone in the surrounding areas. In fact, most of them realized they were far better off, especially compared to those in Olympia and Seattle. There were many firsthand stories about the gangs and the government doing whatever they wanted in the cities. The national news was even bleaker. Chicago was basically a giant prison. New York was largely depopulated, mostly from people leaving in droves, but also from people dying. Los Angeles was pretty much burned to the ground. The rioting and looting that started at the beginning of the Collapse never relented there. Many people fled, but some stayed behind because they believed that the government would make things better "soon."

While the major cities were absolutely terrible, the rest of the country was doing relatively okay for the most part, though it varied greatly depending on region.

The Northeast was almost entirely comprised of major cities and was the Loyalists' center of power. It was in awful shape. The Northeast's rural areas were overrun with people fleeing the cities. It was ugly.

The South was doing quite well. Some of the rural areas of the South were actually prospering. There was no real threat of the FUSA troops or police bothering them. Free enterprise sprang up and took off—as it always does when it's allowed to.

Race relations were good in the South. In isolated rural areas with almost no blacks, there were still problems, but this was a definite exception to the rule. And in some areas that were majority black, there was some anti-white violence. But overall, things were much better than the most would have expected.

There was one exception to the relatively good shape the South was in: the large cities down there. They were in horrible shape. Loyalists from throughout the South flocked to the large cities where their people were in charge, like Houston.

In the cities teeming with the Loyalists, gangs ran everything. These cities had populations—of all races—who were used to things being handed to them. They still were: a little cornbread mix was handed out by a corrupt and oppressive government, and the people in the big cities were grateful for the handout.

The Mountain West was doing very well. Denver and Phoenix were Loyalist strongholds, but other than that, the West was prospering. The federal government was no longer holding them back. They started refining their own oil. In short order, the West was selling gasoline at enormous profits. The feds tried to prevent these shipments because it interfered with their control of vital commodities, like gas. But there was no holding back the free market. Corrupt Limas would let the gas get through—for a cut. That cut wasn't so small, but the gas was getting through.

The Midwest was a mixed bag. The cities were a mess with dependent populations and Loyalists flocking in. The government concentrated its resources on the cities, of course. Some cities were doing okay because they had the first pick of government food and gas. Crime was out of control everywhere, but some of the cities had a decent handle on the gangs. This was because, for whatever reason, some of the local governments in the Midwest did not go into business with the gangs. Some government officials were more honest than others, and there were still decent government officials out there, it was just rare.

Rural areas in the Midwest were doing pretty well. They grew most of the food, which gave them a lot of leverage. The government treated them well. There was no need to kill the goose laying the golden eggs. Large organized gangs were essentially unheard of in the rural Midwest, although there were also isolated small gangs and corrupt police forces, but the gangs in the rural areas were nothing at all like the ones in the major cities.

The thing that continually amazed everyone was that the electricity and water stayed on, for the most part. The United States was not experiencing the full-on breakdown that most survivalists expected. They expected TEOTWAWKI (the end of the world as we know it) with no electricity or water and a total breakdown of society complete with cannibalism and anarchy. Survivalist books and movies reinforced this view of a total breakdown. It made sense: expect things to be the absolute worst they could be. That was a reasonable prediction.

But the United States experienced only a partial collapse. Places like Los Angeles were totally broken down, but places like Pierce Point were only partially broken down and, on balance, doing pretty well. Nowhere in the United States was life "normal" like it had been. In some places, a "new normal" took over. It was worse than the ways things had been, but tolerable, like in Pierce Point.

Grant could identify three reasons why a total breakdown was avoided.

First, the electricity and water stayed on. It wasn't because the government was compassionate or competent. Rather, the government kept the utilities running only because they knew that if they didn't, people would rise up and throw them out of power. Keeping the utilities running was a matter of survival — survival for the government keeping their power.

The second reason was that many military officers refused to carry out unconstitutional orders. The Utility Treaty was the federal government's promise to leave the utilities on. This treaty was possible because most of the military would not follow unconstitutional orders to turn them off. Some military personnel and some police did follow unconstitutional orders, but the majority didn't. Many would simply go AWOL, but an absent soldier or cop is not a threat. A decent chunk of the military, and some cops, joined the Patriots and actively fought. It didn't take too many of them to outnumber the small number of Lima military and cops.

Why did the military largely refuse to follow unconstitutional orders? It was the culture of the military, which insisted on an oath to the Constitution, not to the commander in chief. This was drilled into the military for over two hundred years and it paid off. While many of the younger recruits had no concept of the Constitution, their NCOs and officers did. They led. At the most critical time in the country's history.

A third reason a total breakdown was averted was the vast number of guns and trained shooters in the United States. The Second Amendment functioned perfectly as intended: making a dictatorship impossible as a practical matter. Americans, seeing what was coming as the Collapse approached, bought guns and ammunition like crazy. There were tens of millions of guns out there.

Having lots of guns when the Collapse started was great, but having a long history of owning and using guns was critical, too. The fact that the Second Amendment gave America over two hundred years of active gun ownership meant that people knew how to use guns. Millions of guns, but only a handful of people who knew how to use them, would be useless. The Second Amendment allowed an armed culture in the United States. It meant that people could own guns for generations and teach their children and grandchildren how to use them. The guards at Pierce Point were a perfect example. In an instant, dozens of well-armed and fairly well-trained civilians were available for duty. Some were even extremely good snipers hiding in the woods two hundred yards from the gate. Those skills came from years of hunting and shooting, which would have been impossible if there hadn't been generations of shooting in America. And these generations of shooters would have been impossible without the Second Amendment.

If any one of these three things—utilities staying on, most military not following unconstitutional orders, and the Second Amendment—had not happened, America would have suffered a total breakdown instead of just the partial one. All three were critical.

Of these three things, the Second Amendment was slightly more important. This was because common ownership of guns and the knowledge of how to use them bolstered each of the other two factors. The utilities stayed on because the government feared what would happen if they turned them off—they feared an armed population rising up. They weren't afraid of people with golf clubs.

Similarly, the military and law enforcement knew that they couldn't take over an armed population. The proof of this was the Northeast where civilians were almost totally unarmed; the military and police had no trouble whatsoever taking over in that part of the country.

It was now winter. With the change of seasons, people focused on different things. During the spring and summer, people had reacted to the new conditions they were suddenly facing; they were focused on surviving. Their time and energy was devoted to getting food, arranging for medical care, and defending their communities. They were dealing with the immediate situation at hand and getting through that day or that week. Most people thought it was just temporary, like a big Hurricane that managed to affect the whole nation. It was something America would bounce back from. This is America: nothing really bad ever happens here. Not for long, at least. Most people didn't expect the Collapse to last very long, so they didn't bothering focusing on the long term.

But, by fall and now the winter, it was obvious that the situation wasn't a temporary thing. The country had broken down and wasn't getting fixed anytime soon. People were thinking more about a longer-term solution.

The mood in America had changed to that of a more military one. Food, medical care, and local defenses were in decent shape, at least out in the rural areas, but even this was only a temporary solution; maybe it would just get them through the winter. What about next year? The current conditions could not be sustained and everyone knew it, especially the Limas.

They knew that the Patriots would rally in the spring – insurgencies always did – and maybe as early as the winter. The Limas needed to crush the Patriots now, before they gained more strength—and before conditions got so much worse that average people would side with the Patriots because they had nothing left to lose.

Sensing something big was coming, people were increasingly taking sides. It was easy to be an Undecided throughout the summer when there was food. Not so in the fall and winter. Many were finally forced to take sides: the Patriots for a long-term solution, or the Loyalists, to keep getting food in the short term.

Many gravitated toward the Patriots, but some in the North rallied around the government. Each side gathered more followers and became more strident.

It was obvious to most that the two sides could not co-exist; one had to defeat the other. It wasn't like the old days when there was a hard-fought election and then the next day everyone shook hands and went about their lives. The current problems in America could not be fixed by elections. Everyone knew it. They'd seen it with their own eyes.

A civil war seemed inevitable, though most citizens couldn't wrap their heads around that concept. A "civil war"? No way. A civil war had seemed preposterous in the spring and summer at the beginning of the Collapse. Those don't happen anymore in America. Other countries might, but ... certainly not America. However, as summer changed to fall, everyday survival activities evolved into something that felt more military. People were joining together for mutual aid. It was a practical measure for survival. Joining together was like growing your own food. It was just a way to avoid dying, not a political or military statement.

Surviving at the beginning of the Collapse meant defending your local area against criminals. The Pierce Point gate guards were a perfect example. As time went on, the gate guards got more sophisticated. They had observation points, Sniper Mike, and radio communications. The local defenses started to expand outward. It was now necessary to secure the area around your community to create a buffer from threats. In many communities, this meant joining with neighboring areas to have a strong, joint, integrated, numerically superior common defense force. It started looking and feeling a lot like a military force.

This was happening in most communities in the free areas. Almost all of them were little Patriot communities, which resembled Pierce Point to varying degrees. The Patriots planned for this and took maximum advantage of these homegrown, spontaneous little defense forces springing up. The Patriots were prepared to take in these defense forces and turn them into small military units. They had a command structure for them and offered training and some supplies. Pretty soon, the community guards were part of a State Guard. The community guards elected their own officers and sergeants and joined the State Guard, but they could leave whenever they wanted. While they still didn't wear military uniforms and didn't have standardized weapons, they were a military force, right there in people's communities. Gradually, the neighborhood guards had turned into military units. They were irregular units, but they were military units nonetheless.

People could see what was happening. They could feel that a war was coming. A civil war, as crazy as that had sounded just a few months ago. People could feel it.

They were right.

After Grant spoke at the Sunday dinner, Ted pulled him aside. "You smell that?" Ted asked.

"Smell what?" Grant asked, sniffing to see what Ted was talking about.

"I always smell it a few days before I deploy," Ted said. "It's when the fires are burning and shit's about to break look loose."

"Smell what?" Grant asked again.

"A faint whiff of smoke," Ted said.

Chapter 246

Mementos

(December 10)

Morale in the 17th Irregulars was sky high and it wasn't just because the troops were glad to be better off than most of the country and that they were on the side that was growing in strength. It was personal. They had become a family.

Grant, while no battlefield commander, was a great motivator and leader. He knew the power of traditions, mementos, and camaraderie. The Thanksgiving dinner was proof of that. He knew how to create a family out of 104 former strangers.

He turned Sundays into something special at Marion Farm. They took the day off and rested. Grant, who was no longer a young guy, understood that people needed a day to rest physically, mentally, and emotionally. Sunday was that day. Guard and KP duty still needed to be done, but people took turns. Everyone else kicked back.

The troops could sleep in on Sundays. Initially, this was hard for most to do in a barn with ninety people, some of whom snored. But after a few weeks of sixteen-hour days of hard physical work, people could sleep through almost anything.

Those few extra hours of sleep on Sunday morning were golden. Grant, Ted, and Sap noticed the effects of the rest. On Mondays, there were fewer mental mistakes in training and people had a little more energy. By Saturday, they had been worn back down.

Sunday also meant an optional — truly optional — church service. Pastor Pete came out to Marion Farm for a non-denominational 9:00 a.m. service. He and Grant and the Team would then leave the Marion Farm service and go straight to the Grange service at Pierce Point.

Pastor Pete's services at Marion Farm were fairly well attended, although some guys preferred to sleep in even more. Some came one week and slept in another. As time went on, more and more soldiers came to the service. They were concluding that there was a spiritual aspect to what they were doing. For many, there were way too many "coincidences" that put them out there and with these people. They felt that a higher power had brought them together.

Pastor Pete volunteered to be the battlefield chaplain for the unit. Grant and Ted encouraged him to get to know the troops as much as possible before their mission.

The centerpiece of Sundays, though, was the Sunday dinner. They would eat a later breakfast and then have a dinner at about 2:00 p.m., which would be large and leisurely with plenty of time to relax and talk. Franny, the spectacular Navy cook, made sure there was at least one special food at each Sunday dinner. One time, it was homemade ice cream that a big KP crew made with a hand crank. That was a huge hit.

After Sunday dinner, if it wasn't pouring rain, they would play a football game. They didn't hit each other too hard because they didn't want to injure themselves and diminish combat effectiveness. But there was something about tackling their squad leader that was very satisfying.

Much of the bonding from the Sunday dinners came from the conversations over the meals. The squad leaders made sure that the troops rotated around different tables each Sunday so they got to know people outside of their squads.

"Where you from?" Would be the start of a long conversation at a Sunday dinner. It often ended with, "When the war's over, let's stay in touch. Write your contact info in my book."

A soldier's "book" was the little pocket notebook each one had been issued. On one of the FCard runs into Frederickson, Rich had come across a case of little pocket notebooks that had been looted. Someone was selling them. The case of notebooks cost one package of cornbread mix. Rich asked Grant if he had a use for them and Grant smiled. Grant had never thought of a use for little notebooks but the idea hit him when he saw the case of them.

Grant gave a notebook to each member of the unit for them to write down their memories and have their buddies put down their contact info for post-war reunions. Grant wrote a personalized note on the first page of each notebook thanking the soldier for his or her service. They were sincere messages.

A simple little $0.89 notebook — each of which ended up costing a half a teaspoon of cornbread mix — made a huge morale difference. It reinforced that the troops were making lifetime memories and friends during their few months at Marion Farm.

The 17th had their informal symbol, their "gang sign," which was the hand sign DeShante Anderson came up with.

In contrast to the unofficial gang sign, there was one very

official morale item: the 17th Irregulars' unit patch.

With encouragement from Boston Harbor, Ted and Grant were always trying to make the irregular unit feel like a "real" military unit, which was hard without uniforms and the fact that a sizable chunk of the troops were civilians. Boston Harbor came up with an idea: a unit patch for each of the irregular units. Ted wasn't thrilled with the idea; in Special Forces, patches and insignia were for the "big Army," the regular units, not the elite units that tried to blend into the shadows.

But Ted realized the 17th Irregulars were not a Special Forces unit. They were a ragtag collection of military people from various branches—most with no combat experience—and a bunch of civilians. They were exactly the "big Army" kind of people who needed a patch, so Ted changed his usual position and thought a patch was okay.

The design of the 17th's patch was born from practicality. One day, the Team, Grant, Sap, and a few of the infantrymen were out at the makeshift shooting range at Marion Farm showing the troops how to shoot. They were using dry firing to teach the troops basic marksmanship, how to move from cover, fire, and keep moving as a unit. It was like a choreographed dance where they broke it down into little steps and moved through it slow, then faster and finally at real speed. This took days.

For the training exercise, they used targets crudely shaped like a human silhouette. The targets had a little square for the head and a big rectangle for the body.

Grant looked at the target. It was the perfect shape for a patch; a simple shape that was easy to cut out of cloth. There were no tricky corners or curves since they didn't have machines to make fancy patches out there. He looked at his tactical vest. It was black with light brown ammo pouches. Those would be the colors for the patch: a square on top of a rectangle in light brown with a black "17th Irregs" on it. That was it. The patch was invented right then and there.

The troops liked the design. They found some light brown cloth and black paint. Someone made a stencil. Another person cut out the shapes from some cloth they found. Pretty soon, "17th Irregs." patches were on everyone in the unit. Crude patches, but patches nonetheless. Grant and the Team, who still spent much of their time in Pierce Point working their "day jobs," didn't put a patch on their clothes. No one outside of Marion Farm could see the patch, obviously. Except the enemy, when the time was right. They'd see plenty of those patches. About 104 of them.

The unit patch aided in further bonding. It showed the

"irregular" troops that they were in a "real" military unit, just as Boston Harbor had intended. They weren't a gang; they were soldiers. Instilling this was exactly what the patch was meant to do, and it did it very well.

A final memento was used to bring people together. It was the little beads Grant got before the Collapse. They were in Gadsden yellow, the same color as the in Gadsden "Don't Tread on Me" flag. They had a hole in the middle so they could be put on a neck chain or around a Para cord bracelet. A whole strand of two hundred beads cost about $5.00 before the Collapse. Grant got the strand in his preparations before the Collapse because he realized that he might need to identify friendly people in a way that was easy to conceal. A little bead in a distinctive color was perfect. And cheap.

One Sunday dinner, Grant made a speech and handed out a Gadsden bead, as they became known in the unit, to each man and woman. Troops started wearing them as a necklace with some high-strength fishing line they had. The unit's Gadsden bead became like a dog tag. It was a source of pride and a way to identify each other as part of a unit. It was amazing what impact little things, like a bead, a patch, a hand sign, and a pocket notebook could have.

Chapter 247

Physical and Social Sanitation

(December 15)

Marion Farm wasn't paradise, though. Morale was high, but it was no summer camp. The troops were glad to have it better than most, but this was still a secret military camp with semi-primitive conditions.

Sanitation was a constant concern. There were over one hundred people living in close quarters without all the modern conveniences. The farm had electricity and running water, but there were only two toilets and one shower. And, to make matters worse, they were on a septic tank. It was only designed for about six people, not 104. The septic system also meant that only organic matter could go down the drain or toilet. This was a new limitation for many of the troops who were accustomed to municipal sewer systems that could handle anything that could physically fit down the toilet or sink. They had to supplement the sanitation system.

Don, the Air Force RED HORSE guy, was an expert in field sanitation. His old unit would set up makeshift air fields in primitive conditions, sometimes near or behind enemy lines. Sanitation was part of the necessary facilities. Don, and a detail of men, dug some trenches and made crude outhouses far away from the living quarters. They even set up a crude shower. Cold water only, though, which was a new experience for most people. But, for morale, everyone got a hot shower in the farmhouse … once a month, with a five-minute limit. This was about all the septic system could handle without almost immediately needing a good pumping.

But, then again, Marion Farm was essentially disposable. Once they left on their mission, they would hopefully never need the farm again. They would be occupying recently taken cities, not falling back to the farm. They wanted to preserve Marion Farm as much as possible, though, so it could house another unit or some homeless civilians. Overusing the septic system wouldn't render the place uninhabitable, but they still wanted to be as low-impact on the facilities as possible.

Don would give quick classes on sanitation and made sure

everyone knew how important it was. "You're no damned good to this unit—and are actually a liability—if you're pukin' and crappin'," he would say. The military people who had lived out in the field—primarily the infantrymen and the few Marines—understood this. The rest of the unit who hadn't lived in the field thought the sanitation regulations—like washing their hands several times a day, the constant cleaning of everything, and taking their boots off in the sleeping quarters—were weird. But they complied.

A key component of the sanitation plan was in the kitchen. Franny was an expert at sanitation. Food-borne illness could cripple the whole unit, at least for a few days. That was very serious business. Franny had a small thermometer in a narrow little pocket on the arm of his cooking jacket. He would test the temperature of the water used to wash dishes, pots, and pans. He also measured the temperature of foods to make sure they were either hot enough or cold enough to be safe for eating. People could laugh all they wanted about the cook in a military unit, but they all had to eat and not be doubled up puking for days. The cook was the key to both of these vital things.

The sanitation regulations touched on medical issues. Coughing meant using hand sanitizer. If someone got sick, they were essentially quarantined in the infirmary, which was an RV Rich had brought in as a gift from a generous Pierce Point donor who was told he would be helping the "rental team." RV trailers were valuable commodities after the Collapse. RVs with an engine were less so because they required gas or diesel to be moved, but they were still valuable mobile bug out locations, or mobile quarantine quarters.

Every cut that drew blood—every single one—had to be sanitized and bandaged. Some guys thought it was a sign of toughness to work with open cuts. Ted would go bonkers when he found out about someone with an untreated open cut. He had seen simple cuts turn into major infections, which could take a soldier out of the fight, might kill them, and could tax the unit's resources to treat him or her. "There's no damned medevac here," he would yell at anyone who decided to be a badass and not get a cut properly treated.

One of the hygiene issues Grant harped on was brushing their teeth. The last thing he wanted was a soldier to be taken out of action by a totally preventable toothache. "If you don't brush your damned teeth and get a cavity or whatever," Grant would tell the troops, "it's not just your damned problem. It's the unit's problem because we just lost a fighter that we need. Don't be that guy."

Nick was pressed into service as a makeshift dentist. One

soldier came into the unit with a rotten tooth. After Nick had to yank it out without anesthesia, the unit took preventative dental care much more seriously. The screams from that soldier could have woken the dead, which convinced a lot of people to take care of their teeth.

Nick was tasked with medical spying on the troops. He would constantly observe them and check for any potential medical conditions they might have — from cuts, to coughs, to hypothermia, to whatever. He would give an exam to each soldier about once a month. The troops thought this was overkill, but Nick was catching little things that could become big things. One of the civilians was mildly diabetic (non-insulin dependent) and wasn't doing so well with all the carbohydrates they were eating out there, like cornbread and pancakes. Nick got him on a different diet and he was fine. They needed every single solider to perform at full capacity.

Nick was it out there as far as medical help went. In an emergency, like with Tony Atkins, they would take soldiers to the makeshift medical clinic at Pierce Point. Luckily, Nick could handle almost everything that would come up at Marion Farm on his own.

Nick actually did very little first aid work. Most of his day was taken up by observing the troops, doing the monthly exams, and giving first aid classes. But these were very valuable things. The battlefield medic work would come later. Unfortunately.

While medical sanitation sought to eliminate physical threats, like illness, there were also efforts at social sanitation, which was eliminating threats to the good order of the troops. Jealousy and pride were the main culprits, with lust coming in a close second. People — over one hundred people with wildly different backgrounds, thrown together and cooped up in a secret camp — were bound to have some conflicts, despite all the morale boosting Grant and Ted were doing.

Despite the vetting, with over one hundred people, there were bound to be a few assholes. And people who weren't assholes under normal circumstances can easily turn into assholes under stress.

Sure enough, the 17th had a couple of assholes. Ted and Sap picked them out early on and had the squad leaders watching for problems from them. The assholes — Perkins, Roth, Timerzick, and sometimes Patterson — complained about everything. The food wasn't good enough, they wanted to sleep more, they didn't want to do guard duty or KP, etc. They would find minor inequalities and try to set people against each other. Two of them were military and two were civilians. They would try to claim the other group wasn't doing enough or got better treatment. Their squad leaders tried to manage them, but as time went on, the "four assholes" as they became known, were getting mouthier and mouthier. They were given extra guard duty and KP as punishment but that just made them complain more.

"Can we shoot them?" Grant asked Ted one day. He was kidding ... for the most part.

Ted laughed, "I wish. I think that's kinda a 'war crime.'"

"Oh," Grant said, remembering George Washington's writings about the absolute imperative of military discipline, especially for outnumbered and outgunned rebel forces. "We can throw them in jail, though, right?"

"You're the lawyer, what do you think?" Ted asked. He already knew the answer, but wanted to see how Grant would approach this problem.

"Unit discipline is totally within the discretion of the commanding officer," Grant said. "And that's me."

"Yep," Ted said. Of course, if the commanding officer wanted to shoot someone for a minor infraction, that was not okay. Grant knew that there was always a political element to military discipline: go overboard on it and your troops will no longer respect you. Go too light on discipline and they won't respect you, either. It was like being a parent.

"What would you like to do with the 'four assholes'?" Ted asked. Once again, he knew the correct answer, but was testing Grant.

"I will firmly decide to... ask for the suggestion of my senior NCO," Grant said. Which was the right answer.

"Progressive discipline, like more guard duty hasn't worked, so throw them in the stockade for a few days," Ted said. The "stockade" was the mini military jail they had out there. They didn't have a separate building for it, but they made plans for one in the small equipment shed. Might as well make the discipline problems suffer out there. It wasn't supposed to be fun.

"Excellent suggestion, Sergeant," Grant said. "Two days sound good?"

"Sure, that's usually how long it takes them to shut up," Ted said. "We'll have to watch them after they get out. They'll hold a grudge against you, me, their squad leaders, everyone. They might try to frag us." "Frag" was military slang for killing a superior. The term came from Vietnam where a superior might be killed by an "accidental" blast of a fragmentation grenade.

After two days in the stockade, Timerzick and Patterson mellowed out. The stockade had the opposite effect on Perkins and

Roth; they got even mouthier. It was pretty clear the two didn't want to be soldiers.

"Too damned bad," Grant told them when they asked to be discharged. "Are you two out of your fucking minds?" Grant yelled in the commander's office (a bedroom of the farmhouse) with Ted standing there.

"What?" Grant yelled, "Do you think we'll just let you walk out of here and tell whoever will listen about the 17th Irregulars, our plans, our strengths, and our weaknesses? How stupid do I look?"

They were stunned. They had seen Grant lead, and be tough, but not in such an in-your-face manner. They were deflated. They had honestly thought that they could just say they quit and then get released.

"Nope," Grant said, "you two assholes are staying in the stockade until you decide to honor the commitment you made to your fellow troops, to be soldiers and not be pussies."

Perkins and Roth realized they were basically in jail until they changed their attitudes. This was not how they planned for things to turn out.

Grant continued, "Or, if you continue to be assholes after the unit ships out—at which point Pierce Point will already know what we were doing out here—we'll transfer you to the Pierce Point jail and let them hold you until regular Washington State Guard MPs come in and take you away for your sentences."

Perkins and Roth looked at each other and finally started rethinking things. Grant could tell they were looking for a way out. Perkins and Roth needed to save face.

"Here's the deal, gentlemen," Grant said. "You fucked up. Okay? Everyone makes mistakes. You can come back into the unit if you quit being assholes, act like soldiers, and do your jobs. The unit should be disbanded in a few months, anyway. Then you get on with your lives once we win the war. Okay?"

That sounded pretty reasonable to them. Slowly, Perkins and Roth lost their bad attitudes and were re-integrated into the unit. Grant, Ted, and Sap made sure that the unit wouldn't hold Perkins' and Roth's past behavior against them. The guys in the unit weren't happy about the "forgive and forget" policy as they realized that this unit needed to work together and not have personal disputes getting in the way.

Eventually, Perkins and Roth were functioning members of the unit again. They kept to themselves and bitched about everything—but in private, to each other, not to the whole unit, which was fine. People can hate me, Grant thought, and they can hate being a soldier, but they can't hurt the unit.

Ted, impressed that Grant handled the situation so well without military experience, asked him how he knew what to do with Patterson and Roth.

"I'm a parent," Grant said. "It's a lot like that." Grant thought some and then added, "Except my kids won't frag me."

There were other squabbles in the 17th that didn't involve the "four assholes." The women were the source of some problems. It wasn't their fault. Horny guys are horny guys and will fight over women. They just do. But the squad leaders were on top of that and stopped it before things came to actual fighting.

Then one day, the jealous guys stopped bickering. Right after Ted had a talk with them in private, of course. Later, Ted confided to Grant that he had threatened to cut off the parts of their bodies that were causing the jealousy. That was effective.

Two other social issues sprang up at Marion Farm. The first was the fact that—surprise, surprise—a few of the Team Chicks were pregnant. After all, contraceptives were hard to come by.

In contrast to the soldiers at the Marion Farm, the Team, including Grant, had it made in the sex department. They could come and go from the farm and spend the night in their own cabins in Pierce Point. This meant sex, hot showers, and booze (and, one time for Wes, all three at once).

Grant congratulated his guys on their impending fatherhoods. He suggested that they "marry" their girlfriends. By "marry," he didn't mean a legal marriage; there were no more of those, at least out in rural areas. There was no more government to administer legal marriages.

By "marriage," Grant meant one of the "wartime marriages" where people pledged to be with each other. Grant wasn't a prude, but he thought it was important for the Team—who many Pierce Point residents looked up to—to set a good example. They all agreed. The Team Chicks, even the ones who weren't pregnant, enthusiastically agreed. They wanted to be married, even it was only a wartime marriage.

It wasn't just that the Team Chicks wanted to be married for the sake of being married. They weren't exactly Bible thumpers. Instead, they wanted to be married because even just a wartime marriage meant two things to them. First, they would have a permanent link to their boyfriend on the Team. Actually, for the pregnant ones, they would have the most permanent link possible. But they wanted to have an additional connection with their man. He was so much more than a boyfriend. He was their everything in these bleak Collapse times.

Second, being married was "normal." They still craved a semblance of "normal." It was ironic, though. "Normal" in the days leading up the Collapse was people shacking up without getting married, or at least not getting married until their later twenties or early thirties. It was not "normal" for girls in their late teens and very early twenties to get married.

But the "normal" they sought now was the "normal" from a few generations ago, back when getting married that early was just what young people did. It beat spending your late teens, all of your twenties, and into your early thirties partying, which was fine when things were free and easy like before the Collapse. But now, with everything scarce and the constant threat of danger, partying for ten or fifteen years sounded odd and frivolous. Like a bizarre luxury. Oh, sure, occasional parties were still welcomed. Very welcomed, but it just wasn't the focus.

The Team Chicks—and the Team—grew up in a hurry that summer and fall. They went from a big party at the beginning of the Collapse to being serious soldiers, Army wives, and expectant parents. And, despite the world coming down around them, they were very happy about all of this.

Chapter 248

Warrior Song

(December 16)

With all the excitement out at Marion Farm for the upcoming deployment, Grant had almost forgotten about Pierce Point. He was going to Marion Farm every day and frequently spending the nights there. Lisa wondered why he needed to do so much "training" with the Team, but she wanted to believe that he was really at Pierce Point with them, instead of at that rumored Green Beret farm. Every time she thought he might be doing Army stuff, she told herself how crazy that was. She kept telling herself that.

He used the absence from his family to get himself mentally prepared for the second half of his life, which would be without his family once he shipped out with the unit because Lisa would leave him. Or he would die. Either way, within the next few weeks, he didn't expect to be with his family ever again. War was full of shitty situations. He was doing the best he could to get his head in the right place for when it happened.

Given how much time he was spending at Marion Farm, he couldn't devote much of himself to Pierce Point. Luckily, Pierce Point needed very little of his attention. The place was humming along nicely.

Pierce Point's self-help community services were functioning; it was amazing how a small and truly necessary level of "government" was doable even when everything had pretty much ceased to operate. That was because these things were necessary so people made them happen. All the extra stuff government used to do wasn't necessary, and therefore didn't get done when conditions didn't allow. Plus, unlike the FUSA, Pierce Point couldn't print money, so the community only did the things it could do with available resources.

As expected, there were problems and conflicts, but nothing they couldn't handle. The diminishing number of people who still wanted handouts was quieting down for the most part. They mainly sat around their houses and complained to each other about how unfair it was that no one was feeding them. Once in a while, they stole something and were thrown in jail after a quick trial. On one occasion, a thief was shot by a homeowner. The community threw a party for the homeowner.

Conversations about opening up the semi and distributing the food had subsided. The "ants" won the argument over the "grasshoppers."

Grant focused on training. They had perfected marksmanship and small unit movements a while ago. The trainees moved between cover flawlessly and used hand signals to communicate with their squad, which was pretty impressive, actually. They were finishing up on large unit movements and radio communications now. They were getting familiarized with explosives. First aid classes were constantly going on.

At this point, the Team was fully integrated into the 17th. They were functioning as the MP SWAT team Ted had suggested at the very beginning. The Team, while proud of their skills, were very humble and encouraged the infantrymen and others to teach them things. The Team, while they knew how to work with each other extremely well, needed to learn small and large unit movements. They also needed to learn the unit's communication system, both the hand signals for small-unit movements, and the radios for larger-unit movements. They were socially and tactically integrated into the unit, but were still their own group, which was fine. They had a specialized job to do.

Everyone could feel the changes in tempo and intensity out at Marion Farm. Things were getting serious. All that training on the simple things was building into complicated, military strategies. The people who, just a few weeks ago felt that they were at summer camp were now realizing they were a fairly skilled soldier in a unit with a serious job to do.

They felt like soldiers. They looked like soldiers. They talked like soldiers. They smelled like soldiers.

Ted was feeling that familiar feeling again; the feeling of knowing that he was going off to combat soon – the "faint whiff of smoke." He'd done it several times in his career with Special Forces. When he was in the Army and deployed overseas, he would train a local unit for months and then go out on their first combat mission. It was always scary — not just the combat, but scary seeing if the men and women he trained would perform under combat conditions.

Ted felt very good about the 17th Irregulars. First of all, they were fighting for their homes and families. Many had experienced, or at least witnessed, Lima atrocities, so they were committed to this fight. To fixing things.

Second, a large portion of the unit was military or ex-military, with a few ex-law enforcement sprinkled in, too. While most of them had not been in combat before, at least they thought of themselves as military or law enforcement people which meant they were used to following orders. By watching how the military and law enforcement people acted, the civilians had plenty of examples of what to do and how to do it.

Ted tried to create a "military" atmosphere at Marion Farm. Not ridiculous ticky-tacky military things—like shining their boots or arranging their pillows in a particular way—but practical, military things. Creating a military atmosphere had one goal: create warriors. That was what he wanted out of his soldiers.

To aid with this, Ted started playing a song for the unit's morning runs. He would blare it out of speakers around the running track they built among the outbuildings and farmhouse. The song, called the "Warrior Song" by Sean Householder went:

I've got the reach and the teeth of a killin' machine, with a need to bleed you when the light goes green.

Best believe, I'm in a zone to be, from my Yin to my Yang to my Yang Tze.

Put a grin on my chin when you come to me, 'cuz I'll win.

I'm a one-of-a-kind and I'll bring death to the place you're about to be: another river of blood runnin' under my feet.

Forged in a fire lit long ago, stand next to me, you'll never stand alone.

I'm last to leave, but the first to go, Lord, make me dead before you make me old.

I feed on the fear of the devil inside of the enemy faces in my sights: aim with the hand, shoot with the mind, kill with a heart like arctic ice.

I am a soldier and I'm marching on, I am a warrior and this is my song.

I bask in the glow of the rising war.

Lay waste to the ground of an enemy shore, wade through the blood spilled on the floor, and if another one stands I'll kill some more.

Bullet in the breech and a fire in me, like a cigarette thrown to gasoline.

If death don't bring you fear, I swear, you'll fear these marchin' feet.

Come to the nightmare, come to me.

Deep down in the dark where the devil be, in the maw with the jaws and the razor teeth, where the brimstone burns and the angel weeps.

Call to the gods if I cross your path and my silhouette hangs like a body bag; hope is a moment now long past, the shadow of death is the one I cast.

I am a soldier and I'm marching on, I am a warrior and this is my song.

My eyes are steel and my gaze is long, I am a warrior and this is my song.

Now I live lean and I mean to inflict the grief, and the least of me's still out of your reach.

The killing machine's gonna do the deed, until the river runs dry and my last breath leaves.

Chin in the air with a head held high, I'll stand in the path of the enemy line.

Feel no fear, know my pride: for God and country I'll end your life.

I am a soldier and I'm marching on, I am a warrior and this is my song.

My eyes are steel and my gaze is long, I am a warrior and this is my song.

The troops loved it. The military guys loved it the first time they heard it. The civilians were warming up to it. It was not the kind of song civilians were used to.

The Warrior Song played over and over again each morning. Pretty soon, the unit memorized it and sang along. They bonded by singing it together.

One morning, Dan Morgan was at Marion Farm visiting with his former gate guards who were now in the unit. He heard the song and saw the troops running to it. When the run was over, he pulled Ted aside.

"I understand why you're playing that song, Ted," Dan said. "But I hate to hear it. 'A killin' machine'? You're turning decent people into a 'killin' machine'? Is that what we want?"

"Yes," Ted said. He was a little pissed. What was wrong with Dan? Of course they wanted the troops to think of themselves as killing machines. It was better to have them get through the mental process about this now rather than on the battlefield when they might decide that killing isn't for them and then run away — getting themselves and their buddies killed.

"Hey, listen, I'm no pacifist," Dan said. "But I've been in the shit. I know what combat is. I spent three days without sleep defending the Bagram Air Base. I lost a lot of friends. People got maimed. A friend went blind. You ever heard your buddy scream, 'I can't see!'? Have you?"

"I've been in the shit, too, Dan," Ted said. He wasn't going to brag about all his combat experience, but it was extensive. Ted had snuck up on a man and slit his throat from behind. That still gave Ted nightmares.

"Here's the thing," Dan said, "I don't want these guys to come out of this war hating fellow Americans and loving to kill. Like Jennings, there," Dan pointed to one of the Pierce Point gate guards standing several yards away who had come into the unit. "Great kid. Wants to go to seminary and become a pastor. A nice kid like that is singing that he's a 'killin' machine'? We have to live together when this war is over. I don't want them to like what they're about to do."

"Fair enough," Ted said. He was annoyed at Dan, but needed to treat him with respect. "Don't worry, though," Ted replied. "I guarantee they won't like what they're about to do."

Ted thought some more and then said, "This song is just to get them to the mental place where they can do their jobs. Trust me: they'll look back on the lyrics to this song and say, 'Real combat sure wasn't fun.' But it's our job to get them confident on the battlefield."

Dan thought about it. "Yeah, I know, Ted." He looked off in the distance. "I hate war."

"Me, too," Ted said. "The more you know about it, the more you hate it. And we both know about it."

Ted looked Dan in the eye and said, "But you know what I hate more? What those Lima bastards are doing to my country. It's the only thing worse than war."

Dan nodded. He realized that Ted was right. At least Ted understood that war was the second worst thing.

Chapter 249

"Standin' on My Head"

December 17

"It's no big deal, honey," Matt Collins reassured his wife and daughters, as they sat in the Olympia High School cafeteria, which was now being used for "trials" by the Loyalists. "It's just TDF time," referring to the thirty-day sentence he just received in a Temporary Detention Facility, which were the makeshift jails the Loyalists used to house those convicted of petty political crimes. The Loyalists didn't have enough jails or guards to put political prisoners into real jails, as much as they would have liked to. And they knew they couldn't just shoot them because there would be a backlash. The Loyalists were just trying to control the population; they didn't want to cause an uprising.

"I can do TDF time standing on my head," he said with a shrug. "TDFs are a Club Fed. Minimum security. Three meals a day. No biggie." He waved his hand in a gesture that conveyed, "It's nothing."

His wife was silent and then started softly crying. She knew he'd probably be OK, but there were rumors that TDF prisoners were getting communicable diseases and weren't fed very well, but all of them seemed to return after their short sentences. A little thinner, maybe with a cough that wouldn't go away for a few weeks, but they were alive.

"The worst part about this," Matt said, "Is that we lose the FCard. Sorry about that, ladies." He felt terrible about the loss of the FCard, but it was a calculated risk when he started working part-time as a Patriot helper. He smuggled political contraband to people, like when he got Ron Spencer that yellow spray paint for his "I Miss America" graffiti. He did similar little jobs for the Patriots, like the "FEMA Lima" thing. He wasn't a soldier and hadn't killed anyone. Just little stuff.

"Let's go," the guard said as she came over to the family huddled in the corner of the cafeteria.

"See you in a few days," Matt said as he was led away. He turned to his family and, with a big smile he wanted the guard to see, said, "Standin' on my head, ladies. Standin' on my head." His wife and daughters smiled back and waved. Before the trial, his wife and daughters had talked about how they would smile and be strong for him. It would make it much easier for him to do his time and come back home.

Matt felt surprisingly good about his "conviction" and impending time in jail. He had always said before the Collapse, "I'll end up in jail when this thing falls apart." When he said that, back in peacetime, his friends thought he was kidding. But he was serious. He figured that the pathetic government would try to act tough by putting people in "jail" for lots of things, but they couldn't really incarcerate all the people who broke one of the thousands of new laws and regulations in "real" jails – people who couldn't pay the new skyrocketing taxes, gun owners they caught in traffic stops, and political opponents. The bankrupt government couldn't even afford to lock up real criminals.

The whole process of his arrest and "trial" had reinforced his thoughts on how broken the government was. He had performed dozens of missions for the Patriots before he got caught. He marveled at how lax the Limas' security was. On two occasions he made it through checkpoints with obviously forged documents because the "guards" were half-asleep furloughed state workers who were just doing their new FCorps job to get their FCards filled; they had no desire to actually catch any of their fellow citizens. The Patriot agent giving Matt assignments, who went by the name "Mr. Smith," once said, "You cannot overstate what an advantage our opponents' lack of caring is giving us." Matt saw that every day when he was out running missions in Olympia.

Matt got caught the old fashioned way: sold out by someone who had a petty dispute with him. His neighbor, Terry, had been a decent guy before the Collapse. He was a real estate appraiser who worked churning out appraisals for all the home mortgage programs the government was trying. They seemed to believe that constantly refinancing homes was "economic activity" that would sustain massive consumption and deficit spending. Every refinance needed an appraisal so Terry had plenty of work.

All economic activity essentially stopped when D2, which is what the Second Great Depression was called, kicked off. Not even zero-percent home loans could be sustained when no one had jobs paying anything close to a living wage. Rampant inflation also made zero-percent loans impossible – even for the mighty Federal Reserve and its magic money-printing presses – because a loan with no interest paid back in currency that was nose-diving in value could not be sustained. Not even for this government, which was the king of unsustainable economic schemes.

Terry, now unemployed, was bitter. He resented Matt, who was making a decent living in his various black-market endeavors. Matt wasn't a gangster, but he bought and sold FCards and silver, and he arranged to transport people who were trying to get around the checkpoints and get out of town. Terry had played by the rules and now Matt was prospering by breaking them. That made Terry mad.

Terry decided to befriend Matt so he could keep an eye on him and eventually report him – and get a nice bump in his FCard for his efforts. Terry started off slow with Matt and gained his confidence.

"So what did you do last night?" Terry once asked when Matt had been out on a mission.

"Nothin'," Matt said, "just stayed at home." Terry nodded and smiled to himself. He had a cell-phone photo of Matt leaving his house after the dusk-to-dawn official curfew. Now he had Matt lying about it, which meant Matt was up to no good. Now Terry had enough to go to the neighborhood FCorps captain.

It took the authorities weeks after Terry's report on Matt to start to do anything. Only when Terry kept coming to them with additional reports of suspicious activity did they finally do anything.

Matt was woken up in the middle of the night by a loud knocking on his front door. He grabbed his shotgun and ran to the door. There had been numerous home invasions lately and he was prepared for the worst.

He stood in front of the door and racked a twelve-gauge round, the universally understood sound of "don't come through that door." The knocking stopped.

"FCorps!" a man yelled. "Open the door immediately."

Matt thought this was a trick used by home invaders, so he looked through the peep hole. Sure enough, there were three people in those stupid yellow hard hats. They looked like state workers – not hardened criminals. Matt figured it was safe to open the door. He'd bluffed his way past these morons in the past, so tonight should be no different.

"Coming," he said as he ran into the bathroom to hide his shotgun, which was illegal to possess. He wondered if the sound of the racked round alerted the FCorps people that he had a shotgun. Probably not. They were pretty clueless and had probably never, in their world of cubicles and conformity, even seen or heard anything illegal like a shotgun.

"Hurry up!" an FCorps woman yelled as Matt was coming back to the front door. Matt opened the door and the woman barged her way in, followed by two FCorps men.

"Are you Matt Collins?" she asked sharply. By now his family was up and stirring.

No use denying anything, he thought. At least not verifiable things like his name. "Yes," he said. "What can I do for you this evening?"

"We're here to inspect your home," she said.

"Why?" he asked. No one answered him.

The FCorps people turned on the lights and started tossing things around his house. They were vandals in yellow helmets. Matt heard his wife and daughters crying; that was the worst part of this whole ordeal.

Matt was very careful to hide all the evidence of his activities, but he had slacked lately. He had several items not hidden well.

They went into the garage, which is where the incriminating stuff was.

They went right past the cans of yellow spray paint. One of them looked at the coffee can – containing dozens of hacked FCards, which were the fake FCards the Patriots created with artificial balances. They used these hacked FCards to feed their operatives, troops, and supporters.

The FCorps man tried to open the coffee can but, for some reason, couldn't. So he moved on. Matt felt his face turning red so he tried to leave the room so they wouldn't see him.

"Stop," the woman said loudly. "What's this?" she said as she pointed to a pair of bolt cutters.

"Oh," Matt said, "Those are my pruning shears. You know, for landscaping." Who would believe that? But that's the best he could do.

"Where is the registration?" she asked. One of the thousands of new regulations was the registration of every conceivable tool of sabotage, including, apparently, bolt cutters.

"It would take me a while to find it," Matt said. Registrations were still on paper because the government couldn't get all the various databases to work together. For example, the City of Olympia kept its bolt-cutter registrations in one database that was not compatible with another city's, which was not compatible with the state, let alone the federal databases. So everything remained on paper.

"We can look all through the house to find the registration," the woman said. She did not want to be there all night, though.

Matt knew even these idiots would find a lot more evidence against him if they kept searching. He decided to try the best strategy against the FCorps.

"Maybe I could get you guys a little something for your effort tonight," he said, "I know you guys are underpaid with all the budget cuts."

The FCorps people looked at each other, as if they were deciding if they should accept the offer of bribery. They were new together as a group and didn't trust each other enough yet to know that one of them wouldn't turn them in for bribery.

The woman, who was in charge, said, "That's a second violation: attempted bribery."

"Well, I don't have my bolt-cutter registration handy," Matt said. "So what happens now?"

He was handcuffed in front of his family, with zip ties instead of real handcuffs because that's all the FCorps had, and taken to the FCorps van waiting outside. The bolt cutters were taken, too. He noticed that the lights were on in Terry's house.

Matt sat, very uncomfortably, in the van for about two hours. Then they took him to the school and put him in a classroom with five or six others. They locked the door so they had to stay in there. About half of his detention mates looked like petty criminals and the other half looked like regular guys like him. No one talked. They were tired. The mood of the detainees seemed to be one of a giant inconvenience more than fear of going to jail. It was like TSA had seized their luggage and they had missed their flight more than they were going to a real jail.

Matt woke up, his back aching, in a student seat in the classroom. A guard was taking them out and down the hall. He got up and went.

The hall took them to the cafeteria. He looked around to see if his family was in the audience but they weren't; there wasn't anyone in the audience. He sat with his hands zip tied in a cafeteria seat for another few hours – his back and legs in severe pain at this point – watching the so-called "trials." They lasted about five minutes and consisted of the guard reading some vague charges and the "judge," who looked like someone at the DMV, asking the defendant if they had anything to say. Most didn't, but a few started talking until they were cut off after about a minute. All of them were convicted. The standard sentence seemed to be thirty days and the loss of an FCard. A few of the prisoners seemed distraught about going to jail, but most didn't. From what Matt could tell, most of the prisoners were like him: Patriots charged with petty crimes. The Patriots knew the TDFs were a light sentence so they didn't get too upset about having to go there.

After a few hours of sitting there, without any food or water, they took him back to the classroom. Apparently, they didn't have enough "judges" for the remaining "trials." He finally got some water and one chance to go to the bathroom. Still no food. He got the feeling he'd be hungry for the next thirty days or so. It still wasn't that bad, he kept thinking.

Finally, in the evening, he was hauled back into the cafeteria. By now, some people were in the audience. That's when he saw his family.

"Collins, Matthew," the DMV-looking judge called out. Matt looked at the guard to see if he had permission to stand; she signaled that he did. He stood and forcefully and confidently said, "Present." He wanted his family to see that.

"You are charged with possession of an unregistered bolt-cutter," the judge read. That was it; no mention of the attempted bribery. Interesting, Matt thought. None of the other prisoners had been charged with that, either. It was like the FCorps didn't want the bribery issue discussed, which made sense given how often they took money. "How do you plead?" the judge asked.

"Not guilty," Matt said. "The bolt-cutter registration law is unconstitutional," he asserted.

The judge was unfazed. She heard this all the time. Wacko tea baggers.

"I have reviewed the evidence and find you guilty. You are sentenced to thirty days in a Temporary Detention Facility and the loss of your FCard. Bailiff, please take the prisoner away."

The guard motioned that he could talk to his family briefly. That was when he told them he could TDF time "standing on his head." This would be a piece of cake, he assured himself as he went off to jail.

Chapter 250

The Football Field

(December 20)

Christmas was in a few days. The pending Christmas had a strong effect on many people. It got them thinking. No one wanted a horrible Christmas, yet Christmas was looking horrible for most people.

In Seattle and the suburbs, and in the state capitol of Olympia, things had been getting worse the entire autumn. Food was getting scarce. There was not mass starvation, but people were starting to skip meals. Except the connected; they still had plenty. Regular people were noticing that more and more. Crime was through the roof — but instead of gangs, now it was largely regular people stealing food or items to sell for food. Most Loyalists were realizing that the "Crisis," as they called it, wasn't a temporary emergency that they'd ride out with the help of the government. Now, even the most die-hard Loyalists were realizing things were headed in the wrong direction and wouldn't get better soon.

This caused many Loyalists to start thinking long and hard about the future. Would there be more Christmases like this? Would this be their last Christmas? Would Christmas be ruined for their kids? All the traditions of a normal Christmas were now in direct contrast to reality. Going out and getting a Christmas tree? Not this year. There were none. Having a big Christmas dinner? Not this year. Even the most head-in-the-sand people suffering from normalcy bias had to acknowledge that this Christmas would not be "normal."

The reality of a non-normal Christmas had two different effects on the Loyalists and the Undecideds in the Lima areas of the state. For some, the approaching Christmas gave many Loyalists a strong urge to hunker down and make this Christmas as "normal" as possible. They would put up a branch in their house and call it a Christmas tree, give gifts of canned food, and try not to hear the gun shots in the distance.

For other Loyalists, the approaching Christmas meant they had a strong urge to get out of their deteriorating situations and move to a safer place where things might be better. Getting to a safer place meant getting out of their semi-safe situations in places like the suburbs of

Olympia and going to the fortress of Seattle. It only took a few percentage points of the people moving from wherever they were to Seattle to cause a refugee crisis.

The highways were filling up with buses taking people to Seattle. The government controlled which vehicles could use the highways, of course, but private bus companies, which were illegal, were charging enormous fares to take people to Seattle or wherever they wanted to go. The authorities controlling the highways were happy to take the bus company bribes and sell them gang gas.

Nancy Ringman, who ran the Clover Park TDF was noticing all the people going up Interstate 5 from Olympia to Seattle. Her facility was right off of I-5 and inside the "JBLM ring" south of Seattle and north of Olympia. JBLM was the defensive ring surrounding Joint Base Lewis-McChord, which encompassed the area around Ft. Lewis and McChord Air Base.

She also noticed that her FCorps guards were melting away. There always seemed to be one more guard "out for the holidays" at roll call for every shift. The approaching Christmas gave people cover to desert. And they were leaving in increasing numbers.

Then Nancy got a phone call from her boss, Linda Provost.

She told Nancy that the decision had been made to get important civilians — high- and medium-ranking government employees — out of the suburbs and Olympia and closer to Seattle. The Loyalists knew that the Patriots would be sweeping in from the rural areas in a few weeks or months. The Loyalists couldn't hold these extended territories, so it was better to abandon them and concentrate their people in strongholds, like Seattle and its surrounding defensive areas, like the JBLM ring.

"You need to make room for fleeing civilians at your TDF," Linda told Nancy.

Room? Nancy thought. There is no room. They were stuffed way beyond capacity with detainees. They were sleeping on the floor and diseases were spreading among them. Not like Nancy cared. All those teabagger terrorists needed to die. She wondered why they even fed them, which explained why she didn't care that the guards sold most of the food destined for the detainees to the gangs. Nancy got a cut, too.

"Civilians? What kind of civilians?" Nancy asked.

"Good ones, not teabaggers," Linda said. "Civilians with high clearances." "Clearance" was the system of hierarchy the Loyalists used. The higher a clearance, the more connected a person was, and the more they got on their FCard, along with other perks.

"How many civilians?" Nancy asked.

"I show your TDF as having a capacity of 1,250," Linda said. She paused and slowly said, "I need all 1,250 spots for the civilians."

"Where do I transfer the detainees?" Nancy asked. What a colossal headache this would be. All the paperwork and she was shorthanded with more and more of the FCorps staff being "gone for the holidays."

After a long pause, Linda said, "You don't."

"I don't transfer them?" Nancy asked. Well, if she wasn't going to transfer them, what would she do with the detainees to make room for the civilians?

"No, Nancy, you don't transfer them," Linda said. "You … you're smart, you figure it out."

Nancy was trying to process what Linda was saying.

Oh. That. Wow. Well, at least that will simplify the paperwork, Nancy thought, trying not to think any deeper than that.

"Will the DOE regs be waived for onsite disposal?" Nancy asked. "DOE" was the Department of Ecology, the state version of the EPA.

"Yes," Linda said. She was relieved that she didn't have to spell out for Nancy what needed to be done. This was hard enough to do without being explicit about it.

"When do you need this done?" Nancy asked.

"ASAP," Linda said. "You will start getting civilians in forty-eight hours. Make sure your facilities are clean for the civilians. There might have been some illnesses among your detainees. We don't want our civilians to get sick."

"Consider it done, Linda," Nancy said.

"Happy holidays," Linda said.

"You, too," Nancy replied.

Click.

Nancy sat back in her chair and thought about this. She would separate the sick ones from the able-bodied ones. She would split the able-bodied ones into a digging detail and a cleaning detail.

The cleaning detail would clean everything with hot water and bleach. The digging detail would make the ground ready for the sick ones. They could use the football field.

The sick ones would go outside to the football field and … make room for the coming civilians, those loyal people who respected their government. They were the ones who deserved to be taken care of. Not teabaggers who were all about violence and hate. Then the cleaners would go to the football field and join the sick ones. Then the digging detail would join them.

This was the most humane thing to do, Nancy told herself. Civilians needed food and shelter. It was inhumane to deny civilians food and shelter. The current occupants needed to go. To the football field. At least the football field would now be put to good use. She always hated football. It seemed so violent.

Every few minutes, she would painfully realize that what she was about to do was extremely violent; she couldn't reconcile her hatred of violence with ... what would happen in the football field. Then she'd snap back to reality and realize that she had a job to do. Her facility needed to be emptied to accommodate fleeing civilians. Good people who weren't teabaggers.

Nancy summoned her chief FCorps guard and told him the plan. He walked out of the room without saying a word. She never saw him again.

After about ten minutes, she called in the number two guard, Timothy. She forgot his last name, but he was the effeminate one who really hated teabaggers.

Timothy listened to the plan. He only had one comment.

"We don't have enough ammunition to carry it out," he said. "We have, what? About 2,100 detainees?"

Nancy nodded.

"We've had some thefts of our ammunition," Timothy said with a straight face. Of course, the FCorps had sold most of it to a gang. Nancy hadn't seen a cut of that. Oh well. It was too late to care now.

"So what do we do?" Nancy asked.

"We have some .22s," he said.

"What's that?" Nancy asked.

Timothy explained what a .22 was.

"They're quieter and do the job. They use them on cattle they're butchering."

"Oh, okay," Nancy said. "Whatever works is fine with me. Get things ready. And get it done."

Timothy nodded and walked out of her office.

Time for a glass of wine, Nancy thought. It's been a hard day. She picked one from her wine collection that the facility's food contractor had provided her. The wine was a little "thank you" for all the food that seemed to be diverted from the detainees to the contractor. She picked out a bottle that she'd been meaning to open for a special occasion. Upgrading her TDF to a civilian humanitarian center qualified as a special occasion.

An hour — and a bottle of wine — later, Timothy came back and said, "We have a problem."

"What's that?" Nancy asked, drunk and not caring too much.

"Most of my staff left when they heard the plan," he said. He was embarrassed his staff was disobeying him.

"Go get them," Nancy said. "They can join the detainees in the football field." It was that easy to order people's deaths. That easy.

"I have an idea," Timothy said. "Most of the detainees are teabaggers, but some are regular criminals. Some are pretty bad people. We could have the criminals do the work on the football field. We'd let them go in exchange."

Nancy thought about letting hardened criminals go. They'd go into the areas held by the Legitimate Authorities, and that would be a problem. But it had to be done. They had to make room for the incoming refugees. "Excellent problem solving," Nancy said. "Go with it."

He did. About six hours later, the football field was dug up with the help of a bulldozer. Soft pops and some screaming were heard for over an hour, but it was faint. Surprisingly, it didn't bother Nancy, despite her hatred for violence. Perhaps it was because she didn't have to do the dirty work herself, or even witness it. Or maybe it was because she was busy making plans for the new guests. The decent people who deserved food and shelter. She wanted to impress Linda with how well she was making the transition to civilian guests.

There was a ruckus in the middle of the night, but Nancy slept through it. One of the cleaning details found out what was going on and rioted. The remaining guards and the criminal detainees handled it. Luckily, the rioting took place outside. The remaining guards hosed the blood from the rioting off the cement and the rain washed away the remaining blood.

Nancy was asleep on the couch in her office. It was dawn. Someone came in to her office.

"All done," Timothy said. "Exactly 2,114. Topsoil going over them now."

"Great," Nancy said, still in a sleepy haze. She couldn't wait to tell Linda the good news in the morning. Then Nancy fell back asleep. She had worked really hard that day.

Made in the USA
Columbia, SC
16 February 2021